Smith, Joan
Destiny's dream /

D0829781

DATE DUE

A WOMAN OF MYSTERY

Flora touched her mask to make sure it was securely in place. "I'm not a whore!" she said fiercely. Her eyes blazed and her heart hammered painfully.

"I don't believe in make-believe," he answered gently, and took a step closer. "But one does not expect to find horses in a stable, angels in heaven, and available ladies in a brothel. Or did you slip off a cloud and end up in the wrong manor?" He smiled softly.

His dark head hovered above her, so close she could feel his body heat. A strange warmth invaded her bones. He was going to kiss her . . .

JOAN SMITH

DESTINY'S DREAM

LEISURE BOOKS   NEW YORK CITY

A LEISURE BOOK

Published by

Dorchester Publishing Co., Inc.
6 East 39th Street
New York, NY   10016

Copyright © 1988 by Joan Smith

Printed in the United States of America

1

The horses drew to a stop and a pair of brightly curious eyes peered out the carriage window into the coaching yard. So this was London! Flora had never seen so many people and horses and carriages in one place. She looked around in wonder, her ears ringing with the clamor of traffic. The hotel across the street must be five stories high. It was bigger than the church and hotel at home put together. Flora Sommers rose with the other passengers, happy to alight after a long trip. As she clambered down, she turned to say goodbye to her traveling companions. All she saw was their backs. People were certainly unfriendly in London! Or perhaps they were just in a hurry.

Flora was in a hurry too. The shadows of afternoon were lengthening. Her own small body cast a shadow eight feet long on the dusty cobbled yard. It hardly looked like the shadow of a person. With her shawl pulled over her head and her pelisse around her hunched shoulders, she cast a strangely inhuman shadow—headless, shoulderless, anonymous. A gust of cold November wind tore at her clothes and shivered up her spine. She clutched her threadbare pelisse more tightly about her.

"Mine is the cane bag, please," Flora called to the boy unlashing the cases from the carriage roof.

The boy gave her a dismissing look, spat on the ground, narrowly missing her feet, and growled, "Wait your turn, miss."

The other passengers were giving the boy money. Tuppence just for handing down a piece of luggage! London must be paved with gold. She'd done the right thing to come here. As Flora had no tuppence to spare, she waited humbly for the other passengers to receive their luggage before asking for hers once more. "My case, please."

The boy gave her another condemning glance. "It'll cost you," he said boldly.

Flora felt a flash of confused emotion. Terror and fear were blended in it, but there was anger too. What if he didn't let her have her case? It held her worldly goods—her Sunday-best gown, her linens, her flannelette nightie, her prayer book. The tremor of fear passed and anger reigned. Flora Sommers had been haggling with uppity clerks for a year now. She had learned to put on a bold face, even when she was shaking inside.

"It will not! I've paid my fare. You give me my case or I'll report you to the driver."

The surly brute saw angry sparks glinting in a pair of dark eyes and threw her case to the ground at her feet. The chit had the accents of a lady, he thought, though she didn't look like one. The snap flew open and her humble possessions were scattered in the dust. A tear stung her eyes as she scrambled to pick up her clothes. "I'm going to report you," she warned, but he just laughed and jumped down.

As he towered over her, she saw he was no older than herself, but he was a strong, strapping lad. His nose was runny and his shirt and vest were grimed with dirt. There was a cunning look in the cinnamon eyes that roved boldly from her head to her toes.

His voice softened in cajolery. "No harm meant, miss. Can I call you a hansom cab? Where would you be going, then?"

"That's none of your affair," she said bravely, but her mother's warning about "city men" was with her.

"You've come to London to be a maid. Is that it?"

"Certainly not. I'm visiting relatives."

His loose lips opened in a snide grin. "Dukes and duchesses, I expect, from that fancy accent. I'm surprised their footmen ain't here to see you to their mansion."

"I have the address."

His meaty hand came out and his fingers clamped her upper arm. "No hurry, eh, miss?

Why don't you and me have a bite first. I'll show you the city."

"Let go of me!" she said, and shook him off. A passerby stopped and gave the boy an admonishing glance, and the young groom turned sullenly away.

Flora looked her gratitude to the stranger. He was a tall elderly gentleman, wearing a poorly cut jacket. "You shouldn't be alone in the city, miss," he said. "Best get where you're going before the sun sets." His duty done, he turned to leave.

"Please," she called after him. "Could you direct me to Upper Grosvenor Square?"

"You're a long way from there. It's north-west of here, above Grosvenor Square. I don't live in that part of town myself. That way," he said, and pointed vaguely into the distance.

"Thank you, sir," she said, and clutching her straw case under her arm, for the lock was broken, she set off into the twilight to find her mother's cousin, Mrs. Leadbeater.

Mrs. Leadbeater had agreed to find her a position. With Papa dead and five mouths to feed, it was for the eldest to fend for herself, and hopefully send a little money home besides.

The Sommers were gentry, but not landed gentry. Flora knew that her mother had made what was deemed a "bad match" in marrying a teacher. Papa had been the headmaster of the village school at Bradbury in Devonshire. When he died unexpectedly, the family lost the headmaster's house and moved into a cheap apartment. Mama kept house by day for a local merchant, while Lily, who was fifteen, minded the smaller children. Flora was seventeen—an adult almost—and she was determined to relieve her mother's burden.

Flora had left Bradbury in emotional turmoil, sad to leave home and the family, but proud to be on her own, and excited at the prospect of seeing London. Mrs. Leadbeater was the most prestigious of their relatives. She would get Flora a position in a respectable home as nursemaid or kitchen maid. Eventually even housekeeper wasn't beyond her, in ten or twenty years. Flora had shown excellent housekeeping skills. This future might be prevented by marriage, of course.

Mama had smiled hopefully at her eldest daughter when she suggested the possibility of marriage. Flora was the beauty of the family. Her hair had the sheen of burnished copper. As it tended to unruly curls, Flora wore it short, framing her oval face like a crown. Her complexion was pure Devonshire cream, with a tinge of rose in her cheeks. Her eyes were a somber gray, fringed in long, sooty lashes, giving a serious tone to a face that was otherwise only pretty. She needed those eyes to counteract a set of dimples and her little impertinent chin.

Flora always blushed at the mention of marriage. Her small body was just now swelling to womanhood. It would take another year or two for it to reach its peak. Other than those dream fantasies indulged in by all young maidens, Flora was innocent of any doings with men. All her mother's warnings had to do with defending her virtue.

Flora hurried along the street, scanning the signs for Upper Grosvenor Square. The population of Bradbury was six hundred and five—six hundred and four now that she had left. A metropolis of three-quarters of a million people overwhelmed her. The streets teemed with humanity, every member of which was of consuming interest to Flora.

She had never seen such wealth, or such degrading poverty, in her life. She looked up and read a sign saying Charing Cross Road. Dandies in tight-fitting jackets and carrying bouquets gave her dismissing glances. Prostitutes from Haymarket might have been mistaken for grand ladies. They too ignored Flora. Children too young to be out roamed the streets alone. They had the hungry, inhuman eyes of stray dogs, and the same frightened, furtive manner.

Every intersection was a trial. You took your life in your hands to cross in that traffic, which seemed never to stop. Magnificent black carriages bowled along, throwing up clouds of dust and scraps of paper. Through their windows Flora caught glimmers of feathered bonnets, curled beaver hats, and always those uncaring, inhuman eyes. What was the matter with people here? They didn't even look at you. There were curricles and gigs, delivery carts and mounted riders—all in a great hurry to get somewhere. Where were they going? Twice she asked directions, and twice was waved aside.

For an hour she hurried on, reading all the signs and never finding her goal. St. Martin's Lane—surely she had read that same sign half an hour ago. Was she going in circles? Her arms ached from carrying the cane case, and her legs grew numb. Worse than this was the buzzing in her head, due to hunger. The lights and sounds and wave of humanity inundated her, till she felt she was drowning in a sea of rushing people.

Darkness had fallen, but the glare from carriage and shop lamps concealed it till she turned a corner and found herself off the main thoroughfare. She stood at the mouth of a dark alley where nothing stirred but a mangy dog. He growled menacingly and she turned back to the lit street.

There was a small café on the corner. Mother Hyde's Parlor, the sign said. It had a homey sound. A glance through the window showed Flora that the cafe wasn't too grand to enter. The tables didn't have linen cloths covering the deal wood. Candles stuck in wine bottles were the only illumination—a cozy, flickering light. She must have toast and tea or she'd faint. Surely two shillings would pay for toast and tea, even in London.

2

Flora entered warily, and was struck at once with how different the people here were from the people in the streets. They didn't ignore you, but smiled with brightly curious, friendly eyes as she wound her way to a small table in the corner. She removed her shawl and pelisse and sat on the bentwood chair, waiting for service. The young girl who came to tend her was pretty, with flashing black eyes and black hair. Flora felt uncomfortable to see the girl wearing such a low-cut blouse. Her bosoms pushed out over the top in a way that would cause a riot in Bradbury.

"Good evening, miss," the waitress smiled. "Are you alone, or are you expecting someone?"

"I'm alone. How much does it cost for toast and tea, if you please?"

"Are you short of blunt, dear?"

Flora was surprised to be called "dear,"

especially by a girl no older than herself. "A little," she admitted.

"Just new in town, eh? Who sent you here?"

"I arrived this afternoon—I just happened to see the sign, and thought the cafe looked—friendly."

"Oh, we're all one happy family here," the girl said, waving a hand over the room.

As she looked around, Flora noticed that there was indeed an air of great friendliness. Gentlemen strolled in and joined ladies at the tables. It seemed a sort of meeting place for old friends. The patrons, she feared, must be from a higher class than herself. Everyone was fashionably dressed, many of the gentlemen in black evening suits, and the ladies in beautiful gowns. They certainly wore them low-cut in London! There were even some fur stoles in evidence, and jewelry sparkling at the ladies' throats and ears.

"Have you found a position yet?" the waitress asked.

"No, I'm looking. I have a cousin who will find me one. How did you get this job?" Flora asked.

To Flora's surprise, the girl sat down in the other chair to chat. This was more like home! A smile of relief eased the fatigue from her shoulders. "Mother Hyde is always looking for girls. I could put in a word for you, if you like."

"Could you? Perhaps I should see Mrs. Leadbeater first. That's my cousin. Her husband is in banking. She thought she might find me a position as nursemaid or some such thing."

The waitress shook her head and laughed merrily. "Lawks, what a hard future you're choosing, Miss—?"

"Miss Sommers, from Devonshire."

"Devonshire? That's a long ways away. Nursemaids' jobs are hard work, and hard to come by. I'll have a word with Mother. How did you get to London?"

"On the coach. I've been traveling for days. I'm very hungry," she reminded the waitress. "About the toast and tea—how much is it?"

"We never turn a hungry girl from the door. I'll bring you dinner, and don't worry about the bill."

"But I want to pay! Toast and tea will be fine."

The girl rose. "My name's Sal. Sally Mulligan. You just sit tight and we'll take care of you."

Sally nipped away, her hips swaying insouciantly. Flora noticed that she stopped to joke with the customers. She thought how nice it would be to work here. Even the elegant gentlemen in the black evening suits laughed and joked with Sal. While Flora was still pondering this strange oasis of warmth and conviviality, a tall woman advanced toward her table.

Other than the local squire's wife, Flora had had little to do with fine ladies.

She suspected that she was about to have the honor of meeting a countess or duchess as the noble figure approached her in the dim candlelight. Her black hair was arranged in an intricate bundle of curls, pierced here and there with sparkling stones. Her gown was bright blue, the color of a jay's wing, topped with a shawl fringed in gold. Such magnificence stunned Flora into shy silence.

"Good evening, dearie," the apparition said, and sat down, placing her ringed hands on the table. "New in town, are ye?"

Flora struggled to her feet and curtsied. "Yes, ma'am."

"Sit down, child. There's no need to stand on ceremony with Mother Hyde."

"Oh, you are the proprietress!" Flora sat down on the edge of her chair.

"That I am, love," the grande dame said, with a kindly smile. "I hear you're interested in work?"

"I'm looking for a position, yes."

"You're welcome as any of my lasses."

"You have a very nice—restaurant," Flora said, hesitating over the word. The establishment seemed more than a restaurant, somehow.

"Ye couldn't have done better than to come to me," the woman said. She raised her arm, and a carafe of wine was brought to the table. "It's my treat," she said, and poured two glasses. "Here's to ye, Miss Sommers."

Mother Hyde lifted her glass and drained it, finishing with an unladylike smack of her lips.

When Sally returned, she carried a steaming plate of roast beef and vegetables. Flora had never seen anything so tempting in her life.

"I only ordered toast and tea," she told Mother Hyde.

"That's monk's nourishment. You eat hearty, my love."

Flora began cutting the meat and eating it. It was dry and the potatoes were wet, but she was too hungry to care. It had been many a long month since they had been able to afford roast beef at home.

"You're very kind," she said timidly to the woman across from her. But she wished Mother Hyde would go and leave her to eat in peace.

"I treat my gels right," the woman said. "It was fate that brought you here, that's what it was. Leadbeater, is it, your cousin's name?"

"Yes, Mrs. Joshua Leadbeater, of Upper Grosvenor Square."

"She doesn't know you're here?"

"I haven't been in touch with her yet. I walked and walked, but couldn't seem to find her house," Flora said, and sighed wearily.

"London's monstrous. You just stay here tonight, and I'll send a note off to your cousin to tell her you're here." As she spoke, she filled Flora's wine glass.

"Where would I sleep?"

"I have a rooming house out back. I look after young girls like yourself that come to town, all lost and bewildered, not knowing which way to turn."

The idea of returning to the now dark streets of London filled Flora with terror. Within the walls of this happy establishment, she felt safe. Wine was an unaccustomed treat. The first glass eased her worries, the second left a rosy glow of contentment. How very kind this stranger was. Her generosity was doubly welcome after the lonely, frightening trip, the first trip Flora had ever taken alone.

"I don't have much money," Flora said.

The face across from her blurred, but even in its fuzzy condition, it wore a smile. "You can do a few jobs for me." Mother Hyde smiled benignly.

"I am an excellent sheam—seamstress," Flora said, shaking away the fuzziness that surrounded her.

"Seamstress? Oh that's not my line of business, dearie."

Flora smiled in confusion. "I know," she said. Mother Hyde ran this wonderful little restaurant, where strange girls in town were fed without paying.

"Drink up your wine, and we'll chat again later. I see a new gentleman has arrived. He looks a proper swell!"

Mother Hyde left, and Flora looked after

her. She saw, as through a smoky haze, Mother Hyde greeting the two gentlemen. Flora smiled bemusedly. How marvelous London was! She could swear that one of those gentlemen had jumped right off Mama's tin box of sugared cherries, which Papa had given her for their anniversary two years ago. The box was cherished still.

Seen in silhouette, the man's black hair sat just so along his well-shaped head. The sideburns grew low along a lean cheek. A strong, straight nose and high brow lent a noble air to the vision. When the gentleman removed his drab driving coat, Flora saw he wore a black jacket and immaculate white shirt. His shoulders were broad, his body tall and straight.

Mother Hyde spoke to him, and the gentleman turned to look at Flora.

She swiftly looked away, but not before she had seen the man's face in full view. What she remembered, as she moved a piece of beef around her plate, was his eyes. Dark, probing eyes, smiling irresistibly at her, warm with interest—with admiration. She must be dreaming. She looked again. The smile curved his lips, it sped across the noisy room on silver wings and settled in her heart.

Then Mother Hyde took the two men by the arms and led them to a table, where they sat alone, looking at Flora, smiling. She felt flustered and embarrassed, yet honored in some way she couldn't understand. She wished that Mother Hyde would introduce them to her, but knew she wouldn't be able to say a word if this happened.

The man Flora had been watching turned to his friend and spoke. His face was flushed with brandy. His head reeled, but his speech wasn't slurred. "I thought you were insane, bringing me here, Jack, but by God, you know your way around town! That little redhead is an incomparable."

"A man going off to war should spend his last night in the arms of a woman," his friend said dreamily. They were both well on the way to being drunk. "Wait till you see my Iris."

"That's the woman for me." John Beauchamp gazed across the room. The pretty little redhead smiled shyly at him. "She looks young," he said to his friend.

"If they're big enough, they're old enough. She wouldn't be here if she weren't available."

At length Mother Hyde joined Flora again. "All finished dinner, Miss Sommers?"

"Yes," Flora said, and noticed that it was true. Without being aware of it, she had demolished the large plate of meat and vegetables.

"Then we'll finish the wine," Mother Hyde said, and filled her glass again.

"No more for me, thank you," Flora said, and covered her glass with her hand.

Mother Hyde called for coffee. They always

drank tea at home. The coffee was strong and sweet, with a strange undertaste, rather burning, but pleasant. By the time Flora had finished it, she found she was unable to rise and thank her hostess. But somehow, this didn't matter. Nothing mattered. She was in a warm, friendly place, and tomorrow she'd see Mrs. Leadbeater. Her cousin would know whether it was permissible to work in a public parlor.

Sally Mulligan came to the table. "More brandy, Mother?" she asked Mother Hyde.

"Brandy!" Flora exclaimed.

"Hush! No more coffee, Sal," Mother Hyde ordered. She turned aside and spoke in a low voice to Sal. "Take Miss Sommers to the good room and see her settled in for the night. I'll be along shortly. And you can tell the young gentleman half an hour. Make sure he don't leave, mind."

"Which gentleman?" Sal asked.

"Mr. Smith."

"Lud, they're all Mr. Smith or Mr. Jones. Do you mean the handsome one as just come in with Mr. Strong?"

"That's the one. He fancies Miss Sommers." She turned back to Flora. "You run along with Sal, dearie. She'll give you a nightie."

"I have my own nightgown," Flora said. But her head was spinning so fast that she couldn't remember where she'd put her straw case. As she looked around for it, Sal picked it up and took her by the arm.

"Flannelette, I warrant," Mother Hyde said, and laughed.

Her smile faded as Flora left, and a crafty smirk moved in to replace it. This was just the girl she had been waiting for! She could do something with that fine coppery hair and pretty little face. Get her out of her dowdy clothes into a silken gown to show off her bosoms and she might bring in five guineas a night. She had a touch of class, to please such fine gentlemen as Mr. Strong's friend. A very hoity-toity way of talking the girl had. She was a virgin very likely—have to get the draft into her before she handed her over to the gentleman.

She paused a moment over this Mrs. Leadbeater. But anyone residing in Upper Grosvenor Square couldn't matter—they were mere gentry. The girl had come to London alone on a coach—a nobody, in other words. They could never prove she'd reached London. Once the girl was initiated, she wouldn't be too fast to go running to her straightlaced relatives. And if she did, well, no one was forcing her—unless the gentleman got a little rough. It wasn't likely that anyone would bring an action against a friend of Mr. Strong. Who could he be? A gentleman and no mistake about it. Maybe even a lord—she didn't see many of that set, but with Flora . . .

Visions of a bright future lit Mother Hyde's

greedy eyes. She heaved her heavy body up from the seat and went to oversee Flora's dressing.

3

The bedchamber that Flora entered was embellished with Mother Hyde's notions of finery. The thinly piled carpet underfoot was patterned in red roses. At the windows, deep blue brocade hangings hid the unappetizing view of Long Acre by night. The canopy on the bed was also blue, tasseled and trimmed with gold satin ropes. Other than a table by the bedside, the only furnishing was a carved armchair, but to Flora's swimming eyes, the place appeared magnificent.

"Oh my!" she exclaimed softly. "Am I truly to sleep here?"

Sal slid a laughing eye at the girl. "Not sleep exactly," she said.

"I must rest. I'm so tired—so dizzy," Flora murmured, and sank onto the edge of the bed.

Within a minute Mother Hyde opened the

door and glided in. "How are you feeling, dearie?" she asked Flora.

"I feel strange," Flora answered. She knew she should rise to greet the lady, but when she tried to, she found that her knees had turned to rubber.

Mother Hyde adopted a sympathetic pose. "You've had a hard day," she said. "Sal, get Miss Sommers one of my special sleeping drafts—you know the one—while I help her undress."

Flora was alarmed. "I can undress myself, ma'am." But when she tried to do it, her fingers fumbled on the buttons, so she allowed Mother Hyde to help her.

The woman quickly removed Flora's gown, eager to see what new wares she had acquired for her establishment. She pulled Flora to her feet, brushing the girls fingers aside when she tried to hold on to her petticoats. "Now, now, it's just us women," Mother Hyde chided, as Sal appeared at the door with a steaming cup of liquid. Mother Hyde knew the draft went down more easily if it was mixed with coffee and plenty of sugar, and worked more quickly when served hot. The brandy helped to hide the taste of Spanish fly. This potent brew was known among her girls as Hyde's Hellpot.

Sal held the cup to Flora's lips. Flora took a sip and wrinkled up her nose. "It'll make you sleep like a top," Sal said merrily. Flora took another sip. Then the cup was put aside to allow the women to undress Flora. She made a gesture of pushing them away, but a strange lassitude had come over her. They were women, after all. Such nice women.

The last layer of petticoat was drawn off and the old dame gazed with admiration at Flora's naked body. She hadn't see one this fine in many a long year. There wasn't much of it, to be sure, but what there was was fine. The girl had a dainty white set of shoulders, nicely formed and smooth as velvet, and such a tiny waist! Mother Hyde could have spanned it with her own two hands. The breasts were not so large as gentlemen liked, but with the rosy nipples sitting erect, they were attractive.

The chit needed another year or two before she'd be at her prime, and by then she'd have learned a few tricks to please the gentlemen. She had a ladylike way about her—well spoken—that was a pleasant change. Oh yes, Miss Flora Sommers would be a fine addition to the establishment.

"The white gown, Sal," Mother Hyde ordered, and Sal handed her mistress a white satin peignoir, paneled in lace. It was open down the front, held together by a tie belt.

"How pretty!" Flora crooned, running her fingers over the unaccustomed luxury. "It feels as cool as a stream. Is it really mine?"

"For tonight it is," Sal said saucily. "Better have another sip of your sleeping draft, Miss Sommers. What's your first name?" As she spoke, she lifted the cup for Flora to drink the heady brew.

"My name is Flora. It means flower. My—
sishter's name is Lily. Mama called us all
after . . . flowers." Speaking was difficult.

The other two women exchanged a
satisfied look. "Then you shall have the floral
scent," Sal said, and lifted a bottle of
perfume.

She touched the amber liquid to her
fingers, then to Flora's throat and arms,
placing a drop between her breasts. In some
deep corner of her mind, Flora knew this was
an impertinence, but when she tried to
object, Sal began spinning in front of her
eyes. Besides, the cool perfume felt good on
her fevered skin. The scent was lovely, like a
field of wild flowers in spring. With the cool
satin material caressing her shoulders, and
in this beautiful room, she felt as pampered
as a princess.

"Can you do anything with her hair?"
Mother Hyde said. She spoke hurriedly now,
looking nervously toward the door. "Just
fluff up her curls. Lovely hair the chit has."

"Not a chit," Flora objected, then she fell
to the bed and sat glaring at the two weaving
bodies in front of her.

Sal attacked her hair with the brush. Every
bristle of it pierced Flora's scalp like a
needle, so she pushed Sal away.

"That's good enough," Mother Hyde
decided. She went to the bed and took Flora's
hand in hers. "You're going to have a caller,
Flora."

"Mrs. Leadbeater already?"

"No, a gentleman caller. Mr. Smith. He's an influential man. You be nice to him and he'll do something for you."

"Governess," Flora mumbled. Her secret hope was to be a governess, but she feared her education wasn't good enough.

The women quickly picked up Flora's clothing and tidied the chamber. Just before leaving, Mother Hyde took the cup holding Flora's draft. The girl hadn't drunk half of it, but it was potent. It would last long enough. Already the girl's pupils were dilated, and a feverish flush colored her cheeks. Her coppery curls gleamed like a new penny in the lamplight. With the white peignoir falling open at the top, revealing two gentle mounds of white, Flora made a delectable sight. White was her color—this year. Once the bloom was off the flower, she would look more seductive in brighter shades.

The women left and Flora lay down on a pile of pillows, her head reeling. From far away, she heard strange, soft murmurs, a woman laughing—was that a man's crooning voice? What a happy house this was. She was lethargic, yet some restless sensation curled in her breast too. It was a strange excitement she had never felt before. She wanted to run around the room and dance and shout, but she couldn't even sit up. She felt as if she could open the window and fly away home, or off to Paris or any exotic place.

Then there was a tap at the door. It opened quietly and a man entered. Flora recognized him as the handsome man from the cafe, and her heart pounded in excitement.

"Good evening, Flora," he said, and smiled as he advanced toward the bed, which had a troublesome tendency to move before his eyes.

Flora sat up, pulling the peignoir together with her fingers. In a far corner of her mind, she knew this visit was utterly improper. It was outrageous! She wasn't dressed, and there was no chaperone present. She didn't know this man, who smiled at her from his dark eyes, hinting at mysterious intimacies. But he was terribly handsome. So tall and elegant that she felt intimidated.

"Who are you?" she asked. Her voice was husky from brandy, and tinged with fear.

"Call me John," the man said in a deep, warm voice, and advanced till he stood just beside the bed, gazing down at her.

He had never seen such a lovely woman in his life. Who would have thought to find this jewel in an inferior brothel like Mother Hyde's? She was the picture of innocence, with her great gray eyes open wide, two glittering diamonds in her pale face. He preferred younger women to the more jaded type found in some places. His connoisseur's glance flickered over her Titian curls, a small straight nose, little rosebud mouth puckered in consternation. It must be the brandy he'd drunk that made her appear so ravishing.

As he looked, a tip of pink tongue peeped out and touched her lips. This teasing gesture sent a sudden throb of desire through him. His gaze lingered on her open bodice. The breasts, he could see, were not generous but they were well-shaped, high and firm. He felt an urge to cup their softness in his palms, to bury his face in them and inhale her beauty. He wanted to trace the flow of that lithe young body with his hands. His desire heightened with anticipation. It had been too long since he'd had a woman—any woman—and now to be confronted with this startling vision of beauty . . .

"You shouldn't be here, John," Flora said in a light, childish voice, but with the husky undertones of a courtesan arousing ardor in her customer. The way she used her eyes too—how long had this girl been in the business? She didn't look a day over sixteen, yet she had all the tricks down. Shy glances from beneath those mile-long lashes, a little pout on the lips. Wanton encouragement on one hand, tempered by a show of resistance. He noticed how she coyly folded the gown over her breasts, then allowed it to fall open as if by accident. She knew that men liked to conquer their women.

He sat on the edge of the bed and reached for her fingers, which didn't pull away but clutched his in a feverish grip. "There's nowhere I'd rather be," he said huskily. His dark eyes caressed her till she felt weak. "I knew as soon as I saw you that you were the one."

A shy smile trembled on her lips. "I felt

that way too," she admitted. So many strange things were happening that Flora could no longer tell what was real and what a dream.

Obviously this was a dream. The man from Mama's sugared-cherry tin couldn't be here, holding her hands. She felt a quivering stir of excitement deep within her. Some madness was upon her. The very touch of John's fingers burned her flesh like a flame. Yet it was a flame she had no wish to extinguish. She yearned to feel the fire over her whole body. She felt intimations of it as his dark eyes caressed her. Her skin tingled in response.

As if reading her mind, John lifted his hand and pulled aside the satin peignoir. His hand, a long-fingered, artistic hand, downed with black hair, cupped one bosom and squeezed gently. "You're very beautiful, Flora," he said, gazing as if hypnotized. Echoes of his voice hovered in the still air around her.

"Don't!" she exclaimed with a show of real concern, but when he left his fingers on her breast, she didn't mention it again.

"What are you doing in a place like this?" he asked.

Her eyes felt compelled to go on staring into his, till she felt as if she were drowning in their black depths. "Mother Hyde said I could work for her. She's very kind," she answered.

"I'm glad she takes good care of you." As he spoke, his head descended slowly. His hot lips on the sensitive crook of her neck sent goosebumps racing up her arms. His crisp hair brushed her chin, the sensation magnified to a preternatural height.

His body leaned on hers, pressing her against the pile of cushions. A pleasant scent of soap and spice came from him. His two hands grasped her breasts now, gently squeezing. Where was the outrage she ought to feel? She felt only a writhing fire at her vital core. Her hands rose and touched his black hair, tentatively, diffidently, as though afraid he would vanish.

"John," she breathed, soft as a sigh.

She felt his thumbs graze her nipples, puckering them to hardness. Then reluctantly she murmured, "Don't." A low laugh echoed from below her chin. "Please, don't do that," she begged.

"That 'don't' sounds very much like 'do'!" he teased. "You're very good, Flora, my love, but I'm consumed with passion tonight. Don't overtax my patience."

Consumed with passion. It was exactly how she felt, as though flames were eating her from within. "Oh, John," she murmured, low in her throat, and her fingers found their way into his thick black hair again.

John lifted his head and studied her for a long moment, silently, his black eyes burning into hers, as though to memorize this enchanting creature. He wanted to take this image to war with him, to lighten the long hours, but the brandy kept fuzzing her outlines. It gave rise to a blistering hot passion too. His lips seized hers and he began kissing her with ruthless mastery. His strong arms molded her soft body to the wall of his chest. Her lips trembled under his, till he firmed them with a brutal pressure.

A low moan of pain, or pleasure, caught in her throat, echoed in his ears, increasing his ardor. His arms held her so tightly now she could hardly breathe. While one arm crushed her against him, the other hand hovered on her shoulder, brushed up the side of her throat with infinite tenderness, till she felt enchanted, cherished. She wanted to see this man whose touch set her aflame.

She pulled back and gazed at him with eyes hardly focused. A soft tremble moved her lips. Yes, it really was her hero, come to life. "It's really you," she whispered.

John's heart thudded against his chest with a painful pressure, and his urgency swelled. "Of course it's me. I wanted you the moment I laid eyes on you. You're even more beautiful than I thought," he said hoarsely, and kissed her again.

The rough moistness of his tongue pressed at her lips. Shocked, she opened her mouth to object, and was astonished to feel his tongue glide slowly, surely into her mouth, gently at first, but soon taking complete possession. He was probing, stroking her tongue with his in engrossing intimacy, mating ecstatically with it in a ritual of conquest, till she felt herself melting to warm butter under his accomplished assault.

All these new sensations fueled the fever at her vital core, till a raging need caused her to stir in his arms. She couldn't lie still. She wanted something from him, but in her innocence she didn't know what it was. She only knew she felt an aching, wordless void deep within her. She wanted him, wholly, totally, and if she didn't have him soon, she would burn up, be consumed by the passion. Her hips began moving from side to side, rhythmically at first, but soon she was writhing in her desperate need for fulfillment.

John lifted his head and glanced at her in happy surprise. The girl was eager! "This is going to be good," he promised.

He pushed her back against the pillows and hastily began stripping off his clothing—the cravat, then the jacket, the waistcoat, while Flora gazed at him silently from under her drooping eyelids. She admired his broad shoulders beneath the tautly pulled shirt front. He began unbuttoning his shirt, and she stared at his lean stomach, board flat, ridged with hard muscles. She watched as he quickly pulled off his shirt and stood before her, naked to the waist. His shoulders gleamed palely in the lamplight, and on his chest a mat of dark hair curled. How beautiful a man's naked body was.

The sight increased that fiery need deep within her. She moved her hips seductively as his dark eyes burned into her. The negligee fell open, revealing her slender legs and the swell of one hip. The movement calmed her need for a moment, but in the end it had the strange effect of increasing it. A hot pulsing at the center of her femininity escalated to an aching throb. John's eyes lowered to the open peignoir and gazed. She saw a muscle working in his jaw, saw the glitter in his eyes, and smiled vaguely. Was he feeling this thing, this wordless need too?

As they stared at each other, John removed his trousers and underwear together. Flora felt the warmth of a crimson blush stain her cheeks, then her eyes lowered to study him. That erect, throbbing part of his body, nestled in black curled hair, made her breathless. It was horrible and wonderful all at once, but mostly she couldn't stop gazing at it. That was how she felt—throbbing, quivering, pulsing.

"Stand up," he said.

She knew she couldn't do it. She just lay there looking at him, her lips slightly open, her eyes glazed with desire. "You lazy wanton!" John laughed, and grabbed her hands to pull her to her feet.

His hands slid possessively under the negligee and removed it from her shoulders. She stood before him, a pale, slender form in the flickering light. She shyly raised her hands to cover her breasts. John pulled her hands aside.

"I want to see all of you. You have nothing to hide, Flora. You're beautiful all over. Very beautiful," he said in a voice of wonder. His eyes wandered over her pale body, lingering at her breasts, skimming lower to where a tuft of hair hid her more private parts. "Exquisite," he whispered, and lifting one bosom, he touched it with his lips. Was it satin, or velvet? Irresistibly sweet in any case.

Her nipples puckered at his touch. She had always thought that the naked body was something to be ashamed of, but if this fine gentleman said it was beautiful, then she could be proud. She lifted her chin and smiled.

He pulled her into his arms and their bodies touched in a silken caress from head to toe. His skin was smooth and warm, but the patch of hair prickled her breasts. It was all a mixture of heightened, contradictory sensations. Smooth but rough, soft skin with hard muscles below. Tender, yet forceful as his arms crushed her against his nakedness and his lips plundered hers till she felt she was drowning in quicksilver.

The fever continued building till her breath came in short gasps, and her body demanded satisfaction. She rubbed her breasts against his chest, marveling again at the silken smoothness of touching flesh and the prickle of hair. John crushed her against him, his hands taking her measure down the sides of her body. Their legs brushed, and she slid her knee between his legs, where he held it tightly. She felt the throbbing heat of his need pressing against her abdomen, beating like a heart.

When she thought she could no longer stand it, he said, "What are we waiting for?" She was stunned that he spoke in such an ordinary voice. The moment seemed sacred.

He scooped her into his arms and threw her lightly on the bed. In an instant he pounced down beside her, his dark head hovering above hers on the pillow. At this close range, she could see the individual hairs of his eyelashes, the pupils of his eyes, which looked very large. She could even see the pores in his skin.

"You're a sorceress, Flora. I won't last a minute the first time," he murmured.

His warm breath fanned her cheek. She stared into his darkly glittering eyes, then at his sculptured, full lips with a little laugh line at either side. Some vestige of decorum was activated when he took her hand and placed it on his throbbing member. She pulled away, a shadow of fear darkening her eyes. "No!" she gasped.

He laughed playfully and drew her hand back. He held it there with his own. "Don't," she said, and tried once more to free herself.

He thought it was all part of the game. "You really are good," he said approvingly. "But don't pretend you don't want me. And I want you—now." He straddled her and held her there beneath him, looking at the pretty little face that looked back at him. There was a question in her eyes—perhaps even a touch of fear. How dark her eyes were—all pupil.

"You—want me?" she asked, frowning. The fevered heat inside her pulsed in response to him.

"I won't hurt you," he said to assauge her fear. "It'll be good. You'll see."

His hand moved between her thighs, stroking softly, moving higher by slow, tantalizing degrees, till she didn't know whether she was being loved or tortured. His fingers found out her privacy and began moving feverishly. She felt a moistness there. Flora lay helpless, her mind suddenly so fogged she couldn't understand what was happening. Her breaths came in light, panting gasps. She felt she would suffocate from the pressure that was building in her. She began moving, thinking first to move out of the way of those magical fingers that excited her to frenzy, then she found herself moving closer, responding to every touch, pressing against him, squirming and writhing in an uncontrollable frenzy, while whimpering sounds echoed around her.

Soon John lowered the weight of his whole body on her. The fire that was in her flared to an inferno. She felt her arms go around him, flutter over his broad shoulders, then sink to his waist. She clutched him to her, but it wasn't enough. There was an aching, empty need, quivering, driving her on.

"Oh John, John," she gasped. "Help me. I can't bear it. I want . . . I need. Oh John, John." It was a delirium in the blood, a madness driving her beyond reason. Her fingernails dug into his back. She clawed wildly, thrusting herself against him, arching her body up against his, as though to devour him.

"Easy, my darling."

But she couldn't wait. It must happen now —now! Her whole body twitched uncontrollably as he entered her. There was a sharp, painful sting, then a moment's release before he plunged deeper. "Ouch!" she cried, but it was muffled against his shoulder.

Then it began again, the driving madness as they moved together, the rhythm increasing, lips pressing harder. And still it wasn't enough. It wasn't hard enough, fast enough. "John, please. For God's sake."

His hands clutched her to him, grazed down her hips, gathered the soft flesh of her buttocks tightly as their bodies, damp with perspiration, never broke the escalating, irresistible rhythm. He held her still tighter till she couldn't tell where her own body stopped and his began—it was all one with the movement and the throbbing of a jungle drum inside her head. Something unexplainable, blissful, something out of time was occurring as they went on, moving together in the bed, till it finally reached a suddering crescendo of ecstatic release that was like a burst of fireworks inside her head, leaving her limp and panting. John's head dropped beside hers on the pillow. He rolled over and heaved a deep sigh.

Flora lay a moment, gasping. It was better now. It was all right. The aching need was satisfied. The whirling room began to settle down. John reached out and patted her derriere. "I told you it'd be good," he said contentedly. "Next time it'll be even better. Give me half an hour. Shall we have some wine?"

Next time? She shook away the wisps of confusion. What had happened here? What had he done?

When Flora didn't answer, he reached out and touched her. She lay so still he thought she had fallen asleep. But a body asleep was soft. She felt rigid. "Flora, are you all right?" he asked, and lifted himself on his elbows to look at her.

He saw her large eyes staring at him from a white, pinched face. "Who are you?" she demanded fiercely.

"The game's over, my little hellcat. Just be gentle now. I don't feel like fighting." But as he looked, he saw that she was even paler than before. She was trembling.

A rumble began shaking her inside. "I'm going to be sick!" she croaked, and pulled the sheets aside to flee to the water closet behind the curtains. John heard the sounds of retching and wondered if he should go to help her. She must have had too much wine. She'd probably prefer to be alone. He glanced to where she had thrown back the covers and saw a few drops of blood on the sheets. Blood! Good God, was the girl a virgin? Mother Hyde should have told him. He had no taste for deflowering virgins.

She certainly hadn't seemed inexperienced. The girl was a wildcat in bed. She had given that little yelp when he penetrated her, but a well-schooled whore continued that act for years. He had had some difficulty entering her, but the way she was thrashing around . . . a virgin wouldn't be that hot. Women did bleed for other reasons.

John was thirsty, but he knew that a girl who had just cast up her accounts wouldn't want wine. He pulled the rope, wrapped himself in a sheet, and when a servant came to the door, he asked for a pot of tea. Then he went to the curtain and called, "Are you all right, Flora?"

A small voice called back, "Go away!"

She heard a light chuckle. "Not bloody likely! I'm staying the night. I'll do better next time. I've ordered tea. It'll make you feel better."

"I said go away!" Her voice was higher, edged with panic.

Behind the curtain, Flora looked into a mirror over the washstand and wished she were dead. The brandy and Mother Hyde's draft had been spewed out, leaving her weak and in a cold sweat. She looked like a death mask, her dark eyes sunk in her head. What had she done? She must have been intoxicated. She shouldn't have had that second glass of wine. She only had one at home ever, and that was usually watered. Her bare shoulders in the mirror reminded her of her nakedness. That man—John—was still out there, and she didn't have a stitch of clothing to put on.

Worried by the silence, he called "Flora?" again.

"Bring my gown, please," she called, more quietly now.

He brought the satin peignoir and handed it behind the curtain. Flora wrapped it around her. The cool satin didn't feel so good now. She was trembling. But it wasn't only with the cold. She was ruined. After all her mother's careful warnings, she had been ruined her first night in London. How had it happened? She could hardly remember what that man looked like. A glitter of dark eyes fluttered in her memory, a flashing smile— then a pair of naked shoulders, a mat of curly hair, and that other pulsing thing . . .

No, it must be a dream. But the stinging pain between her legs was real enough, and the lingering warmth of semen. Oh Lord, what if she was pregnant? And she didn't even know the man's name. Just John. She was quite sure his name was John.

She heard the tea arrive, heard John pacing the room and finally pushed the curtain aside. He had wrapped himself in a sheet and looked like a Roman senator. He looked arrogant and noble. Those dark eyes were as she remembered. The naked shoulders too. But she saw no attraction in him now. He was the embodiment of her downfall. He was a rapacious man who had barged in and taken advantage of an intoxicated girl. Why had he done it? How could she explain to Mrs. Hyde? Mother Hyde, who was so kind.

She must find out who he was and have him arrested. She timidly drew back the curtain. John turned and smiled at her. "Feeling better, Flora?" he asked.

He looked like such a nice man when he smiled. How could he smile after what he had done? "No, I feel awful."

"I think you had too much wine. I'm a little bosky myself, but in an hour—"

"What's your name?" she asked stiffly.

"John."

"John what?"

"What does it matter? We'll probably never meet again," he said, rather wistfully. "I'm leaving for the Peninsula tomorrow. I came here tonight to celebrate."

"Going to the Peninsula!" she gasped. How could he be made to pay if he were in another country, Portugal or Spain, miles away? Maybe even dead before long. "You can't!"

He reached out and touched her hair. "You make me wish I could stay," he said gently, "but my ship leaves tomorrow." He noticed her glazed stare. "What's the matter, Flora? Have you fallen in love with me?" he asked archly.

"In love? I hate you. I hope you get killed in the Peninsula! How dare you—" Her voice broke, and tears began to run slowly down her cheeks.

He gave her a disgusted look and picked up his trousers. "I came here to be entertained, not to see a Cheltenham tragedy. Next you'll be telling me you never had a man before."

"I didn't!"

"Then what are you doing, posing as a whore in a cathouse?" he asked nonchalantly over his shoulder. "It seemed to me you knew what you were doing."

Flora didn't answer. She just stood staring, trying to make sense of what he had said. A whore! That's what he took her for. What would a whore be doing at Mother Hyde's? At this place where everyone was so nice? But she remembered that even in the cafe, it was women who sat alone, and men who approached them. The women wore those immodest gowns, advertising their bodies. Words and pictures began flashing back to terrify her. "You're going to entertain a gentleman. Be nice to him and he may do something for you." The white satin gown, arranged to fall open at the slightest movement. A whore's gown. Mother Hyde ran a brothel!

Flora's cheeks burned with shame. She turned her head aside. She didn't want to have to look at John, and didn't want him to see her. He finished dressing and went toward the door. "I left you something extra. Thanks, Flora. Maybe we'll meet again after the war."

Then the door closed, and she was alone with her thoughts, and regrets. She walked toward the bed. He had left a guinea on the bedside table. A guinea, in exchange for her virtue. Yes, she really did hope he was shot in the Peninsula, or drowned on the way there, so that the one person who knew her shame should cease to exist. ▪

4

She must escape! She couldn't tackle Mother Hyde alone, but with the Leadbeaters' help, this wicked placed would be closed down and Mother Hyde put in jail before she ruined any other innocent girls. Ruined! The word ran through her mind, trailing a dozen stories of betrayed women doomed to a life of degradation.

What had happened to her? What madness was in her body to have made her assist at her own ruination? Surely a few glasses of wine didn't turn a girl into an animal. Sal had mentioned brandy . . . And that last "sleeping draft"—it had tasted bitter. She still felt ill from its effects. She looked for her clothing, but it was gone from the room. She had nothing to wear. Naked, and in a state of terror, Flora sat on the edge of the bed and cried.

Eventually her eyes closed and she fell into

a troubled sleep, which brought a phantas-
magoria of evil visions—men that turned into
monsters, witches forcing foul brews down
her throat while she lay helpless. There was
blood in the dream too. John lay on a ship
deck with his chest blown open. Someone
threw him overboard, and she watched his
body sink slowly into the green, rolling
ocean, staining it with his blood. A guinea
was thrown on top of his sinking body. When
she awoke, the sun was shining through the
open drapes.

With clear, disillusioned eyes, Flora saw
the room for what it was—a garish, tawdry
room where whores entertained their
customers. Her eyes turned to the night
table. The guinea was gone—stolen by
Mother Hyde or someone. Her head ached
violently, and she was so thirsty she wanted
to drink a gallon of water. She poured a cup
of the cold tea from the night before and
drank it without milk or sugar. It made her
feel a little better physically, but with
physical ease came an overwhelming
realization of her predicament.

Before she put the cup down, the door
opened and Mother Hyde entered. By the
light of day, Flora saw that the woman was as
vulgar and gaudy as the room. Her black hair
must have been dyed, for her face was lined,
with deep crowsfeet at the corners of her
crafty black eyes.

Anger and desperation lent courage to
Flora. She had nothing more to lose. "I'm

going to the police and have you arrested," she announced firmly.

The woman gave an oily smile and sat on the edge of the bed. "Now, it wasn't so bad, was it, dearie? The gentleman seemed very nice to me."

"Where are my clothes?"

"I gave them to the poorhouse. I don't dress my girls in fustian. Sal will bring you a nice silk gown with ribbons and lace. White's your color, dearie."

"White is for virgins," Flora said in a cold, hard voice. She felt she had aged a dozen years in one night. Her youth had been stolen away from her, leaving her embittered.

"You're not that any longer, are you, Miss Sommers? My, what would the Leadbeaters say if I had to tell them what you was up to last night? Do you think they'd let the likes of you into their house, or recommend you to friends with young children to be tended? Oh my no! A girl's honor is like a bubble. Once it's been burst, it's gone forever."

Flora felt crushed at the truth of this, but her temper flared at the smirking old woman who sat calmly pleating her skirt. Flora lifted the tea cup and threw the remains of the tea in her face. "You witch! You won't get away with this!"

Mother Hyde's black eyes snapped, but she controlled the impulse to smack the girl across the face. "Temper, temper, dearie. You're a whore now, like it or not, so you might as well make the best of it. My house is

better than peddling your wares on the
street. You asked me if you could work here.
Why, you saw yourself last night how happy
my girls are. You mentioned it in particular.
There's worse places you could be than
Mother Hyde's house."

"I want my clothes—and my guinea!" Flora
said.

Mother Hyde pulled her bulky frame up
from the bed and straightened her skirts.
"And you shall have them, Miss Sommers.
You have the soul of a whore—wanting your
pay for your services. I'll have your things
brought in, but you think over what I said.
What's done is done, and spite don't butter
any parsnips. If you haul me into court, you'll
have to go too, and advertise your shame to
the world." She cast a triumphant sneer at
the dejected girl on the bed. "I pay my girls
well," she said, and left the room.

"The soul of a whore." Flora didn't want
that guinea. She just didn't want Mother
Hyde to have it, but she wouldn't accept it.
She'd throw it away sooner than put it in her
pocket. And she'd pay for last night's dinner
too.

It was a quarter of an hour before Sal came
tapping at the door. She came in carrying
Flora's clothing, the guinea, and a tray of
breakfast. For this occasion, Mother Hyde
had loaded on gammon and eggs, things not
usually served. "How are you today, Flora?"
Sal asked, with a laughing eye. "You look as

awful as I felt after my first taste of Hyde's Hellpot."

Flora turned an accusing eye on the girl. "You helped her!" Flora said. "Why did you do it? What have I ever done to you?"

"Oh, Flora, don't take it that way," Sal begged. Tears formed in her eyes. "I was trying to help you. You don't know what it's like out there on the streets at night. If I'd let you go out that door alone, you'd be in worse shape than this today. Girls get kilt and robbed and beaten and worse. Mother Hyde looks after us. Didn't you care for the gentleman you had? He seemed very handsome to me."

"What did you give me to drink?"

"It's some black powder Mother Hyde buys. It makes you want a man so bad, doesn't it? Nearly drives you up a tree. Lud, you should have seen me attack the old codger I had my first time. She only uses it if the girls are skittish," Sal added leniently.

Flora took the guinea and looked at it. "I don't want this," she said. "Here, you can have it. And I'll pay for last night's dinner too —as much as I can." She emptied every penny from her purse and handed it over to Sal.

Sal pocketed the money, blinking in surprise. "You earned it fair and square," she pointed out.

"I will not accept money for—that."

"What else have the likes of us got to sell?"

Sal asked.

Flora took her clothes and turned her back before putting them on. Sal watched her silently. She liked Miss Sommers. She hoped she'd stay, and turned her wiles to this purpose. "Where can you go, Flora? Mother Hyde will tell the Leadbeaters what happened. Don't think she won't."

"She'll be thrown in jail if she does."

"Oh no, you asked if you could work for her." Flora gave her a scathing look. "All she did was offer you a room and introduce you to the gentleman. That's not against the law. He didn't force you, did he?"

"No."

"Then what's the crime? And think of your mama, Flora!"

Though Sal didn't realize it, this was the most powerful argument she could have used. Flora dreaded to have her mother learn what had befallen her. Not that her mother would accuse. Worse, she'd blame herself. No, she couldn't tell her mother, and that meant not telling the Leadbeaters either. She must find some position on her own and write home as though all had gone well.

She'd worry about the Leadbeaters later. They weren't so eager that they'd be looking for her. But whatever position she found, it certainly wouldn't be as a whore. Her cheeks still flamed to remember that word on John's uncaring lips. Worse, she had acted like one.

"Leave me alone, Sal," she ordered. The girl smiled and left. Flora ate the breakfast.

She had earned it, and heaven knew when she would have another meal. This done, she went quietly into the hallway. Her blue pelisse was on the coat rack. She took it and the shawl, which she put around her head, then went quietly out into the street.

Long Acre by day was only slightly less unappealing than by night. The streets were narrow, dirty, peopled with groups of ruffians. She ran as fast as her legs would carry her till she had run far enough to be out of that district, then slowed to a walk. She stopped the first decent-looking woman she met and asked directions to an employment agency.

The woman looked at Flora's flushed face and ill-fitting pelisse. "People who can afford servants don't hire the likes of you," she said rudely and walked on.

Flora bit back the retort that sprang to her tongue. Fighting with strangers would do no good. The woman was probably right. Very well then, she'd lower her sights. Inns hired serving girls. She walked till she came to one. It was a small, dingy tavern called the Castle Arms. She went around to the back door and tapped before entering. The man who answered it glared and said, "What do you want? Go away, girlie."

"Please, I want to work. I won't charge much."

"What kind of work do you do?"

"I can cook, or clean. I'll do anything."

A lascivious light gleamed in his rheumy

eye, and his eyes examined her in an insultingly blatant way. He reached out and pulled back her pelisse. "Anything?" he asked hopefully.

She pulled her coat from his fingers and fled out the door. For the remainder of the morning she went from place to place. Any establishment that was even slightly respectable wanted experience and references. It was only at the others that she elicited any interest. It seemed that the only work open to a girl in London was the sort Mother Hyde provided.

By afternoon Flora was dog tired. She had no idea where she was, and she was weak with hunger. Even the slop cooking in the worst inns smelled good. But still she plodded on, looking for work, any work. As the shadows of evening fell, she walked more quickly, with no destination in mind, but only wanting to get away from where she was.

When darkness began to fall, she was desperate. She looked up at a sign and saw the familiar St. Martin's Lane. She'd been here last night, at about this same time. But last night she had had a little money in her pocket. The hunger was gnawing at her vitals. Now it was growing dark, and she had no money and nowhere to go.

She blinked back a tear and kept on walking. It was just half a block up St. Martin's Lane that the two bucks out for mischief accosted her. They came at her from behind, each grabbing her by an elbow and lifting her feet from the ground, carrying her along as easily as if she were a rag doll. "Where do we take her, Mick, your place or mine?" one asked, laughing.

"What, take this trollop home to Mama? We'll have her in the alley."

Flora didn't know whether they were serious or only having a joke at her expense. Sal's warning came back to haunt her. The streets were dangerous, she said. Men might rob or beat you or worse—even kill you. She opened her lips and with the last of her strength let out a howl of protest. The bucks dropped her, exchanged a startled look, and burst into laughter.

Flora took to her heels and ran as if her life depended on it. But this time she knew where she was going. Mother Hyde's was back a block and down an alley. It was a horrible place, but it was at least a known evil. There were worse places a girl could end up.

5

"So you're back," Mother Hyde exclaimed when Flora was taken to her. She hadn't been very worried that the chit would make trouble, but she was relieved all the same, and was ready to treat Flora fairly in spite of that cup of tea in the face. She liked a girl with spirit. "I thought you'd come to your senses. Have you had dinner?"

"No, ma'am," Flora said meekly. She didn't volunteer that she hadn't had lunch either.

"Sit down and eat, then, and we'll talk after. Come to my office. Sal will show you the way."

With a satisfied smile, Mother Hyde strode off to welcome new arrivals, and Flora sat at the same small table she'd occupied the night before. Again it was Sal who served her. "I'm glad you came back," Sal said, smiling as she set the steaming plate on the table. "Did you go to your cousin?"

"I decided not to," Flora said briefly. The aroma of roast beef made her weak with hunger. Without further conversation, she dug in and cleaned her plate, oblivious to lumpy gravy and wet potatoes. No wine was offered this time, nor did she want any, but the food gave her courage. While she ate, she made plans, and when she had finished, she felt strong enough to take on Mother Hyde on her own terms.

Sal directed her to the office. Flora couldn't remember going out through the back of the restaurant last night into the private house beyond. This time she knew she would be staying here—for a while at least—and got her bearings. Sal took her down a dark passage into a front hall, carpeted in red with a chandelier overhead. There was dust on the furnishings, and the carpet was spotted. The air was rancid with the smell of tobacco and food and human sweat.

"Mother Hyde's office is in here," Sal said, and knocked on a dark oaken door just off the lobby. Without waiting for a reply, Sal opened the door and the girls went in.

Mother Hyde looked up, her eyes snapping angrily. "You know you're not to come in here till I tell you!" As she spoke, her fat, white hand moved across a desk surface, scooping golden coins into a tin box. She closed the lid with a snap, put it into a drawer and locked it.

Flora looked around the office and was struck with the opulence of the place. It was

all done in the worst of taste, but money had
been spent—a lot of money. Mother Hyde
liked that bright royal blue. Her drapes were
blue, the red carpet was sprinkled with blue
flowers, and the satin sofa against one wall
was blue, striped with gold. Rather than
relieving the strong colors with something
pale, she had chosen gaudy ornaments in red
and gold. There were large urns holding
dried flowers, various vases and bibelots,
and over the desk a huge portrait of a nude
woman lying down. Flora stared at it, dis-
cerning a resemblance to the harridan
behind the desk. Good gracious, it was a
painting of Mother Hyde, done years ago
when she was young and rather pretty.

"Run along, Sal," Mother Hyde directed.
She nodded to Flora to have a seat. "I'm glad
you've come to your senses. Now let's talk
business. I'll give you the same salary I give
all my newcomers. A guinea a week, plus
your room and board. Mornings you clean or
work in the kitchen, every second afternoon
you're free—afternoon business is light—and
evenings you're a hostess, seven days a
week." But hostess, Flora knew, meant
whore. She realized that Mother Hyde hadn't
accumulated that pile of gold by paying her
girls a large part of what they earned, but
that wasn't her concern at the moment.

"I have a different suggestion," Flora said.
"I'll work any hours you want cooking or
cleaning, but I won't be a—hostess."

Mother Hyde gave a sneering laugh.

"That's the business I'm in, Miss Sommers. I have all the free maids and cooks I need. You work under my terms or you don't work here. Go back to the streets. You've had a taste of them, and come back with your tail between your legs. You're a pretty thing. I'll relieve you of the morning work. Most of my girls don't get that privilege till they've proven themselves."

Flora's insides were knotted in fear, but she lifted her chin at a pugnacious angle. She took a breath, clenched her hands into fists in her lap and said bravely, "No."

"Two guineas a week then," Mother Hyde bargained. Mr. Smith had been highly pleased with Flora the night before. Hadn't he come prancing back that afternoon, looking for her again? He was very put out to hear she wasn't in. In fact, the man had appeared downright suspicious. Mother Hyde was glad to hear he was leaving the country that same day.

Flora began rising to her feet. She had no idea where she'd go or what she'd do, but she knew she wouldn't sell herself, even for two guineas a week, which sounded like a fortune to her. "We have nothing more to discuss," she said with simple dignity.

The fat white hand fluttered toward the chair. "Stay," the old lady ordered. She knew that Flora had some quality her other wenches lacked. She wouldn't have called it "breeding," but the word "class" came to mind. The girl would soon tire of scrubbing and laundering. Inside of a week she'd be begging for a customer. Let her hang around, then. "Do you cook?" she asked.

"Yes, and I could run a house better than you run this one." As she spoke, Flora put out a finger and wiped it along the desk surface. It came away coated with dust.

Mother Hyde felt an urge to laugh at the prissy little face before her. By God, she did like this strange creature. "We could use someone with a little management, especially in the kitchen," she admitted. "I swear Maggie McMahon burns more meat than she serves. All right, Miss Sommers, I'll give you a try. Go down to the kitchen and tell Maggie I sent you. After you've finished there, she'll show you to a room."

"Thank you, Mrs. Hyde."

"My girls all call me Mother."

"I'm not one of your girls. I'm kitchen help." Mother Hyde's black eyes glittered dangerously, but her smile was still in place when she raised her hand and waved Flora out.

Flora gently closed the door behind her and exhaled a great sigh of relief. Her knees were shaking and her heart was knocking against her ribs. She didn't know what she would have done if Mrs. Hyde had refused her terms. She looked around and saw a dark staircase, presumably leading to the kitchen. She hurried down it and opened a door into a bright, hot room of incredible confusion. A table eight feet long was piled high with dirty dishes. A slatternly woman was bent over the stove, her hair hanging in her eyes as she lifted a roast of mutton from the oven. It was burned very dark and appeared quite dry. The woman looked up when Flora entered.

"Who would ye be, then?" the slattern asked in a voice touched with a lilting Irish brogue.

"I'm Miss Sommers, and I'm here to help you, if you're Miss McMahon."

"Mrs. McMahon, missie. You're a new face in this hell hole, I think. Come over and let me get a look at you."

Flora picked her way around the assortment of pots and pans littering the floor. When she saw a gray cat licking one, she felt ill to remember she'd eaten food from this kitchen. She turned her eyes to her new mistress, a woman of about forty-five who took no concern for her appearance. Her hair was an indeterminate rusty-gray, thick with grease and hanging lank along her face. She wore a blue dimity gown and an apron that had probably been white once upon a time. At the moment it was grimed with grease and gravy and vegetables of various hues.

"You're a tiny slip of a thing. Do you know anything about running a kitchen?"

Flora looked at the disaster around her. "More than you do, from the looks of this mess," she replied bluntly.

"Good, then you can come and give me a hand with this mutton. A wee drap of gravy might bring it back to life."

A blast of heat emanated from the stove. "You're fire's too hot," Flora ventured.

"It's always too hot or too cold," Maggie grumbled.

Flora reached for the handle of the flue. "You can adjust the draft this way," she pointed out, giving it half a turn.

"Mercy! Fancy you knowing that. Do you know how to make gravy as well?"

"Yes, if there are any drippings in the pan," Flora replied. The drippings were nearly all burned and stuck to the bottom, but she removed the mutton and poured water into the pan from the boiling kettle. "Where do you keep the flour?"

Maggie floundered around the counter and brought the flour. She watched as Flora prepared the gravy, magically achieving a lumpless brown sauce in two minutes. It even tasted good. Maggie sliced the mutton, and as she was finishing, a boy came to the kitchen to carry the food off to the restaurant. There were other orders to be filled. The food was prepared in large quantities and taken to the restaurant kitchen by a group of youngsters hired for the purpose. They boiled peas and peeled carrots, sliced bread, and made endless pots of coffee and tea.

In two hours the orders had ceased coming in, and the two women sat at the table, exhausted, but already friends. "I'll make us a spot of tea," Maggie said. Flora got cups and milk and together they sipped slowly, letting their feet and legs rest after their Herculean effort.

"Why ain't you upstairs at this hour?" Maggie asked.

"I don't work upstairs. I'm kitchen help," Flora said proudly.

Maggie examined the little face, still pretty in its flushed and disheveled condition. It was the eyes that set it apart—intelligent eyes, and spirited too. "You mean she hired you to help me? Don't you believe it, Miss Sommers. She has her eye on you for a hostess."

"She's wasting her time. I won't do it."

"It's a living," Maggie said tolerantly. "I did it for ten years, till I lost my looks. So did Bonnie—that's Mother Hyde. She was Bonnie Banyon in those days. Quite a lively one. She got a half-pay officer to marry her, and when he ran off on her, she sold up his furniture and opened this place. She was always tight as bark to a tree, but she's got worse lately. Greedy! I don't know why she wants money so badly, unless it's for that young Jack Dandy she keeps hanging around."

A surprised laugh escaped Flora's lips. "You mean she has a beau!"

"If you can call him that. He only comes when he wants something from her. His name's Mark Dryden. She calls him her business manager—French for paramour. He brings gentlemen friends in—it's an excuse for her to give him a commission. She charges a guinea an hour for most of the girls. Elsie and Rose get two. They're our prima donnas, the sluts."

She noticed Flora's shocked expression at this plain speaking. Maggie admitted she had fallen into rough talk since coming here. She used to be nicer.

"Is Mrs. Hyde rich?" Flora asked, remembering that box of gold coins.

"She's been raking in the blunt for fifteen years. She must be worth fifty thousand pounds if she's worth a penny."

"That much!" Flora gasped.

"It'd be more if she knew how to hang on to it. Bonnie's a fool with her money. She gives a lot to Dryden, and gambles it away on business ventures that haven't a hope of succeeding. But she's worried about her old age now. The gambling's tapered off."

Flora listened, taking an interest in these people who would be her daily companions till she had enough money to leave. When the tea was done, she cast an disheartened eye at the table full of dirty dishes.

"The boys do them," Maggie told her. "I'll leave the rest of the mess till morning." As she spoke, she rose to leave, scooping the gray cat up in her arms and putting him out the door. "This fellow used to sleep in my room till I replaced him with a canary," she said.

"Shouldn't we cover the meat and put the perishable food in the cold pantry?" Flora asked.

"The girls come slipping down during the evening between customers and have a bite. There won't be much left by morning," Maggie laughed.

It went against the grain to walk away from such a scene of chaos, but Flora didn't feel up to tackling it that night. Her bones were weary from her tiring day. Her eyelids were sagging as she took her last look at the awful kitchen. Tomorrow she'd restore it to order. "Mrs. Hyde said you'd show me to a room," she said, and yawned behind her hand as they went upstairs.

"You can have the cubbyhole next to mine. You won't want to be in the main wing, listening to the carousing. Drinking and cursing and singing and playing the out-of-tune piano." Maggie stopped and opened a door for Flora. "The room isn't what you're used to, I daresay?" Maggie asked, with a curious light in her eye as she looked at the demure girl beside her. Almost a lady, to judge by her manners and speech. Maggie remembered with surprise that she'd been a lady herself once. She really should fix up her hair and take better care of herself.

"It will do just fine," Flora said. "Thank you, Mrs. McMahon. I'll see you tomorrow morning."

"Call me Maggie. Everyone does."

"My name's Flora."

"That's pretty. Good night, Flora."

Maggie smiled and went to enjoy a few moments with her canary before covering it for the night. Little Tweety had been her best friend the past few years. Flora rather reminded her of the bird, so delicate and pretty. Good-natured too—she'd be a regular ray of sunshine in this hell hole.

Flora went into her new room. It was extremely spartan and very cold. The only furnishings were a trundel bed with cotton sheets and a coarse blanket, and in the corner a dresser with the paint all chipped. A lick of paint would fix that. There was no carpet on the floor, no curtains at the window, only a bedspread hung on a string. But the place wasn't too dirty. She was so tired she hardly cared. At least it was a haven from the streets of London. She undressed quickly and got between the sheets wearing her petticoat. She thought sleep would come quickly, but as she lay on the pillowless bed, her mind was seething with pictures all whirling around in a storm.

She had made it to London, made it through one day and two evenings. She had found a job, and she had made a friend— Maggie McMahon was nice. Even Mama would like her, except of course that she was so terribly slatternly, and used to be a "hostess." Even mentally, Flora shied away from the blunter word, but her cheek still burned crimson to remember her shame.

Last night at this time she had been with John, acting like a wild animal. What must he have thought? As if she didn't know! And now John was on a ship, going to the Peninsula.

How strange life was. What incredible things happened to people in the city. Going off to war, and being seduced, and Mrs. Hyde making fifty thousand pounds by selling girls' bodies to men. She wouldn't stay in this place for more than a few weeks, just till she got her bearings.

It was cold aboard the *Gallant* as the ship edged its way through the Channel. A raw wind filled the sails and caused a worrying creak in the masts and rigging. As the white moon rose high in the black sky, most of the officers left the deck and went below to pass the evening at cards and drinking. John Beauchamp's head was still aching from last night's debauch. He remained above, enjoying the cold, clean air. There'd be plenty of heat in the Peninsula. At the prow, looking out toward the endless, heaving ocean, his thoughts flew forward to Spain. Had he been a fool to come? Life was pleasant and easy in England. Perhaps too easy. A man fell into bad habits.

His thoughts turned to the past, and he wandered toward the stern of the ship, looking back toward England. Life went on there without him. At home his uncle would be reading the journals. His friends would be out carousing and drinking. Somewhere on that black dot of island, a little redhead was entertaining some other gentleman, as she had entertained him last night. A stab of discontent goaded him at the thought. Such a pretty girl, and so young. A vision of her widely spaced eyes and coppery head had been in and out of his mind all day.

What was it about her that haunted him? Not just her eagerness—there were plenty of eager women around. No, it was her air of innocence, her remorse after the fact that intrigued him. The guilt that made her lash out at him. Somewhere deep inside that girl there lurked the remnants of a proper upbringing. How had someone like that ended up in a whorehouse, and at such a young age? She seemed more suited to be a man's wife.

He'd go back to Mother Hyde's and see if she was still there when he returned from the war. If he returned from the war . . . A stronger breeze blew across the water. John shivered into his coat and went below.

6

The next day Sal announced that she was pregnant.

"But what will happen to you?" Flora demanded, aghast at her friend's condition.

"Mother Hyde will pick out some well-inlaid gent as the father and dun him for money," Sal explained. "She sends the kids to a wet nurse in the country. She has a laying-in room on the third floor. She doesn't turn us out when we get preggers. But I'm not showing yet—I'll work another month or two. I just wanted you to know. I'm glad you're here, Flora. I haven't told the others. It's nice to have somebody I can talk to about it. I'm scared," she added. "I'd like to keep my baby—but not here."

The conversation took place in the kitchen after the evening rush was over. Maggie McMahon was there too, the pot of tea on the table between them. The clean, tidy kitchen bore evidence of its new mistress. In the space of one day, it had been tacitly established that Flora was in charge.

Maggie, with her hair neatly brushed and wearing a clean apron, reached out and patted Sal's hand. "We'll see you through, Sal. Never fear. You're not alone. You can't keep the kid here, but you can visit it in the country if you have it boarded nearby. Why, you could visit it every weekend. Flora and I will help make the nappies and gowns."

"I'm not staying here!" Flora objected.

There was an outburst of aggrieved regret, and many reminders of how hard life was on the streets. But in the end it was Sal's tears that convinced Flora to stay till after the child was delivered. It seemed the right, the Christian thing to do. And even as kitchen help, Mother Hyde was paying her a decent salary, more than half of which would be sent home to her mother. Kitchen help in a regular family home paid less than half that.

By slow degrees, Flora began to fit into her new life. She met the other "hostesses," and found them interesting. Other than the moral blind spot about their line of work, they were just ordinary girls. Not well-educated, but not mean either. Some of them even went to church with Flora on Sunday. Jennie White-head was the youngest. She reminded Flora of her sister Lily. Elsie and Rose, the prima donnas, didn't try to convince her to join the sorority of hostesses. Mother Hyde urged them to encourage Flora, but they suspected too much competition from that quarter. Besides, the food was so much better since Flora was in the kitchen.

Rose Darrow, nee Emma Frumm, was a proud beauty, but Elsie Pringle was likeable. She often talked to Flora with the hope of improving her grammar. "Lawks, I'm twenty-four, Flora, and hardly know my letters. I seen Mr. Laverty smirk last night when he asked me to read the newspaper to him and I could hardly stumble through the headline."

"Saw," Flora said. "I saw him smirk. I haven't time to teach you to read, but I'll help you with your grammar, if you like, Elsie."

"I'd like it ever so!"

"You'd like it very much," Flora corrected.

The rest of the house began to undergo a noticeable improvement as well. Things looked better. The rooms were always clean and tidy, and when the girls had a gripe, it was to the kitchen, to the youngest and smallest inhabitant, that they went for advice. Flora had established a subtle sway over Mother Hyde. She had learned that an appeal to her purse was the most successful appeal.

"Serve the girls meat for lunch when there are no gentlemen present?" Mother Hyde demanded hotly. "What do you think I'm made of, money? They have meat for dinner, and that's more than they'd have at home."

"But on tea and bread they become hagged in a hurry, Mrs. Hyde," Flora pointed out. "You don't want them falling ill on you. And only think if they should complain to their customers! It wouldn't be pleasant to have your hostess in a sulky mood. Why, the gentlemen would take into their heads to go somewhere else."

"You'll put me in the poorhouse," Mother Hyde grumbled, but the girls were given stew for lunch.

When Elsie fell ill, it was to Flora that she went for assistance. "I can't entertain anyone tonight, and that's a fact!" she said, thumping down on a chair at the table. "Mr. Jackson is asking for me, and Mother says I must see him but I ain't up to it."

"You're not up to it," Flora said automatically.

"That's what I said."

Elsie did look wretched tonight. Her blonde hair and fair complexion needed good health to look their best. She had circles under her eyes, and her cheeks were pale.

Flora ran up the now familiar staircase and went tapping at Mother Hyde's office door. "Elsie has fainted, Mrs. Hyde," she said, for exaggeration was sometimes required. "I'm putting her to bed with a posset. I hope it isn't contagious. You'd best keep the other girls away from her—because of the customers, you know. If word gets out you're spreading an infection, you'd have to shut down your business."

There wasn't a word of objection on that occasion. Mother Hyde knew that Flora was a cunning little rascal, but she knew she was often right too. The house was much better run now, and Flora was a demon for work. In any case, infection was Mother Hyde's bogey-man. Elsie went to bed and slept for two days, and returned to work refreshed.

When the time came for Sal's confinement, Flora was still there, still talking of leaving, but less frequently now. Sal's baby was a boy; she called him Johnnie, and grandly informed Flora she could be his aunt. He was staying with a wet nurse at Ilford, just north of London.

Flora had written home that she had found work as a cook for a wealthy lady. Mrs. Lead-beater never wrote to inquire of Mrs. Sommers what happened to Flora, and Mrs. Sommers never again wrote to her cousin. The letters to and from Bradbury were limited to one a month—franks cost money. Money was more plentiful at home now with Flora's addition, but every penny still counted. Mrs. Sommers hoped to be able to send her son to university.

After the baby was farmed out and Sal was back at work, Flora made one more bid for freedom. She went, neatly dressed, to answer several ads for kitchen help at prestigious homes, but always the lack of a character reference defeated her. In the end, she stayed on at Mother Hyde's, consoling herself that the money was good, and needed at home. It wasn't such a bad life. She had friends, and she was doing something useful.

Two years passed, and she became familiar with all the secrets of the place. Girls came and went, sometimes returning to the country to marry an old beau, sometimes being taken under the wing of a patron, set up as his mistress. These were the successful graduates. Rose, one of the prima donnas, got herself a baronet and had her own flat. She came back to visit, lording it over Elsie.

"You'd best look sharp for a gentleman too, Elsie," she said grandly. "You ain't as young as you used to be."

"Ain't?" Elsie asked, arching a dainty brow. "No, I'm not as young as some, but I'm younger than you, Rose. I ain—I'm not using rouge, at least."

Flora learned that when Mrs. Hyde's beau was visiting, she wasn't to go into the office unless rung for. Mark Dryden reminded her of the villain in a stage play. He wasn't ugly, but he managed to make a handsome face and body unattractive. His blond curls were as dainty as a lady's. He had pretty blue eyes that could turn to ice if you crossed him, and a nose as long and sharp as a razor. He was tall and thin and rather foppish in his dress. He took money from Mrs. Hyde, then insulted her for the way she made that money. And worst of all, after one of his visits, Mrs. Hyde invariably returned to the theme of Flora becoming a hostess. This had never quite died, but it was dormant.

One evening when he was visiting, Mrs. Hyde rang for dinner. Flora prepared the tray herself and took it up to the office, politely knocking before entering. Mr.

Dryden sat lounging on the sofa in an elegant black evening suit, his feet sticking out into the room, with a cheroot in his fingers. The office always smelled for days after one of his visits. Mrs. Hyde sat beside him.

Flora arranged the tray and turned to leave. "I see you're still using your prettiest girl as a waitress," Mr. Dryden said to Mother Hyde, but his pale eyes lingered on Flora's face, then slowly toured her body. She felt her flesh crawl when he looked at her like that, as though undressing her.

"Will there be anything else?" Flora asked coolly.

"I could bring you some really first-rate customers if you had more girls like Flora," he added. "We'd have a nabob's establishment, instead of this den." He looked around the ornate room with a disparaging eye. "If you must be an abbess, Bonnie, you could at least run an elegant house."

"I'm doing pretty well as it is," Mrs. Hyde remarked. Her attitude was apologetic, conciliatory. Why did she put up with this barnacle?

"You call this pretty well?" he sneered. "Last year we only made—"

"You can go now, Flora," Mrs. Hyde said rather quickly.

Flora was glad to escape, but she was curious enough to listen outside the door. "What has that girl got on you?" Dryden demanded.

"Nothing. Flora's too much help around

the kitchen to turn to other work. Besides, she refuses to do it. I've asked her a dozen times, Mark. Are you a little short of money, dear? Is that it? I could advance you a hundred, if that would help."

"I haven't had a new jacket in months," he sulked, like a little boy.

"I'll have the hundred next time you call. Will you come tomorrow evening?"

"Why don't you give it to me now, Bonnie?" he asked, and laughed a nasty, knowing laugh. "Afraid to let me know where you keep your gold? I'm not a thief, you know. I know you don't trust the banks. Is it here in this room?"

"Mark!" she exclaimed, and laughed. "As though I didn't trust you. I just want to make sure you come tomorrow night."

"I'll be here at seven. I could use a hundred and fifty. I lost a little at the Newmarket races."

"I guess I can manage that much. Let me pour you some wine," Mrs. Hyde said, and the conversation turned to other matters.

Flora nipped downstairs, thinking about that talk. Where *did* Mrs. Hyde hide her gold? It must be in that office somewhere. It wasn't in the desk, as the others thought. She often helped Mrs. Hyde with her letters—the woman could scarcely read or write—and the box wasn't in the drawers. Maybe she kept it in her bedchamber. It was only a fleeting thought. Where Mrs. Hyde kept her money was of little interest to Flora. She had a dozen things to do in the kitchen.

When she went to bed that night, she took the newspaper with her. She turned first, as she always did, to the news of the war in the Peninsula. The words Talavera and Cadiz were familiar to her as scenes of battles. She often wondered if John had taken part in them. She still didn't know his last name. He was a friend of Iris's beau, Mr. Strong, but for a month Flora had been too shy to ask Iris his name, and when she finally did ask her, Iris didn't remember. Mr. Strong had stopped coming in the meanwhile, so she never discovered his name, but she read all the war news and often thought about him.

Every time she saw a "John" in the list of casualties or mortalities, she wondered if it was him. Was he Captain John Chalmers, wounded at Cadiz? Lieutenant John Forsythe, killed in action? He deserved to die. He must have known she was young, and a virgin. A man-about-town would know all about Spanish fly. The girls told her that was the secret ingredient in Mother Hyde's hell-pot. What kind of creature would take advantage of a young girl? If men wanted sex, they should get married. Maybe he was married. Plenty of their customers were. It made her despise him even more.

Sometimes Flora went to sleep dreaming of getting revenge on John. She imagined seeing him in a public place with his wife or some fine lady friend. She'd walk straight up to him and point an accusing finger. "This is the man that ruined me!" she would announce.

She still flushed to remember that night and the wrenching, aching need that had consumed her. She never felt anything like that again, but sometimes when she was alone in bed at night, she felt faint stirrings of the same sort. She remembered, as in a dream, John's lips burning hers. The image of his dark, caressing eyes was sharp and clear after all this time. She felt again his hands on her body, taking liberties in spots she never touched herself, and a languorous desire overcame her. It was lonesome and unsatisfying. She hadn't felt this hollowness before, or this guilty pleasure. She nursed the wrong that John had done her, and shored up her resolve for revenge.

7

The winter of 1811 was a hard one in England. The Thames was frozen solid from London Bridge to Blackfriars. Enterprising merchants renamed the river Freezeland Street, and set up a Frost Fair to amuse the idle. It was just the sort of entertainment to please Mother Hyde. It gave people like herself an opportunity to rub elbows with the ton. She decided to go and see the Frost Fair, and took Elsie with her for company, and in the way of business. Elsie's flirtatious smile usually brought a few gentlemen to the house.

They dawdled along Freezeland Street, enjoying the clamor of the holiday crowd. They lingered at the stalls to try the meat pies and gingerbread, but it was the gambling wheel that soon caught Mother Hyde's interest. She remained there an hour. She lost five guineas and came home with a wretched sore throat.

As Mr. Dryden was visiting friends in Surrey he wouldn't be calling that night, so she decided to spend the evening in bed. She rang for Flora and said, "You'll have to take over the office tonight, Flora. I can't go downstairs."

"Me?" Flora stared as though the woman had asked her to jump off St. Paul's. "I can't do it! I won't!"

Although Flora was virtually in charge of running the domestic side of the house now, she never appeared in public. She would make deliveries to Mrs. Hyde's office and occasionally met Mr. Dryden there, but shunned the regular customers. She didn't want to see them, and more importantly, she didn't want them to see her. In the bottom of her heart, she still hoped to get out of this place one day. What an embarrassment if some future employer should recognize her as an inhabitant of a brothel!

"Somebody's got to see that the customers pay."

"I've been telling you for a year you should hire a man," Flora scolded. "You need a man about the place for when a customer gets rowdy. You remember the trial we had getting Mr. Makepiece out when he was bosky."

"Mr. Dryden doesn't think it's a good idea," Mother Hyde said.

Mr. Dryden's word was law, but Flora suspected that Mr. Dryden was just afraid that

Mrs. Hyde would find herself a more obliging boyfriend. It made no sense to be without a man in an establishment like this.

"You'll have to do it tonight, Flora. There's no one else. And don't put on that black gown you got for church. Borrow something stylish from one of the girls. I charge a guinea a visit —two if it goes over an hour, and extra for wine or food. And no more credit to Mr. Stanton. He owes me twenty-five pounds already."

Another piece of folly on Mrs. Hyde's part, giving credit for six months at a time. But this was a mere passing thought. "I can't wear one of those gowns!" Flora objected. They were lovely and fashionable, but they exposed half the girls' bosoms.

"What are you ashamed of? It's what the ton ladies wear. That's what you'd really like, eh, Flora? To be a grand lady," Mrs. Hyde jeered.

"Don't be ridiculous," Flora scoffed. "I just don't want to meet the customers. What if I should meet one of them again when I go to my cousin's place?"

Mrs. Hyde shook her head. Mrs. Leadbeater was a familiar threat that Flora frequently mentioned, but there wasn't much chance of Flora's ever meeting the woman. "If that's all that's stopping you, wear a mask. You'll find one in my dresser. I wore it to Vauxhall with Mr. Dryden last autumn when—" The woman fell into a fit of coughing.

Flora could see that Mrs. Hyde really was too ill to go to the office that night. Her face was flushed, and her chest sounded heavy. "All right," Flora said, "but you'd best get cured in a hurry. I don't want to make a habit of this." She went to the dresser and found a black-feathered half mask in a drawer.

"Bring me up the cash later. And no funny business. I want a record of everyone who comes."

Flora's eyes sparkled and she answered boldly, "Have I ever stolen anything from you?" There was no ceremony between these combatants now. Each knew that the other was her match.

"You're about the only one I trust," Mother Hyde admitted.

"I'll have Maggie bring you up a posset," Flora said, and left to make her preparations.

Flora didn't want to wear one of the low-cut gowns, but it seemed sacrilegious to wear her church dress for such a base purpose. She borrowed Sal's green silk, and carried the mask to conceal her face. As she stood in front of her mirror, the woman she gazed at didn't look anything like the girl who had come to Mother Hyde's more than two years before.

Her short, curly hair had grown long and was now worn up behind her head. In her tarnished mirror, the color even looked darker. The last trace of childishness had vanished from her features, revealing the high cheekbones, the straight nose and proud chin. But it was the eyes that told the true story. They no longer bore that glow of youthful innocence. They were the disillusioned eyes of a fully mature woman who knew the way of the world. You couldn't live in a place like this and keep your illusions. The girls talked when they came to the kitchen. Flora had gotten over being shocked at what she heard.

Her body had matured too. The gown she wore tonight would have hung loose two years ago. Now her breasts filled the bodice. A rim of white velvet breast peeped daringly out at the top. Flora examined herself with a curious, detached interest. I actually look pretty, she thought. I wonder what John would think if he could see me now. He was the only man she'd ever known, and came easily to her mind as a judge. But how out of place she looked in her spartan little room.

It was still the same room she'd been shown to that night by Maggie McMahon. It had curtains at the windows now and a spotted carpet from the dining room. The dresser was painted blue and a table held the little creature comforts Flora had bought from her wages—a few books, stationery, a pretty brass-handled brush and comb set. An extravagance, but her hair was her best feature. The girls said if you brushed it every night, it would grow full and thick, but Flora's hope was that brushing would reduce the curls to waves.

She felt as nervous as a bride when she

went to Mother Hyde's office and sat behind the old oaken desk to await the first customers. The business end of the transactions was carried out as briefly as possible, which was not as briefly as she would have liked. More than one of her callers tried his hand at taking Flora to bed, but she put them off with a joke. The mask that was meant to conceal intrigued the gentlemen, especially when they looked at the copper crown above it, the impertinent little chin below, and the youthful, kissable set of lips.

It was late when Mr. Pettigrew arrived. Flora knew his reputation—none of the girls liked him. He was called a gentleman, but he was an overbearing brute. He came every Friday night after work at Whitehall, where he was a solicitor in the records department. He had had every girl in the establishment, had a complaint against each one, and was intrigued to discover a new hostess.

"Where's Mother tonight?" he asked, staring boldly at Flora's bosoms even before he examined her half mask.

Flora felt a strong urge to strike him. "Mrs. Hyde is not feeling well. I'm handling the business for her. I think you know all the girls, sir. They're all busy at the moment except Elsie and Dora."

"*You* don't appear to be occupied. You have the advantage of me, madam," he smiled boldly. Something in his look reminded her of a cinnamon-eyed boy who had thrown her case in the dust the day she arrived in London. He had the same cunning look. "I don't believe I've met you?"

"I'm not a hostess," she said curtly. "Will it be Elsie or Dora?"

"I'd like a change," he said, and stuck his hands in his pockets, leaning back and examining her insolently.

"Then you will be going along to another establishment, I take it?"

"You're a bold wench! Take care or I'll tell Mother on you, miss!"

Flora rose to her feet and stared hard from behind her mask. "Mr. Pettigrew, you're wasting my time. I have told you which hostesses are free at the moment. If you don't want one of them, you can either wait in the saloon or leave the premises."

His voice came out sharp and loud. "Who are you?" he demanded.

"That's no concern of yours."

"You have a good accent. A lady fallen on hard times? Come now, my dear, you can tell Petti." He spoke in a friendly voice, but she could see the anger in his eyes and wished he would leave. Why did Mrs. Hyde not have a man on the premises to handle obstreperous people like Pettigrew?

"Please go," she said, and began walking toward the door to open it for him.

He reached out and grabbed her arm. "You're a shy little thing," he said, and reached playfully for her mask.

She pushed him off briskly. "Get out!" she shouted.

"Your temper matches that red hair! Come upstairs with me, my dear, and I'll make it worth your while."

Flora only wanted to get rid of him. "You couldn't make it worth my while, Mr. Pettigrew. You're only a solicitor," she said, and tried to brush past him.

He reached out and grabbed at her mask. Flora raised her hands and pushed at his chest. Caught off guard, he thumped against the door, making it impossible for her to flee. When Pettigrew recovered his balance, his face was red and the last pretense of good humor had vanished.

"Only a solicitor, is it, Miss High and Mighty? And you are only a whore!" He advanced toward her with a wild light in his eyes.

Flora ducked past him and finally got hold of the doorknob. Before she had wrenched the door open, he whirled her into the room and advanced on her, an ugly smirk on his face. Flora's only hope of rescue was to shout and hope that one of the other gentlemen was just arriving or leaving. "Help!" she called. "Somebody help me!"

Mr. Pettigrew laughed and lunged forward. He grabbed her by the shoulders and held her against the wall with a strong, rude hand. Her head caught the corner of the picture frame behind Mother Hyde's desk, pushing it askew. His arms were strong, but Flora writhed violently, so that he couldn't hold her against the wall and remove her mask at the same time. He was extremely curious to get it off and see who was hiding there. That crown of flaming hair suggested the name Caroline Lamb. Caro had the reputation of enjoying risque stunts. What a weapon to hold over her prestigious family, the Melbournes!

One large hand moved to Flora's breast and squeezed hard enough to make her yelp in pain. Just as his other hand rose to pull aside the mask, the door opened and a young gentleman plunged in. He moved with the swift, purposeful precision of an eagle. In her turmoil, Flora saw only the black blur of his jacket at first. She soon observed, with a wave of relief, that he was an excellent bruiser. One blow on Pettigrew's jaw and he sank to the floor in a limp heap. The new arrival leaned down, pulled him out into the hall by the scruff of his neck, and closed the door behind him. Then he turned back to face Flora, dusting his hands.

"The natives are restless tonight," he smiled. She watched in silent horror as his smile dwindled to curiosity. He stared hard at her. His eyes widened in astonishment, but not wider than Flora's.

She was looking at John.

8

For a moment, she thought it was an illusion.
The strange buzzing in her ears lent an air of
unreality to the apparition. Many nights he
had appeared in her dreams, and often his
face was in her mind when she was awake.
That handsome face, hated and reviled as the
instrument of her downfall! The breath
caught in her throat, and a hand rose instinctively to her heart, hammering violently
against her ribs.

It couldn't be! The face was darker,
thinner. The hair was shorter—but it was
him. She'd never forget those black eyes, not
if she lived to be a hundred. His complexion
was weathered from Spain, he was thinner
from his hard work. Of course a soldier's hair
would be short. Why was he staring at her
like that? My God, had he recognized her?

"Why are you wearing a mask?" he asked.
His voice showed no recognition. It was the

same deep voice as before, pleasantly polite.

That was all he was staring at then, the mask. Her next thought was that he must not recognize her. Shame burned hot at the memory of their past intimacy. She tried to speak, but only a light, strangled sigh came out. Her mind was seething with images. His dark eyes, even darker than she remembered, stared at her with questioning amusement. She glanced at his hands—long and artistic, as she remembered them—taking outrageous liberties with her naked body. Oh God! This couldn't be happening! He couldn't be back.

"Here, have a glass of wine," he offered, and poured her a glass from Mother Hyde's desk decanter. She watched in silent turmoil as the red liquid swirled like blood in the glass.

She accepted it with trembling fingers, still speechless. After a sip, she said, "Thank you," in a faltering voice, pitched low to conceal her nervousness.

Her mind was a maelstrom of confusion. Why was he here? A wild feeling surged that he had come looking for her. She didn't know whether it was a hope or a fear, but she knew it set her trembling in every atom of her body. Vivid memories stirred at his presence. Beneath that sparkling white shirt, his chest spread broad, muscled, with that patch of curled black hair. How could he not recognize her?

"Where's Mother Hyde?" he asked, quite nonchalantly.

Of course, he had only come to buy some entertainment, and that angered her too. Flora felt an impotent rage in her breast. She clutched at her throat and said, "She's ill tonight."

John gazed at her, a question in his dark eyes. "Did that lout hurt you? Do you need a doctor?" he asked.

She shook her head. "I'll be all right. Thank you for rescuing me."

"You need a muscleman here. Does this sort of thing happen often?"

She shook her head mutely and took another sip of wine to give herself time to think. She had to get him out of the office at once, before he recognized her. Revenge could wait—*must* wait, till she recovered from the shock. "Did you come for a hostess?" she asked.

A smile quivered on his sensual lips. It stretched to a grin, rose up to his eyes, which suddenly glowed with a fire that Flora remembered. "I didn't actually, but if you'd care to remove that mask, we might arrange something." His voice hummed with innuendo.

As he spoke, his eyes flickered over her hair and face. What a beautiful shade of hair. A little lighter than Titian, darker than new copper. It reminded him of that hellcat he was looking for. But that was the only resemblance. This woman was older, more striking, and much less hot at hand. The word "cool" seemed appropriate. He could tell from her chin and firm jawline that she was young, but still much older than the young girl with the red, curly hair.

Her breasts were luxuriously full, as he liked them. In her agitation, two white mounds rose and fell enticingly. The hostesses at Mother Hyde's didn't wear the concealing Empress gowns favored in ton circles. What they did wear gave customers a much better idea of their charms. This one had an enviable little waist, flaring to full hips. He felt a surge of passion as he studied her.

Flora touched her mask to make sure it was securely in place. "I'm not a whore!" she said harshly. Her eyes blazed and her heart hammered painfully.

"I don't believe in calling names," he answered gently, and took a step closer. "But one does expect to find cows in a stable, angels in heaven, and available ladies in a brothel. Or did you slip off a cloud and end up in the wrong milieu?" He smiled softly.

His dark head hovered above her, so close she could feel his body heat. A strange weakness invaded her bones. He was going to kiss her! She moved behind the desk for safety, and John sat casually on the edge of it, leaning toward her, gazing at her with a mischievous smile dancing in his eyes. This playful flirtation was a side of him she hadn't seen before.

Flora took courage that he didn't recognize her. The anger still burned that he had come to buy a woman, and she decided to repay him. "It's true that pigs usually wallow in mire too, is it not? And gentlemen usually frequent a brothel to hire a whore. Why are you here, if not to sample the merchandise, sir?"

He put his head back and laughed. "It's good to be home! Maybe I just came to hear some plain Anglo-Saxon talk after my travels abroad."

Flora wanted to hear about his experiences in the Peninsula, but didn't want to reveal any knowledge of John.

"You didn't have to come here to hear English spoken," she answered reasonably.

His black eyes smoldered over her body. "Maybe I wanted to do more than talk," he said. A bold, assessing look examined her.

He has changed, she thought. The John she remembered wasn't quite so forward. Of course war was bound to change a man. "Actually I came looking for a little hellcat that used to be here. The hottest girl I ever knew, but finding you here put her out of my mind. Take off your mask." Though his words were a command, his tone made them a suggestion.

"I would prefer not to." A hellcat, that's what he thought her. A rough and ready companion in sex. She writhed in embarrassment. But perhaps it wasn't her he meant . . .

"You have beautiful lips—and an adorable chin," he said. His voice, fogged with desire, was soft as an echo. She felt a betraying quiver deep inside. He lifted a finger and ran it lightly over her lips, which tingled in response. She felt them tremble, and her breath came in light, shallow gasps.

"What are you hiding? A pair of squinty eyes? A flat nose?" he teased. As he spoke, he gazed into her eyes. They were clearly not squinty, but their shape was concealed. He saw only a dark glitter behind the mask.

She turned her face away and held onto her mask with one hand. John's hand fell from her lips to her shoulder, where it burned like a brand. A tide of remembered desire surged through her. She hated this man. Why did her treacherous body turn limp at his touch?

"I'm an officer just returned from Spain," he said. "I read in the journals just today that we're welcomed everywhere with open arms. Now, you wouldn't want to slight a returned hero?" he asked archly. "Especially one with his pockets jingling."

Jingling with guineas, the established price for a whore. "We charge a guinea, sir. You will be welcomed with open arms by any of our available hostesses," she said stiffly.

"But not by the reigning abbess, eh? Wounded to the quick, Miss—whoever you are!"

Abbess! It went from bad to worse. He thought she was the proprietress of this whorehouse.

"Is it the price that has offended you, madam? I can spare more than a guinea, if you provide some extraordinary service." He stood waiting, with a gleam of passion growing in his eyes. "Well?"

"I'm not for sale."

"Everything is for sale if the price is right." On this cynical comment John rose and turned toward the door.

Flora instinctively rose too, as she made a particular point of maintaining her good manners. John heard her movement with surprise. He stopped and turned to look over his shoulder. Was the haughty beauty having second thoughts about his jingling pockets? She was a remarkably handsome woman, and it had been a long time . . .

"I'll see you out," Flora said. Her voice was tense with anger, but she didn't want another scene. She just wanted to get rid of him. She moved swiftly toward the door.

As she reached for the handle, John's arm shot out and encircled her waist. He pulled her into his arms and gazed down at her— proud Titian head arched back on an entrancing curve of ivory throat, which fell to that tantalizing hint of bosoms. He felt an urge to lift them out and taste their texture. They were heaving in vexation, and that increased his interest.

"Don't make my trip completely futile," he murmured. His voice was ragged with impatience as he lowered his head to kiss her. She tasted the wine on his lips.

With both arms against his chest, Flora pushed with all her might. It was like trying to move a house. He stood solid, tightening his grip and increasing the pressure of his lips on hers while she struggled vainly. By insensible degrees, Flora stopped struggling and gave in to his persuasion. Her hands, trapped between their bodies, slid out and went around his waist.

The remembered passion swelled in her, filling her lungs till she could hardly breathe. The madness was back, the aching need for him that two years hadn't stifled. It was an addiction, this craving to feel his body against hers. She was depraved from having known him. Her breasts above her gown tingled from the roughness of his black jacket as she pressed shamelessly close to him. She was minutely mindful of the chest beneath it, patched with springy hair.

John was back, holding her in his arms as she had so often remembered, and dreamed. She admitted that this was the reason she held on to her shame and grief and vain thought of revenge. It was this exquisite, burning longing for his love that kept the memories alive. His lips were ruthless, demanding a response. His hard chest molded her softer body to its outlines. One hand played over her back, sliding up past the top of her gown to inflame her naked flesh, igniting the old flame to a fury.

But this time she knew what it was she wanted from him. His knee moved familiarly between her legs, stirring memories of their ecstatic intimacy. Without the aid of Hyde's Hellpot, that quivering excitement inside her coiled, ready to lash out and overwhelm her. This was madness beyond indiscretion. All he wanted was a whore.

She wrenched her head free, but his arms held her tightly. His lips chased along her throat, leaving a tingle of heat behind. They lit on the lobe of her ear and grasped the tip, where the rough moisture of his tongue sent shivers of desire shooting through her. His breath seemed to enter the very core of her being, setting off a violent quake. "Quite sure I can't convince you?" he asked. His voice was like honey, sweet and thick.

"Let me go," she said, but her voice was weak with reluctance.

His fingers moved to the top of her gown, where they lay on her velvet skin, rising and falling with her breath. She felt his warm fingers curve into the opening, caressing one breast with infinite tenderness. "This is no way to treat a hero," he chided softly, and seized her lips again.

Flora wrenched her head aside. "Heroes don't boast! I don't see any wounds, any limbs missing!" she charged.

"I am completely intact, and willing to prove it," he taunted.

"Go away!"

"I don't give up that easily, madam abbess. I'll go now—I have a pressing appointment— but I shall return." He stepped away and jabbed at his cravat. "When will Mother Hyde be back at her post?"

"Soon." As soon as the word was out, Flora

realized it was unwise—he'd be back to bother her again. He said he hadn't come to hire a hostess, and this seemed to be true. If she could find out what he wanted, she might be rid of him once and for all. And if, as she suspected, it was herself he had come for, she must convince him the hellcat he remembered wasn't there. Any thought of revenge had dissipated. She only wanted to be alone, free from temptation.

"Perhaps I could help you?" she asked.

"How long have you been here?"

"More than two years."

"Perhaps you *can* help me then. There was a girl here at that time. Her name was Flora." Flora's heart began pounding. She felt a nearly overpowering urge to reveal herself, but pride or shame prevented it. "I—I just wanted to know what happened to her," John said, frowning.

"Why?" The word leapt out of her mouth before she had time to consider it.

He tossed his broad shoulders and smiled. His bold facade faded, and a rather wistful smile alit on his lips. "I don't know. She was a taking little thing. Pretty. I've often wondered what happened to her . . . how she came to be here. I just wanted to see her again. I daresay it was foolish of me."

"We don't have anyone here by that name," Flora said firmly. "I believe she returned home and married a tenant farmer."

"Where?"

Flora quickly removed her imaginary self

to the farthest corner of the island. "In Scotland."

"She wasn't Scottish. She had a good English accent."

A jolt of alarm shook her. She must be more careful! "I believe you're right. She was from the lake country—somewhere up north near Scotland. She used to speak of it."

"Married, eh? That's good. Well, it's been pleasant—er, chatting to you, Miss Incognita. A catchy trick, hiding your face, but I think I'll recognize you, if ever we meet again. And certainly if we ever kiss again," he added mischievously, then he grinned and left.

Flora reached out and locked the door behind him. On shaking legs, she went to the desk and sank into the chair. It was almost incredibly bad luck that John should have come the one night she was in the office. Yet it might be good too. If Mrs. Hyde had been here, she might have told him the truth—that Flora was still here. The old nagging to don a silk gown and become a hostess would start up again. And if it was John who was asking for her . . . would she have the fortitude to resist?

Before long, Flora felt a burst of pleasure that John had remembered her. He'd thought of her often, he said. He remembered her accent. Yet he seemed happy to hear she was married, so it didn't seem that he wanted to continue any relationship. She knew by this time that virgins were rare in a place like this. Maybe he'd known she was one, and felt a little guilty. Well he might! He hadn't changed. He was still chasing whores. Why did she feel this urge to defend him?

She poured a glass of wine and sat alone, thinking. When had he come back from the Peninsula? Why? Officers didn't usually return during a campaign unless they were wounded, and John seemed to be in one piece. Who was he? Was his name even John? "John Smith" was a basket name for any gentleman who wished to remain anonymous.

She knew every secret of his beautiful body —knew his most private, personal details, yet she didn't know his name. With a confused shake of her head, Flora looked at the head-and-shoulders clock on the table and saw it was midnight. On busy evenings Mother Hyde's Parlor remained open late, but custom was slow in this spell of bad weather. She'd close now and take the money upstairs.

As Flora rose, she noticed that the painting of a young Bonnie Banyon had become knocked askew, and straightened it. Something seemed to catch it and hold it aslant. She lifted a corner of the frame and saw a locked door behind it—a small, metal door with a hinged lock on it. The money! *That's* where it was kept. With a little laugh, Flora lifted the picture an inch from the wall and hung it straight again. It wouldn't do for Mrs. Hyde to know that her great secret had been discovered.

The hallway was empty when Flora went

out. Everyone had left, and she removed the mask. Elsie was sitting in the parlor with Dora, having a glass of wine while they waited to see if their services were required any longer.

"It's midnight," Elsie said. "Can we go to bed now? I'm dog tired."

"Yes, run along. I'm going to lock up. Did Pettigrew kick up a ruckus when he left?"

"He skulked out like a dog with his tail between his legs, the old lecher," Elsie laughed. "I wager Lord Hywell gave him a taste of the home-brewed. Fancy Lord Hywell paying us a call. What did he want? I was hoping he'd ask for me."

Flora frowned a moment, trying to think who Elsie meant. "Lord Hywell? Good God— is that who he is?"

"The tall, handsome gent that threw Pettigrew out."

"Gentleman," Flora corrected unthinkingly.

"You kept him all to yourself, eh, Flora?" Dora tossed in with a knowing look. "I bet Mother's sofa saw action tonight, even if Dryden didn't come. What's Hywell like?"

"Don't be ridiculous. He was just looking for a girl that used to be here years ago, before he went to the war."

"Was it Rose he wanted?" Elsie asked jealously.

"No. About Lord Hywell, how did you know his name?"

"Old Mr. Stanton dropped in—just to say

hello. His pockets are to let. He said that was John Beauchamp, the new Earl of Hywell. His uncle died, and Beauchamp was sent for, off in Spain. Quite the hero, folks say. He led some charge of the Dragoons in Spain. He's the Hywell heir. Ever so old a family, and rich as nabobs."

Flora heard this with mixed emotions. One little corner of her heart was happy that John had given her his own name. He hadn't hidden behind an alias. Almost before this occurred to her, she thought that if he was an earl, a peer of the realm, he would never have anything to do with a girl out of a brothel. Oh, he might call a few evenings and hire her, but it would never be more than that, and that would be worse than nothing. He would soon marry some duke's or earl's daughter, and set up as a fine lord in the House of Parliament. He'd be utterly beyond her reach, and her revenge.

"What are you looking so stunned for?" Dora asked. She studied Flora with narrowed eyes and leapt unerringly to the truth. "He's the man who seduced you, isn't he?"

Flora didn't confirm it in words, but her stricken face was answer enough.

"Flora!" Elsie exclaimed. "You mean it was *you* he came looking for? Oh, ain't it romantic, Dora! Just like a stage play. He might take you for his mistress, Florie. Set you up in a grand flat, with nabobs calling on you. Wait till Rose hears this. She'll be jealous as a green cow."

"He didn't know it was me. I wore this mask," Flora said, lifting it to show the girls. "I told him Flora wasn't here. Don't tell him otherwise, and don't let the other girls tell him either, if he comes back. I don't want him to know I'm here."

"Whyever not?" Dora asked.

Flora didn't feel up to correcting her. "Because I don't."

"He'll not be back," Elsie prophecied. "He was never a regular. Mr. Strong just brought him once, for a bit of a spree before he went off to the war. I think you're daft, Flora. Well, if you're locking up, I'm for bed." She rose, yawned and strolled away with Dora.

Flora took the money up to Mrs. Hyde, who was still awake. "How are you feeling?" Flora asked, when she'd reported on the night's doings.

"A bit warm."

"Why don't I call a doctor?" Flora felt the woman's cheeks, and was worried about her fever.

"I'll have him in the morning if I don't feel better."

Flora wanted to explain about Lord Hywell, but Mrs. Hyde was distressed. It could wait till morning.

"Would you like some broth, or tea? I'll go to the kitchen and get it."

"No, I'm all right. Maggie brought me some broth an hour ago. She was griping about being alone, but traffic was light tonight. I'll be back on duty tomorrow. Thanks for handling matters for me, Flora."

A "thanks" from Mrs. Hyde was a rare thing. "That's all right," Flora said. She felt a bothersome twinge of sympathy for the woman.

Mrs. Hyde was a conscienceless old viper, living off the avails of prostitution, but she had her moments. She did take better care of her girls than most abbesses, Flora admitted. And she had stopped using Hyde's Hellpot when Flora urged the girls to revolt. There were many occasions when the kitchen rang with merry laughter. Prostitution wasn't seen as a vice by Mother Hyde; it was the only line of business she knew. As Maggie McMahon said so leniently, "Somebody's going to do it. It's the world's oldest profession, and the second most profitable, after making guns for men to kill each other."

"You're welcome," Flora said. "Sleep tight."

In her own room she removed the green silk gown and hung it up carefully, but when she went to bed, memories swarmed over her. John Beauchamp. He had a whole name now—and a title. Earl of Hywell. Lord Hywell. There was no point harping on it. He didn't really care for her. He didn't even recognize her. All that was left was revenge, and a nobleman was above and beyond paying for his crimes.

She'd done the right thing to tell him Flora wasn't here. The Flora he knew wasn't here. What was here now was a shell, not that hot-blooded vixen he'd come back to see. That was it—he had mistaken her for that lustful wench created by Mother Hyde's poison. Her cheeks were hot with shame, as hot as they'd been when he first called her a whore. But she hadn't taken the brew tonight, and still she wanted him.

9

After thinking of John for more than two years, planning her revenge, and finally seeing him last night, Flora was no longer sure whether it was love or hate she felt. She only knew it was a dangerously violent passion. She was afraid his sudden reappearance would take over her life. As events turned out, she was much too busy for that. In the morning, Mrs. Hyde's sore throat had turned putrid, and the fever had risen to a threatening level.

The doctor came and put Maggie McMahon and Flora in charge of her care. Maggie put a sign on the door stating the house was closed temporarily. Every time the knocker sounded, Flora wondered if it was John. A dozen times in one afternoon she found her thoughts straying to him, but there was always something to distract her—the restorative pork jelly to be made, the kitchen to oversee, and the patient upstairs demanding constant attention.

The girls huddled together in the saloon, showing more concern for Mother Hyde's health than Flora expected. "How is she?" Elsie asked anxiously.

"She's doing poorly," Flora admitted.

A shadow of fear clouded Elsie's eyes. "Flora, what will happen to us if she dies?"

"Why, you'll be free to go and make a decent life for yourself," Flora answered.

"Go where?" Elsie demanded.

"Back on the streets," Jennie said resignedly.

By the second evening, it was beginning to seem that Mrs. Hyde was not going to pull through. Flora sat with her in the dark room, worrying about the heavy rumble when Mrs. Hyde breathed. Such a heavy chest sounded very serious. Mrs. Hyde beckoned Flora to her bedside.

"Mark was supposed to be back yesterday. He said he'd call. Send for him," Mrs. Hyde whispered, and gave his address.

Flora wrote a note explaining the situation and sent one of the kitchen boys off with it. He returned an hour later. "Mr. Dryden said to say he's out," he reported.

"You mean he was there and sent that message?" Flora demanded, incensed.

"He was just on his way out the door to a party, Flora. He said it was important. He couldn't come tonight, but he'll come tomorrow."

Flora went back upstairs. "Mr. Dryden wasn't home, Mrs. Hyde," she said. "I had the note left. He'll come tomorrow."

A pair of dark, disillusioned eyes stared at Flora from the pillow. Set in that hagged face, surrounded by a cloud of black hair, they were the saddest sight Flora had ever seen.

"He was due back last night. He doesn't want to come," Mrs. Hyde said. "After all I've done for him, he won't come. If anything happens to me, Flora—"

"Don't talk so foolishly," Flora scolded.

"Hear me out. It's too late for bandying words," Mrs. Hyde said. She spoke harshly, but her voice soon faded to a croaking whisper. "I want you to take over the place when I'm gone, Flora. I left it to you in my will. I was going to give Mark the cash, but I'll not. If he can't spare me a minute when I'm dying, he don't deserve it."

"I don't want it!" Flora said angrily. "What would I want with a place like this?" My God, what would people think of me? she thought.

"Somebody's got to look after the girls."

"Give it to Maggie."

"She'll stay on and give you a hand. Maggie couldn't even run the kitchen. How could she handle all my business?"

Flora wanted to object further, but Mrs. Hyde had broken out in a sweat, and Flora had to try to give her the medicine left by the doctor. At nine it was Maggie's turn to take over the sickroom and Flora went to the kitchen to eat.

The doctor went up to Mrs. Hyde while Flora was in the kitchen, sitting with a pot of tea and a plate of toast in front of her, thinking over what Mrs. Hyde had said. She was outraged that she should be left a brothel. Surely it was illegal! A woman couldn't be forced to become an abbess. If Mrs. Hyde left her anything, she'd refuse to accept it. That's all. *Working* in a whore-house was bad enough. She wouldn't *own* one.

As she sat on, thinking, a few of the girls came down and sat around the large table. They spoke in low, worried tones about their future. Flora listened, but added nothing. She didn't want anyone to know the stunt played on her.

"What'll happen," Elsie warned, "is that Mark Dryden will take us over. I won't work for him, and that's a fact."

"It'd be better than the streets," Jennie pointed out. "In the middle of winter—I won't leave, not if Satan hisself takes over."

"Himself," Flora said automatically.

"I've been out in the cold before," Sal said, and shuddered at some private memory. "I'll have to stay, much as I hate to. I've got to save money for little Johnnie."

"There's a Mr. Johnson in Swallow Street that has a very fancy house," Elsie mentioned. "I wonder if he'd take us."

"You, maybe," Jennie said jealously. Elsie was the beauty of the place. "I'll be out on my butt, and so will Sal and the rest of us."

Flora listened and felt a surge of pity for these girls. She felt guilty, and guilt lent her voice a sharp edge. "For goodness' sake, have you no gumption? Why don't you go back home where you came from?"

"My da kicked me out when I was fifteen and said he didn't want to see my face again," Jennie said.

"What home?" another asked. "They don't let you stay at the orphanage past sixteen."

"Get a decent job as a nursemaid or servant, then," Flora said. But she knew from her own experience that this was nearly impossible.

"The first job I had, the son used to sneak into my room at night," Dora said. "I told his da, and he boxed my ears and threw me out on the street. If men are going to use me, I'm going to get paid for it."

"I hate men!" Flora said angrily.

It was an hour later when Maggie came down to the kitchen. Her face was pinched and white. "She's dead," she announced. The circle of pale, frightened faces fell silent. "The doctor's calling the undertaker. We'll have to arrange for the funeral, Flora."

"Yes," Flora said. She felt as if a stone sat on her chest. All these foolish girls—what would become of them? Why was it *her* duty to see that they survived? It wasn't fair!

The funeral was arranged quietly and discreetly. A note was sent to Mr. Dryden, who didn't deign to answer. Maggie said there

were no relatives to be informed. Mr.
Banyon, if he was still alive, was beyond
contact. Mrs. Hyde hadn't heard from him in
years.

The afternoon after the funeral, the lawyer,
Mr. Baker, came to the house in Long Acre.
Like everything else in Mrs. Hyde's life, he
was third-rate—a tall, shifty-eyed man in a
shiny jacket threadbare at the elbows. Flora
and Maggie were invited into Mrs. Hyde's
office for the reading of the will. Maggie was
left Mrs. Hyde's jewelry and personal effects.
The remainder of the estate, including the
business with all its assets, was left to Flora
Sommers.

"I'll sell the house and split the money
between the girls," Flora said.

"Oh, she doesn't own the house. It's
rented," Mr. Baker told her.

"Rented? Then what *did* she own? What
exactly has she left me?"

"The business—goodwill, the furnishings,
her carriage. All the goods and chattels, and
any investments she may have made. Mrs.
Hyde didn't inform me in detail, but there
must be a list of investments somewhere. Let
me know when you find them, and I'll see to
the transfer of them to your name."

"She didn't have any investments," Maggie
said.

"Well then, it'd be just the furnishings of
the place, and any cash you come across,"
Mr. Baker explained.

Maggie and Flora exchanged a questioning

look. The cash!

Mr. Baker left with the reminder that he'd be happy to continue as the solicitor for Mother Hyde's Parlor. "Will you keep the name?" he asked, mildly curious.

"Neither the name nor the business," Flora said firmly.

When he was gone, Flora moved to the chair behind the desk. "We'll split the money up evenly between the lot of us," she said. "Twelve ways, between the ten girls, you, and myself."

"That's not what she wanted, Flora. Can you see Jennie Whitehead with her pockets full of money? She'd blow it in a day, or hand it over to some dandy to fritter away on her." Flora thought of Jennie, who bore that peculiar resemblance to Lily. "They don't have your common sense. That's why Bonnie chose you to look after them. What'll become of them if we close the house?"

Flora's face was pale and torn with doubt. "I won't be an abbess, Maggie. Don't ask it of me." Really, if it weren't for John, she was almost of a mind to do it.

"There's worse things a body can be."

"Then let them work for someone else."

"Bah, there are dozens of houses full of girls like our lot. More than enough girls to go around. Bonnie has established a niche for herself. It seems a shame to close it down. I'm going upstairs to clean out her room. I'll put the jewelry away safely while I'm about it. Most of the stuff is only glass, but the garnets are real."

"I'll give you a hand packing her things. We'll clean and air the room too."

It was while they were at that lugubrious chore that Dora came running upstairs, all in a clamor. "Flora! Mark Dryden's downstairs raising a dust, wanting to know why we didn't tell him Mother was dying."

Flora rose angrily and marched down to the office. She knew by the aroma of cigar smoke that he was there. She opened the door to find Mr. Dryden rifling the desk. His face was livid with anger, his pale eyes flashing, quivering nostrils narrowed to slits. "You're too late, Mr. Dryden. She's already dead and buried."

He bridled up and demanded, "Why wasn't I told?"

"You were told she was ill. You were told the time and place of the funeral. Having failed to come when she wanted you, it's a little late now. This visit has the air of the vulture seeing what he can pick from the corpse." She looked at the open drawers and the papers in his hands.

"I'm the heir," he said loftily. "Watch that tongue, Miss Sommers, or you'll find yourself on the streets—where you belong. I'm in charge of this brothel. My first act is to dispense with your services. And my second will be to throw half the chits Bonnie hired out along with you. I plan to run a higher-class establishment."

Flora felt an urge to throw him out by the

scruff of his neck, but as he was a foot taller than she, this was obviously impossible. "You'll have to run it from some other house than this. I am Mrs. Hyde's heir, sir. The lawyer was here this morning, putting me in legal charge of the estate."

A stream of profanities poured from his mouth. "Don't think you're going to do me out of what I've earned. You and your prissy, simpering, wheedling ways. I've catered to that old hag too long to take this sitting down. I know she's got money here, and I mean to have it! Just try and stop me!" As he spoke, he began pulling drawers out and throwing them to the floor. He opened a cupboard and tossed the collected debris of a decade around the room. There were pictures and souvenir mugs from fairs, fans and discarded masks, chapbooks and broadsheets.

"If you don't get out this minute, I'll call in a constable," Flora said boldly, but inside she was shaking. What if he knocked the picture from the wall and found the money? She really needed a strong man around the place. When she took over, she'd hire one.

Flora didn't recognize the exact moment when the decision was made, but at some deeper level of her mind she had come to accept that she couldn't abandon the girls to such creatures as Mr. Dryden. She felt a wrenching inside to know that she was putting herself forever beyond respectability. Her association with Mother

Hyde's had been innocent and kept very quiet. To become an abbess herself was entirely a different matter.

With his anger spent, Mr. Dryden turned a cold eye on Flora. "I'll fight this will, Miss Sommers. I don't know how you got around Bonnie, but I was to be her heir. You used some threats—"

"If you care to have your behavior dragged through the courts, Mr. Dryden, I'll be happy to oblige you. To tell the world how you came sweet-talking a woman old enough to be your mother, begging money from her, and then not even coming to see her when she was dying! That's where you made your mistake, sir. That was the thing that changed her mind about the will—your neglect!"

His eyes narrowed to slits. "You may have won this round, but I'm not through yet. I can ruin you. Do you think any of my friends will come here when I've told them about this?"

"We don't want any friends of yours! And most especially, we don't want you."

Mr. Dryden swore one last string of oaths before butting his cigar on the desk and storming out. Flora sat on the chair, trembling. It seemed she was now the proprietress of an abbey. She had best get busy.

10

Flora had been mentally improving the management of Mother Hyde's for years, and now she was in a position to carry out her reforms. There would be stricter control of clients and a pair of sturdy footmen hired to eject the unruly. There would be no more business done on credit. And if the money box allowed, there would be some renovations to the house as well. She didn't want to spend her nights in this horrid office, with every stick of furniture reminding her of Mother Hyde.

A moment later, Maggie came to the door. "I found this key under Bonnie's pillow, Flora. I wonder what it can be for?"

Flora took it with a little smile. "Close the door, Maggie. I think I know," she said, and removed the picture from the wall.

"So that's where she kept it!" Maggie said, and laughed.

Flora unlocked the door and pulled out the tin box. It was so heavy she had to use both hands, and behind it there were other boxes. Three in all, each stuffed to the top with money—gold coin and paper money. When the counting was done, they sat staring at a desk bearing approximately fifty thousand pounds in cash.

"You're rich!" Maggie gasped as she read the total.

Flora looked around the squalid room. "Maybe even rich enough to move to new quarters and set up a more elegant parlor," she said pensively. Yes, if she left this place, John wouldn't know where to find her. She half wished he would come, but he hadn't, and it was for the best. "Elsie mentioned Swallow Street as a good address. Somewhere in that area. We'll get new outfits for the girls, and serve a slightly finer sort of wine and dinner, I think."

"You won't make much, giving the clients all that."

"Oh yes we will. We'll charge more. I want a higher-class clientele. I wonder when the lease comes up for renewal. It must be here somewhere in this mess Dryden left behind." Dryden—a worry niggled at the back of her mind. But he wouldn't sue—he daren't. He didn't have a leg to stand on.

The lease came due the end of March. That gave her six weeks to find a better address and prepare a new house to reopen business in the spring. The timing was perfect, just a few weeks before the official spring Season, when the ton would be in London. On all her errands Flora wore a heavy black veil, like a lady in mourning, though her purpose was to hide her features. She chose the name of Mrs. Belmont and called herself a widow. The house eventually chosen was a block east of Swallow, just on the fringes of society.

A large brick house in the Georgian style, it would look elegant once it was repainted and the windows were cleaned. Flora fell in love with the interior. A black and white marble floor in the entrance hall lent an air of luxury, as did the twin Adams fireplaces in the saloon. There were chandeliers in several rooms, and niches built into the hallway to hold statuary. It was almost like being a bride, choosing draperies and carpets and furniture. But a nagging pain in her heart reminded Flora that this was as close to being a bride as she'd ever come.

By accepting her new role as proprietress, she had removed herself forever from the possibility of marriage. The widow's veil she wore did symbolize a death, the death of a dream. At night Flora worried about her future. What if Mama found out? But she never would, and look at all the money she'd be able to send home. Mama could quit working, and eventually even move into a house. Mrs. Hyde's money, Flora felt, wasn't hers to spend as she wished. Along with the legacy from Mrs. Hyde went the duty of looking after the girls.

The house she rented had been used for a purpose similar to Flora's in the past, and had some unique features. The room Flora chose for her office had a peephole hidden behind a picture of the Three Graces, which gave her a view of the saloon without being seen. As she was touring the house one day, she had discovered an even more intriguing item. One of the bedchambers also had a secret door into a hidden corridor. Midway along the corridor, there was a slatted window where voyeurs could observe the act of love in the next room without being seen. In the bedroom, the trellis was covered with silk vines and flowers and looked harmless. It was horrible—sick! Flora had the door to this secret corridor nailed shut and painted over. She took the room leading to the secret corridor for her own, to make sure the girls didn't discover it.

The girls were all delighted with the new arrangements and eagerly took to their lessons in speech and propriety which Flora had imposed. Flora enjoyed the lessons; it reminded her of home, teaching her sisters. And there were no customers to plague them either. Flora had not reopened Mother Hyde's Parlor after Bonnie's death. There was too much to be done.

Spring finally arrived, after that long, hard winter. The fruit trees blossomed forth in full abundance to make up for their long chill. Birds sang again and the sun shone brightly in the sky. Flora saw it all through her widow's veil as she hastened to and fro on errands.

Elsie, a little cleverer than most, came up with an idea to draw customers to the new house.

"Why don't you let me and some of the girls ride in Hyde Park in the carriage, Flora?" she suggested. Flora had hired a full-time groom. Mrs. Hyde had only hired one as needed. "It'll whet the gentlemen's curiosity. If they speak to us, we'll tell them when we're opening, and where."

"All right. We'll need to do a good business to pay for all the expenses I've incurred."

"What are you going to call the house? Mother Belmont's Parlor?"

"No, parlor isn't elegant enough for the aviary we're setting up here. I'll think of something."

"What's an aviary?" Elsie asked.

"Why, it's where birds roost," Flora told her. "Since my ladybirds roost here, I call it an aviary. That's what we'll call the house—the Aviary."

"And you'll rule the roost!" Elsie laughed. "What will you wear the first night, Flora?"

"My green, I think."

Flora had had a few gowns made up for her new role. As she was pitching herself into the business with all her energy, she didn't hesitate to select gowns as daring as her ladybirds'. With her coppery tresses, she chose rich shades of green, peacock blue, and gold.

Two stout footmen, Tom and Willie, were hired. They were the least elegant items in the establishment, but Flora knew the necessity of strong arms in case of trouble. She had blue livery made up in an effort to make them look presentable. There were other servants hired as well. A cook and cook's helper, an upstairs maid to tend to the rooms, and a downstairs maid and a laundress, for the standard of cleanliness was to be high.

No formal advertisement for such an enterprise as Flora's was made, but the girls' rides in the park and word of mouth had done the job well. There was considerable curiosity amongst the ton to check out the new establishment. As the great evening, April first, drew near, Flora was exhausted. The strain was not only physical, but mental as well. Was she doing the right thing? Surely she wouldn't feel so guilty if she were. Prostitution couldn't be right. Yet it existed, and the alternative for her friends was not a better life, but a worse one in some establishment that would exploit them.

Maggie McMahon had long since changed her appearance from the slatternly woman with the greasy hair hanging about her face that Flora first encountered in Long Acre. Flora was surprised to see how elegant Maggie appeared on the opening night, with a fashionable black gown showing off her still-pretty shoulders and her hair dressed high on her head.

"You're not dressed yet!" Maggie exclaimed when she found Flora lying on her bed, thinking. "Who will greet the callers?"

"I can't do it, Maggie. I haven't the courage to show my face to decent people as an abbess. Will you be the hostess?"

"What would I say?"

"You won't have to say much. The gentlemen will pay you, and go into the saloon to make their choice. You can use the little waiting room to handle the money. I'll be in my office if there's any trouble, but I don't want to face the crowd. It's lily-livered of me, I know, but—"

"Well," Maggie said forgivingly, "we're not all cut out for everything, and you've done a grand job of organizing, Flora. I'll be out front. I'm rather looking forward to it," she admitted, and laughed. "It's been a long time since I've been on display, meeting people. I may run into some of my old customers. It'll be great fun. You'd best get dressed."

Flora felt ashamed of herself, asking Maggie to do her job, but she just couldn't face it. She'd watch the saloon from the peephole in her office, and she'd dress with care, in case anyone should come to her door. The green shot-silk gown she chose reminded her of the one she'd worn the night John came back. Was that why she'd selected it? It clung tightly to her body, showing off her high, rounded bosoms and small waist. In the lamplight, her white skin looked like alabaster marble against the dark silk. She dressed her own hair in a swirl of curls and stuck a white gardenia amidst her tresses. As she gazed in the mirror, she was glad she wasn't to be seen. She looked like one of her own ladybirds. And not the least attractive either, she decided, running her palms down the sides of the gown.

She headed toward her door, then turned back. The mask borrowed from Mother Hyde was on her dresser. She kept it as a reminder of John's visit. "Coward," she murmured as she picked it up to take with her.

Flora stopped a moment at the head of the curved staircase and looked down to the lobby, admiring her handiwork. The marble floors gleamed like new. The crystals of the chandelier had been washed and polished. Dancing prisms of color reflected on the marble floor, and on the scattered tables, large bouquets of flowers sat, perfuming the air. It was like a picture from a book, and she had done it all. But she hadn't managed to add the one thing that would complete the picture. There was no gentleman waiting at the bottom of the stairs to greet her. Instead there were Tom and Willie, nervously pacing, looking like a pair of bruisers dressed up for a masquerade in their elegant blue livery.

Flora swept down the stairs, planning to go into the saloon for a last word with the girls before any customers arrived. Just as she reached the landing, the door knocker sounded, and she scurried back up the stairs and into her office. She went directly to the peephole and moved the picture aside to survey the first arrivals. They were three fine gentlemen in evening dress. How elegant they looked, how different from the motley crew that came to Long Acre. She looked with quick interest to see how they reacted to her ladybirds. Really the girls looked lovely, in their new gowns, with their hair artfully arranged, and practicing their new manners. She wished she could hear. She hoped Jennie wasn't dropping her aitches, or Elsie saying she was "ever so pleased" to make their acquaintance.

Before long, she quit worrying. The gentlemen seemed very well satisfied with her hostesses. Other gentlemen arrived, in such large numbers that they had to sit in the saloon, where they were served wine while waiting for free hostesses. Flora should have bought playing cards to entertain them. She jotted it down, and went back to her peephole. Tom went through the room with a platter of hors d'oeuvres and Willie with a decanter of wine to fill glasses.

Maggie came to Flora's door at regular intervals to announce who had come. "Lord Everton and a Mr. Walbeck. A lord, Flora! Imagine. He didn't blink an eye at the price either. I think we should charge more. He gave Tom a guinea tip."

"Good for him!" Flora smiled. "How's Jennie behaving?"

"Fine as a lady, but I do wish she'd stop calling Everton 'your grace.' I never should have told her you don't call a duke 'milord.' She's got firmly in her noggin that all lords are called 'your grace.' Mind you, Everton doesn't seem to mind the promotion.''

Flora peered through the hole again. "Tom's overdoing it with the hors d'oeuvres. He's bothered Mr. Walbeck three times in five minutes. Tell him to slow down, Maggie. And if you can slip Sal the word to stop twiddling at her hair, do it.''

"I will. Everything's going smooth as silk, Flora. I knew you could do it. What do you say we have a bottle of champagne to celebrate?''

"All right. We'll do ourselves proud and have a bottle of the best. I could use some wine. I'm as nervous as a broody hen.''

"I'll fetch it.''

Maggie left, and Flora, a little more relaxed as the evening wore on, sat at her desk, mentally counting up the number of customers and the amount of money made. There was a tap at the door. Maggie couldn't be back yet. It must be Tom or Willie. "Who is it?'' she called.

There was no answer. Tom or Willie would have answered—too loudly; they hadn't gotten over the tendency to shout yet. The door knob began to turn slowly. Flora reached for her feathered mask and slid the band over her head. She rose from her chair nervously. The door opened, and John Beauchamp stepped in.

11

John stood in the doorway gazing at the proud woman who ruled now in this elegant house, with her head held as high as any duchess. Her Titian hair glowed in the lamplight. For an agonizing moment they stood measuring each other like combatants, then John stepped into the room and spoke.

"Still hiding behind your mask, eh?" he asked sardonically. His words were tinged with anger—directed not at the masked lady before him, but at himself. Why had he come running back? Why did he feel this unreasonable lust for a woman in a brothel? Good God, he was a peer now. High born debs vied for his attentions, but still he found himself, when alone, thinking of this copper-crowned, proud wench who withheld her favors from him even though she was in the shoddy business of selling girls.

But she was beautiful. Her delicate

shoulders were formed as classically as a
statue by Phidias. The silk of her gown was
pulled taut across her chest, just low enough
to give a view of those swelling mounds that
moved in agitation till it was all he could do
keep his hands off them. And her face, what
he could see of it, was perfection. That little
chin, lifting now in anger—not pretended
anger either.

Flora stared, her throat too dry to speak.
Why was he here? And beneath the agitation,
a flush of triumph swelled. He had come to
see her! Not the old Flora, who was only a
phantom, but *her*. She watched silently as his
eyes examined her face, then dropped to her
breasts, where they lingered. He couldn't
recognize Flora in her—she had changed too
much. No, it wasn't recognition that moved
the muscles at the back of his jaws. It was
desire, and an effort to overcome it. He
wanted her.

"Lord Hywell!" she said, and curtsied.
"How did you know. . . ?"

The presumption of her, stating as fact
what he had planned to conceal! She knew
what had drawn him—herself. "I have the
use of my wits," he answered, schooling his
voice to ennui. "You've been parading your
girls through Hyde Park to give a preview of
coming attractions. Mother Hyde's is closed,
and when a new house opens with the same
women—it doesn't take a genius to figure out
who's running the place."

"I'm sure I never accused you of being a

genius," she agreed mockingly. "But I didn't run Mother Hyde's."

"You were in charge the last time I was at Long Acre."

"I wasn't in charge!"

"And aren't in charge here either, I suppose? You should have the courage of your convictions, madam. It's hypocrisy to make your livelihood off prostitution and hide behind a mask, as though ashamed of your calling."

"I'm not ashamed!" she shot out, guilt demanding a hot denial. "It's *you* should be ashamed—coming to a place like this. Every time I see you, you're in a—a—"

"A brothel," he said, imbuing the word with opprobrium. His black eyes were glowing with accusation. She didn't belong here. This woman belonged on a throne—or in his bed. "It's true a man doesn't go to a butcher shop to buy cheese. I go other places as well—I don't spend my entire life slumming—but somehow, I never chance to meet you at the Royal Chapel or in the Queen's Drawing Room. Perhaps the blame belongs to the mask—Queen Charlotte doesn't approve of masquerades. Why don't we remove it and see what it's hiding? I hear whispers abroad that you are a lady." He came a step closer. Flora retreated to safety behind her desk.

Her hand flew to her mask. "I have two brawlers standing ready to remove anyone who makes himself a nuisance. I suggest you leave, Lord Hywell."

"So you've discovered who I am. I'm not here to make trouble. Miss—dammit, I don't even know your name!" he said impatiently.

"My name is Mrs. Belmont." Flora lifted her chin and dared him to contradict her.

"I know what you call yourself. As you wear a disguise, I assume the name's an alias. What's your first name?"

Flora's mind went blank. The only name she could think of was Mrs. Hyde's name. "Bonnie," she said.

"It suits that red hair." Was she from Scotland? The hair and the name suggested it, and she'd mentioned that little Flora had gone to Scotland. Perhaps the girls were relatives—Flora's hair had been close to that same lovely shade. John was alive with curiosity. He wanted to know how a well-spoken girl had come to this place; he wanted to know everything about her, but he sensed her anger, and knew that anger was usually founded on fear. Why was she afraid of him? He must set her fears to rest, let her know why he had come. Because if he didn't possess this woman soon, he would go mad. She had become a fever in his blood.

He took a step back and glanced around the room. "This is much better than the parlor at Long Acre, Bonnie," he said in a pleasant tone. "I admire your taste. I wish you would sit down."

"Why?" she asked suspiciously. But her fear was receding. She was inordinately pleased to hear his small word of praise. He smiled then, softly, intimately, and Flora felt a warm glow suffuse her body at that look.

"Because a gentleman can't take a seat while a lady is standing," he answered. That "lady" had come out instinctively, and Bonnie hadn't even noticed it. She'd heard herself called a lady before, then, he surmised.

Flora glanced at the door. Maggie would be coming any moment with the champagne. She could have a few minutes with John—moments she'd cherish forever. She longed to learn all about him. She sat daintily and took a deep breath to calm her nerves, but it made a shambles of John's when her breasts nearly heaved out of her gown. She thought that John would sit on the chair behind him, well away from the desk. Instead he advanced and pulled a chair close to her. Flora immediately jumped up. "Over there!" she said, pointing to the corner.

John rose. "But I can't see you over there, Bonnie, my love." His hand came out and clasped hers loosely. She could have pulled away if she wanted. Instead she looked at him and a small smile curved her lips.

"You'll have to behave yourself," she scolded like a little mother, and pursed her lips.

"I shan't forget where I am. When in Rome, you know," he warned, but in a teasing way.

And when in a brothel . . . It was impossible —there could never be any understanding

between her and John. "If you're going to act
like that, you may leave," she scolded.

John laughed. "You are irresistible, Bonnie
Belmont!" Without another word he pulled
her into his arms and kissed her very
thoroughly indeed. This time, Flora didn't
resist. She only had a moment, and she had
been so lonesome for so long. It felt good,
being cradled in John's arms, his lips
singeing hers with a hot kiss. He was no
schoolboy, to be satisfied with lukewarm
embraces. Already his tongue was easing
between her lips, plundering her mouth,
begging, demanding.

A hot swelling in her chest left her weak.
She lifted her hands to his head, reveling in
the crisp texture of his hair, like raw silk. She
slid her hands down the column of his proud
neck, and his arms tightened around her. Her
fingers splayed hungrily over his cheeks,
feeling the structure of his jaws, wanting to
memorize him for future repining. A moan of
desire echoed in his throat at the gentleness
of her touch, like a butterfly, yet her lightest
touch inflamed him. He moved his lips over
her cheeks, fanning them with his soft
breath.

"Bonnie," he said, his voice husky, "let me
make love to you. Where can we go to be
together? I've thought about you constantly
since that night. I went back to Mother
Hyde's half a dozen times. First no one
answered, then there was a crape knocker on
the door. I feared I'd lost you forever." He

hadn't meant to reveal his desperate seeking, but knowing she wanted him too, he had forgotten his pride.

Flora felt a thrilling rush at his words, but it was soon followed by regret. She would never let him know she was that wanton who had behaved like a wild animal—that woman he'd called a whore, and who had behaved like one. His respect meant too much to her. Flora leaned her head back to look at him. It was hard to see through the feathered mask. She thought John was going to ask her to remove it, but he just smiled and placed his lips on the beating pulse of her stretched throat. His lips slid lower, down to the hollow between her breasts, where they burned like live coals.

"John!" she warned, with a look to the door.

He looked drugged. His face was flushed, and when he spoke, his voice was fogged. "Damn the door. This is a whorehouse, after all. We're not going to shock anyone," he said, and plunged one hand down the front of her gown.

His words stung like a nettle. She was still a whore in his eyes. She'd never be anything else. She tried to pull away, but he had one arm around her waist, forcing her against him. While she struggled, he lifted one white breast from the gown and took the rosy tip between his lips. His teeth grated with rough gentleness, then he opened his mouth and, with one hand steadying her breast, took more of it into his mouth, hungrily, as though to consume her.

The disturbingly familiar touch of his fingers on her breast, the clinging damp of his cheek on her sensitive skin were like charms. Flora gasped at the exploding sensation that followed. She felt as though fireworks were being lit up inside her. She stirred in his arms, knowing she should pull away, but her arms went around him and she held her breath as he moved his tongue over her breast languorously, with slow, sensuous sweeps, tasting her, relishing the flavor. She could hardly breathe as he moved his lips higher, up over her throat, to settle on her lips in a bruising kiss as she clung to him.

"Take me to your room, Bonnie," he breathed in her ear when he had finished.

Flora closed her eyes and shook herself back to sanity. "I don't do that, John. I'm not—"

"Couldn't you make an exception—for me?" he whispered.

How could she refuse him? More than anything in the world, she wanted to be in his arms, naked. She wanted to hear him say he loved her. Then she thought of her mask—you couldn't make love in a mask. "I'm afraid not," she said, but with no conviction.

"I won't tell anyone, if it's your dignity that's bothering you. I want you all to myself. I'll make it well worth your while," he promised rashly. Now why did that turn the woman to stone in his arms?

"You're trying to *buy* me!" she squealed.

"I didn't expect you to give me your favors gratis."

"Oh, you—pig!" Flora let out a cry of disappointment. She pulled away and glared at him. Was this the man she had cried bitter tears over? The great war hero, embellished with brave virtue? Her eyes were an angry glitter behind her mask.

John tossed up his hands in confusion. "I don't understand! What did you expect?"

In the middle of the argument, the door opened and Maggie came in with the champagne.

Flora straightened her shoulders and stared at John. "You remember Lord Hywell, Mrs. McMahon? He came to rent a girl," she said, using the harshest words she could find, "but blundered into my office by mistake. Perhaps you'd show him to the saloon."

A blaze of frustration leapt in his eyes. "I know my way out," John said, and turned to let himself out the door.

Flora flew to the peephole, but he didn't go into the saloon, and she was glad. If she had seen him walk off with Elsie or Dora or one of the other girls, she would have died.

"What was all that about?" Maggie asked doubtfully.

"Nothing important. Just a little contretemps. There are bound to be a few of them the first night. Nothing for us to get upset over. Let's have some champagne.''

But the thrill was gone out of the night. It was a great success, a social triumph and a monetary bonanza. The gentlemen scattered pourboires like rain. Everyone was delighted except Flora, though she tried to act as pleased as the others. It wasn't till she went to bed alone that the burning of her cheeks was cooled by tears. What was the use? He only wanted her body. He didn't love her. Elsie or Jennie would do him as well. But a voice whispered that there were hundreds of bodies for hire in London. Better bodies than hers—yet it was hers that he came back after.

She wished he wouldn't come back, and feared that her wish would be answered. John was a proud man. He wouldn't come begging. She'd gotten rid of him for good. Well, that was fine. But if he didn't come back, the sunshine would be gone from her life. She was glad he'd seen her in better surroundings, that he knew now her taste wasn't the taste of Long Acre. He had said he liked the room. That little consolation warmed her heart. It would be so nice if they could share a house together, a home that she'd make pretty for him. But that was mere weakness—a lord didn't marry someone like her. Here was she, wasting her time day-dreaming instead of planning. She had to plan now for all her girls.

The next day, Flora asked Elsie to buy her a full-length face mask when she went out to

Bond Street to spend some of her newfound wealth. Elsie returned with a gold papier-mache mask that was formed to resemble a human face. It covered her face from hairline to chin. It was very pretty, and offered total concealment.

That evening, Flora wore her peacock blue gown. As she dressed, the image in her mind was John, hovering at her shoulder. And when she sat in her office later, she listened for the sound of footfalls outside her door. Perhaps John would come again. Surely he would come back.

The next night she repeated the same thing in the gold gown. Then she rotated the gowns again, and a week was suddenly past.

Over the next month as the Season got underway, it seemed that everyone in London came to the Aviary except Lord Hywell. Maggie was constantly running to the door, and every time Flora's heart hammered violently. The news, though good, was never the news she wanted to hear. "We have a duke and a marquess just come in together. They heard about us at White's Club. We're the talk of the town, Flora."

The talk of the town—what would John think off that? He would despise her, as she secretly despised herself. Flora and the girls read all the social papers now. Flora read that Lord Hywell attended this and that party. She read with a feeling of pride that he had taken his seat in the House of Lords, and made his maiden speech. She wished she had

known, for she would have gone to the ladies'
balcony to hear him. He spoke about the
plight of the Luddites, the frameworkers in
Yorkshire who were in revolt. She had
thought he'd speak about the campaign still
being waged in the Peninsula. It was odd that
he could have forgotten his comrades there.
But he seemed to be good at forgetting.

12

At Whitehall, Lord Bathurst, new Secretary of State for War and the Colonies, raised his walruslike face and said, "Ah, Hywell, thank you for coming." He motioned Hywell to a seat and began rooting around his littered desk for some papers. "You've been wanting a look-in on the Peninsular campaign since coming back from Spain. There's a matter of some urgency you might handle for me." Hywell leaned forward in his chair, his face alive with eager interest. "Ah, here we are. It's about supplies for Wellington. A man can't fight a war without arms, eh? As a soldier you must know that."

"The uncertainty of supplies was always a problem," Hywell nodded. "I'd be happy to do anything I can to regulate them." To sit behind a desk filling orders wasn't really what he wanted to do, but he knew it was necessary.

"They're regular enough," Bathurst scowled. "Every lot we ship out is pirated on us, regular as a clock. The situation is desperate."

"Pirated—in this day and age!"

"Modern piracy, and the French pirates seem to know exactly when a new shipment is on the way. We have a leak in our department—how else could they be lying in wait for us? Now, I want you to look into it, but it will be better if your status remains a secret. Officially, you'll continue with the Luddite business—someone will write up a speech for you to give in the House from time to time, but I want you to get to the bottom of this other matter. Hire whatever staff you need, and discover who is selling us out."

They discussed the matter for an hour, at the end of which Hywell left, well satisfied with his new unofficial position. The urgency of his mission filled his days and nights, and he welcomed every chore. It kept him from running back to Mrs. Belmont like a puppy. But after a few weeks, he found he could no longer control the impulse to see her.

A month had passed, and at the Aviary so many men had to be turned from the door that business settled down to a regular set of first-class customers, who occasionally brought new friends. Tom and Willie were so adept at keeping the customers under control that no one had made it into Flora's private sanctum, though they often peeked in the door. It was on a Friday evening in midseason that Flora stood at the peephole examining her girls and the guests, for they mingled like any polite party before slipping upstairs. Her gold mask was on her desk, ready to pick up if required.

Elsie had spoken to her about the mask at lunch that day. "Lord Chalmers says you're the favorite on dit in the drawing rooms, Flora," she said. "Everyone is wondering who hides behind the gold mask. Some think it's Lady Caroline Lamb."

"How did anyone see me?" Flora asked.

"Why, they peek in at your door when Maggie or Tom or Willie are going in. They've had a glimpse of you, no more. We let them know that Mrs. Belmont doesn't wish to be disturbed," Elsie said, pulling a dowager's face.

"They never question that I *am* Mrs. Belmont?" Flora asked.

"What's to know?" Jennie laughed. "I mean it's not as though you really were some fine lady who had to hide her shame. No one in London would know Flora Sommers. I think you're too cautious. You miss out on all the fun in the saloon. Last night we played charades. I made two quid off Chalmers."

"From," Flora said automatically.

Jennie made a moue. "Chalmers likes it when I talk Cockney. I'm teaching him rhyming slang. He asked for his 'tit for' last night when he was ready for his hat. 'Tit for tat'—it means hat," she explained when Flora looked puzzled.

"The aristocrats have always amused themselves at our ways," Maggie said. "They say the young Duke of Dorval has had his front teeth sawed off so he can whistle through them like the coach drivers. And to hear some of the bucks talk, you'd think they'd never been to school. Between thieves' cant and stable talk, they sound like the backhouse boys at home in Ireland."

Elsie nodded in agreement. "I think you're right. They like to come to us because they can relax and feel superior. They know nothing shocks us. Chalmers says he much prefers girls like us. His wife pokers up if he says 'damn,' so he says 'demme' instead."

Flora listened, wondering. Was that why John frequented brothels? Was that why he wanted her, someone to whom he felt infinitely superior, so he could behave in ways he wouldn't behave with a real lady? He must have settled on someone else, since he never came back.

As she stood at the peephole, these memories drifted aimlessly through her mind. She saw Tom pouring wine for Mr. Walbeck. Maggie was just bringing in a newcomer. Flora didn't recognize him, though she recognized most of her customers by name and reputation now. The regulars included a good sprinkling of Members of Parliament, and Mr. Walbeck from the Privy Council. There was old Chalmers calling for his brandy; Willie brought him the bottle to save steps. Oh dear, they weren't all three supposed to leave the lobby at one time—Tom and Willie, and Maggie. Someone might come and no one would hear him knock.

If it was a newcomer, he might just stroll in and end up at her door. It had happened a few times before, no doubt adding to the on dits about her mask. Flora slipped on her gold mask, just in case. There, Willie was going back to the lobby, with a coin in his pocket for delivering the brandy decanter. London really was paved with gold, if you were in the right neighborhood.

Later that evening, there was a tap on her door, and Flora called, "Come on in, Willie." It had to be Willie. He'd be coming to bring her tea, on a large silver platter, accompanied with sweets from the refreshment table, as he did every night at eleven. Willie was a little early night, she noticed.

She opened the door and stood with only the mask between her and John Beauchamp. Before she could push the door closed, he stepped in and stood looking at her, his head cocked at an angle to study her.

"A new face tonight, eh, Bonnie? I think I prefer the half-mask."

Surprise at seeing him left her breathless. Why did he always have to catch her unprepared? She wanted to be cool and sophisticated, but heard herself exclaim, "John!" in a voice that revealed all her eagerness. Impossible as it was, John looked more handsome every time she saw him. His hair had grown a little longer. He wore it brushed forward in the stylish Brutus do. His dark tan from Spain had begun to fade, though he was still more weathered than most Englishmen. But there was a greater change than either of these. He looked—tired. She noticed little lines at the corners of his eyes and along his forehead. "So you decided to bring your business back to the Aviary," she said, and looked sharply to see his reaction.

John rubbed his hand wearily across his forehead. "I've been working till half an hour ago. I don't think I could do justice to a woman tonight."

Her quick sympathy was easily aroused. "Why did you come, then?" she said.

"Do you have to ask? To see you. Just to see you, Bonnie. May I sit down?" As he spoke, he looked at her in a way she hadn't seen before. The admiration hadn't disappeared; it was still there, but overlaid with some new emotion. A softer light glowed in his black eyes tonight. It looked like lonesomeness, friendship, even longing, and she was powerless against it.

Flora went behind her desk, and John took the chair that was sedately placed on the other side of it. "What has been keeping you so well occupied?" she asked. "Is it the Luddite riots?"

A quick gleam of interest flashed across his mobile features. One eyebrow tilted in a question. "How did you know I was involved in that?"

"I saw a mention of it in the journals," she answered offhandedly. "We *do* know how to read here, you know," she added testily.

John's smile softened. So she did take some interest in his affairs! He knew what brought that swift, defensive answer, and was determined not to offend Bonnie tonight. That would defeat his plan before he had time to present it. "I haven't come for a verbal sparring match tonight, Bonnie. Let us not begin by exchanging insults and innuendo."

There was a tap at the door. Willie with the tea! "Come in," Flora called, then jumped up to help Willie with the door. John's eyes followed as she moved away from him. How tiny her waist was, how gracefully she moved, like a flower swaying in the wind.

Willie entered and stopped dead at the sight of a gentleman in Mrs. Belmont's private sanctum. "Eh? What's this then?" he asked suspiciously. "How'd this gent slip past me? Want I should show him the door?" he asked Flora.

"That's quite all right, Willie. Lord Hywell is a—" She hesitated a moment over what word to use.

"A friend," John supplied, and felt gratified to hear the pleasure in her voice when she continued.

"A friend," she agreed. "We're just having

a chat. Perhaps you would get another cup for him."

A grunt of disapproval rumbled in Willie's throat and a very suspicious eye measured Hywell's body. Willie was built like St. Paul's, with massive shoulders and a little lantern of a head. He felt a strong wish to pit himself against the Corinthian in the chair. A fine set of shoulders the lad had. Hywell was known as a member of the fancy, which amused itself with boxing.

"I hear you knocked Gentleman Jackson off his feet," Willie grunted.

"That was some time ago—a lucky punch," Hywell said modestly.

"If you want to test your dabs with me, just you try getting tricky with Mrs. Belmont, lad."

"The cup, Willie," Flora reminded him, and he left.

After Willie left, John gave a little laugh. "Your butler certainly has the knack of making a fellow feel welcome. What's that bull doing in your dainty china shop, Bonnie?"

"It's the custom to have a bull protect the heifers, is it not? Willie's our official protector, caster out of unruly gentlemen who have too much to drink."

John listened closely to Bonnie's conversation. He didn't hear the breath of Scotland in it, but the undeniable accents of a lady. Her speech wasn't the uncertain mixture of elegance and bad grammar usually heard in women of her sort. He listened closely, determined to draw her out and discover something about this intriguing charmer.

"That comment about a bull protecting heifers sounds like farm lore. Are you a farmer's daughter?"

"No," she said unhelpfully.

He wished he could see her face. That damned gold mask concealed even her mouth and chin. You could tell quite a bit about a person's expression from the lips. Was she smiling, knowing she'd kept her secret? Was she nervous? But most of all, he wanted to see more of her than just her exquisite shoulders.

"I wish you'd remove that mask," he scowled.

Flora wanted to take it off. She wanted John to see that she'd improved from that hoyden who'd attacked him before. She waited a moment before answering. "We all wear masks, John," she said pensively. "Mine is recognized as such. Gentlemen smile at their wives, then come here to betray them. Princes wear a crown and behave like yahoos. You can't judge anyone by his face," she said, rather wistfully.

Willie returned with the cup. He gave Hywell another threatening glare and said to his mistress, "I'll be right outside the door if you need me, lass."

"She won't need you," John smiled.

"Thank you, Willie." Under her mask, Flora smiled to see Hywell's surprise at this polite threat. "Willie, on the other hand, is a diamond disguised as a pebble," she added after he had left.

"No, disguised as a mountain."

"We'll split the difference. Willie is a rock," she laughed. John listened to the throaty sound, mentally congratulating himself. She was becoming quite easy in his company.

Flora poured tea from her silver pot into the dainty Wedgewood cups. John watched the graceful ballet of her arms and hands in a performance that would do credit to a princess. "Milk, sugar?" she asked. The domestic chore, the wifely question, caused a pang of regret in Flora. This is how she wanted it to be with John and her. Polite, civilized.

"Yes, please," he answered, and politely said "Thank you" when she handed him the cup. Then he stared, waiting. She couldn't drink her tea in that full face mask.

Flora realized the same thing as soon as she lifted her cup. She set it down again. "I'm not very thirsty tonight," she said. The feeling of domesticity was ruined. She realized how evanescent this moment's seeming normalcy really was. There could never be any normal relationship between her and John.

"Nor I," he said, and set his cup back in the saucer. "Bonnie, let's go out somewhere," he said. "Let's get away from the Aviary tonight.

You said every time you see me I'm in a brothel."

"You're the one who used that word!" she reminded him.

He smiled to see how well she remembered every detail—as well as he remembered it himself. "It's what you meant. Let's go somewhere and dance and drink wine and—I don't care where. Let's just get way from here."

The offer came like a bolt out of the blue. Flora had never been "out" with a gentleman in her life. She felt a tingle of excitement at the prospect, yet almost immediately difficulties occurred to her. He couldn't take someone like her to a polite ball—certainly not in a mask. She had learned at home how to perform simple country dances, and she knew the steps of the new waltz from trying it with the girls, but she'd never waltzed with a man. To dance in a man's arms seemed almost as scandalous as making love, yet it was done in polite circles—even at the rigidly polite Almack's Club, with the hostess's permission. "Where could we go?" she asked uncertainly.

"You're outfitted for the Pantheon masquerade. If you insist on wearing that mask, you limit our choices. Why don't you remove it?" he suggested, casually.

She knew that the Pantheon masquerade assemblies were a little less than respectable. They were where such women as herself were entertained, but Elsie said the place was quite magnificent, and it did solve the problem of the mask.

"The Pantheon sounds fine," she agreed.

"I expect that means you plan to wear the mask?" he asked, defeated.

"But of course, John! I wouldn't want to destroy the reputation of a sterling gentleman by letting him be seen in company with me," she teased.

"If I weren't willing to be seen with you in public, I wouldn't have invited you out! Don't lay it in my dish!" he riposted.

He looked, but saw only the mask. Behind it, Flora felt a sting of anger. Yes, willing to be seen at the Pantheon, where all the fine gentlemen took their mistresses! What did she expect? That he'd take her home to meet his mother? To Carlton House to meet the Prince Regent, perhaps?

"I'll have to go upstairs and get my pelisse," she said, and whisked out of the room.

She sent for Maggie and explained that she should take over the business affairs for a few hours.

"You're going out?" Maggie asked, her eyes starting from her head in astonishment. "Who with?"

"Lord Hywell. We're going to the Pantheon. Oh, Maggie, don't chide me. I know I shouldn't do it, but I must."

"Why shouldn't you?" Maggie demanded in a purely rhetorical spirit. "I'm delighted you've decided to have a bit of fun. Hywell,

eh? The last one I would have expected—''
She looked a question at Flora.

"It's not what you think. I just—feel like
dancing. I hope I don't waltz all over his
toes."

Maggie continued to look doubtful. "I hope
you don't waltz yourself into trouble. Have a
good time—and don't hurry home," she
added with a suggestive little laugh.

"Home"—to the Aviary. Flora wished she
never had to come back here. She went
upstairs, and on impulse added the half-mask
to her reticule. John wouldn't be able to kiss
her if she wore the full face mask.

13

John was waiting at the bottom of the stairs, as Flora had pictured him waiting the night the Aviary opened. With a greatcoat thrown over his elegant shoulders, he was the embodiment of any girl's dream—so tall and handsome, sprinkled with magic prisms from the crystal chandelier overhead that added a touch of unreality. Best of all was the anticipation glowing in the depths of his jet eyes. He put out one hand to greet her; she placed hers in it and they went silently out the door, smiling. John's mood, thought he was careful to hide it, was different from Flora's. He had hoped she'd remove that silly mask. It made her seem a stranger, a riddle—less than a woman. Before the night was over, he meant to throw it out the window and see her whole face.

Flora felt like a fairytale princess climbing into a chariot as she entered his shiny black carriage with a crest emblazoned on the door. Inside, the squabs were not the customary leather, but luxurious velvet. A metallic twinkle around the door hinted at silver appointments. She was both relieved and disappointed when John sat discreetly on the banquette opposite instead of beside her. The seat was chosen so he could study her gestures. He meant to learn all her secrets tonight. The carriage turned north toward Oxford Street.

"I expect you've been to the Pantheon often?" he asked nonchalantly.

"I've never been there, but I've often heard the girls talk about it."

"What do you do for entertainment, Bonnie?"

The dullness of her life might sound like a bid for pity, and she didn't want John's pity. "I read and play the piano," she answered vaguely.

He noted these genteel occupations, the usual pastimes of a lady. "I mean for social entertainment, as you don't amuse yourself with your customers. I can't believe you find much in common with your employees."

"A woman in my position doesn't have many friends."

"It sounds a lonely sort of life," he said sympathetically. "Why do you place this awful embargo on yourself—not going out, not making friends? You could enjoy a very successful social life. You must have heard of Harriet Wilson and her sisters—why, they're the toast of London. One meets them at the opera and the theater.''

That he placed her in a class with the most notorious courtesans in London infuriated Flora. But what was the point of protesting once again her distance from her employees? She was what she was, and the fault wasn't entirely John's, so she wouldn't let it spoil this evening.

"I've been very busy till now," she said. "Perhaps later I'll get out more.''

He leaned across the space between them and took her hands. "You know where you can always find an eager companion," he said.

It was a short drive to the magnificent Pantheon, on the south side of Oxford Street. The road was full of carriages letting down passengers. Flora looked at the elegant patrons and felt a tingle of excitement. She felt as if she were going to attend her first ball, and she looked as fine as any of the other ladies, too. Great torches lit the entrance to the Pantheon. John sent the carriage off and together they went into the building. It was ablaze with light from dozens of chandeliers, which sparkled on the array of gilt and glitter below. Couples, mostly in dominoes and masks, paraded to and fro, talking loudly and laughing.

"It's magnificent!" Flora exclaimed in delight. "I thought I had made the Aviary grand, but this is beyond anything."

John smiled at her excitement, and felt

again a strong wish that he could see beneath
that mask. As they walked in, a couple
accosted John. "Hywell, out on the town, I
see," the man smiled. This couple weren't
wearing masks.

"Lord Harrod, Lady Harrod." John smiled,
but he didn't make any motion of introducing
his companion. Lady Harrod stared at Flora
quite rudely and finally asked roguishly,
"Anyone we know, John?"

"An incognita, and she wishes to remain
that way," John laughed, and hurried on.

A lord and his lady—that's why John didn't
care to introduce her! She knew well enough
that a lightskirt was not presented to respectable women. Flora's pleasure of the night
was in danger of being ruined till John said,
"Lady Harrod would have insisted on having
that mask ripped off you if we'd stopped.
She's known as the London Intelligencer."

Flora didn't believe it, but she knew he was
trying to spare her feelings, and she accepted
it.

"We'll get a box upstairs so we can look
down on the crowd," he suggested.

Soon they were ensconced in a booth and
ordered a bottle of wine. While waiting for it,
Flora said, "I think they're working you very
hard in Parliament. You look a little tired,
John."

"This is doing me more good than a week's
holiday."

"I was surprised to hear you're working
for the Luddites. Of course, my sympathies

are always with the working man, but I had
thought you'd be taking some part in the war
effort.''

John didn't suspect any ulterior motive in
the question. He felt a troublesome urge to
tell her the truth about his important work.
He wanted to hear her praise and pity, but no
one except Bathurst and his immediate
colleagues knew what he was doing. "The
frameworkers are in a sort of war too,'' he
answered vaguely.

"But the real war is more—oh, not
important, but it's a matter of life and death
every day. It must be hard to just turn your
back on your friends in the Peninsula.''

"There wasn't anything open in that
department,'' John said brusquely. Flora's
oblique criticism left him tender.

She sensed his reluctance to discuss it.
"Perhaps something will come up later,'' she
said. Then the wine arrived before he could
answer.

"I'm parched,'' Flora said, watching him
pour the ruby liquid into the glasses. John
looked across the table with a mischievous
smile. "Now you will have to remove your
mask, milady!''

From behind the sheet of gold a teasing
voice answered. "Turn your head—I don't
want to shock you with my crowsfeet and
wrinkles!''

John obediently turned away, angry with
himself for the excited pounding of his heart.
At last he'd see the mystery woman! When he

turned back, she had replaced the gold mask with her feathered half-mask. "Bonnie!" he howled. "That's not fair! I want to see the woman I'm with, dammit!"

"But all the ladies here wear masks, John. I wouldn't want to look out of place," she laughed. Her laughter was an intoxicating, throaty warble. Her smile was enchanting too. Pearly teeth, not straight and hard-edged but beautifully softened to curves around the bottom. Her whole body was a design of curves—from the chin, along the graceful line of her throat, down to those breasts that he ached to touch. There wasn't a straight edge anywhere. He gazed entranced as she laughed at his consternation.

"You win," he sighed, "but if you see me memorizing your body, you know where to lay the blame. I must have some memory to take home with me."

The lambent admiration in his eyes made Flora giddy with excitement. She lifted her glass. "Let's propose a toast, John," she suggested. "What shall it be?"

He studied her and slowly lifted the ruby wine to touch hers. "To us, I believe is the customary one on such occasions as this."

"What occasion is that?"

"The beginning of an affair," he said, and drank, his eyes regarding her intently over the top of his glass.

The glass trembled in Flora's hand. It was what she had been secretly hoping, wasn't it? She longed to reach out and touch him. She

had come out with the hope that he'd kiss her
—why else had she brought the half-mask?

"To us," she murmured, and drank. She
watched as John's alert, wary expression
softened to a smile of triumph. How dark his
eyes were, like two glittering black
diamonds. No, diamond was the wrong word.
They weren't cold and hard. They were hot,
smoldering, when they caressed her lips and
shoulders.

He rose from his seat and sat beside her on
the bench, one arm around her, pulling her
against him. It felt so strange to be cuddling
in public, but in this place she saw couples
doing a good deal more. There was one hussy
sitting on her gentleman's lap, kissing him
hotly, and his hands going places they
oughtn't to go in public. She noticed that
John was looking at them to. As he looked,
his hand moved to her breast and gathered it
in his hand, sending a shiver through her.

"This is horrid!" she exclaimed, and
pushed it away. "No wonder decent ladies
don't come here. It's like Sodom and
Gomorrah!" She felt suddenly hot, and the
noise was deafening.

John lifted a brow at this show of prudery,
but his plan was succeeding, and he didn't
intend to let slip the word hypocrisy. "Some
things are best done in private," he agreed.
"Shall we dance instead?"

Flora took another sip of wine to give her
courage and rose. They went below to the
dance floor, where a waltz was just

beginning. He gathered her in his arms, holding her close against him. Flora had only heard of the waltz. This was the first time she had seen it, and in this déclassé place all the gentlemen were clutching their partners against them. It wasn't the way the dance was performed at more polite parties, but Flora had no way of knowing this. John's arm tightened till she could feel his body against hers, strong and masterful and exciting. He lowered his head and his chin brushed her curls.

"No wonder the waltz has caused a scandal if this is how it's done!" she said in a weak voice. "I'll probably walk all over you. We didn't do the waltz in—at—" She drew up short on the word Bradbury.

John clenched his jaw in annoyance. He had been listening closely to hear what might slip out. "Where?" he asked nonchalantly.

"At home," she said.

"Where's home, Bonnie? I don't believe you ever mentioned where you're from." He tried to make the question light, but he felt her stiffen in his arms.

"What does it matter where I'm from? I'm here now." I'm an abbess, she added silently, and the only place you can be seen with me is in a den of iniquity like this.

He pulled his head back and looked at her lips, pursed in an adorable pout. He felt a strong inclination to seize them, but he wanted more than her lips, and his aim was to soothe her. "Then let's enjoy ourselves, here and now," he said gently. "It doesn't really matter to me where you come from, you know. It's where we're going that matters."

"Where's that?" she asked, rather angrily.

"As you said, what does it matter? We're going together, Bonnie. I'm not going to lose you again. We're going to be together." His arms folded around her, both arms now holding her in a protective shelter from the unruly crowd that bumped around quite at random. The disinterested crowd created a sort of privacy. Flora placed her head on his shoulder and sighed.

John continued talking, his words soft as a lullaby in her ear. She felt his lips move, tickling her temple as he continued with a series of delightful escapades. "I'm going to set you free from that Aviary, my little love-bird. We're going to Astley Circus to see the horses, and St. Paul's and the Royal Exchange, like visiting tourists. I'm going to show you all the sights of London, and when we've seen London, we'll go to Bartholomew Fair and duck for apples, and for long drives down country lanes. We'll have picnics at the seashore—would you like that?"

A bright panoply stretched before. Could it really be like that? Had she found a friend, after all the loneliness? The aching inside eased insensibly. She felt like a blossom stroked by the sun, felt herself open to him. "Could we really do that, John?"

The yearning in her voice, as wistful as a

child with her nose to the candy-store
window, pulled at his heartstrings. A surge of
tenderness welled up in him. She seemed so
small and vulnerable in his arms. He wanted
to take her away and lock her in an ivory
castle. "Why not?" he said. "We can do
anything we want."

"I've never done anything I wanted," she
said. "I've never even seen the seashore."

He smiled down at her with a twinkle in his
eyes. "Mind you, you'll have to take off your
mask. We wouldn't want to frighten the fish."

Her head twitched painfully at that. She
was deluding herself. Those normal pastimes
weren't for her—certainly not with John. But
she had a carriage now, she could go with
Maggie in the afternoons, or on Sunday. Of
course it wouldn't be the same. She wouldn't
be in John's arms. His soothing voice
wouldn't be whispering in her ear, promising
a bright future, sounding as though he loved
her. She felt bathed in a golden glow, warm
and cherished.

They went back to their table after the
dance and had more wine, then danced again.
A lazy, languorous mood came over Flora as
she drank the wine—more than she was used
to. Tea was still her preferred drink. "Do you
want to dance again?" John asked.

"It's such a melee down there. Let's not."

"The party's beginning to get rough.
Bonnie, let's go now," he said, and took her
hand, squeezing her small fingers
possessively.

"Yes, let's leave. Oh I feel dizzy," she said, as she tried to stand up.

"We'll drive through the park before—"

"That might be a good idea," she nodded. She didn't want to go home tipsy.

As they waited for the carriage, John was silent. He was wondering where he could take her to make love to her. Obviously not home, where an aunt and three eminently respectable cousins, one a bishop, were visiting. The Aviary came to mind, only to be rejected. He didn't want their liaison to smell of the brothel. That damned Aviary—she wouldn't want to give up such a profitable venture, but he'd be stapped if his mistress would continue as an abbess. One had some standards! A closer examination of his true feelings forced him to admit it was really jealousy that gave rise to this insistence. He didn't want her surrounded by men. He'd have to come down heavy to repay her for giving it up. How much could it make? Her rates were ridiculously low. That annoyed him too, that people were taking advantage of his Bonnie.

14

When the carriage came, John showed Flora in before directing the driver to Hyde Park and from there to a little inn on the Chelsea Road. When he got in, he sat beside Flora, with her head on his shoulder and his arms around her. Again that sense of tenderness came over him as he cradled her small, soft body in his arms. She was no better than a child. Something niggled at the back of his mind, but his eagerness to solve the riddle of Bonnie Belmont overcame it. He wanted to protect her, and it nagged at him that she didn't really need his protection. She was a wealthy businesswoman, engaged in the most shameful trade imaginable.

"How did you come to open the Aviary, Bonnie?" he asked. He wanted to hear a story that would remove the taint of degradation.

"Mother Hyde left me some money."

"But how did you come to be with Mother Hyde in the first place?"

She lifted her head from his shoulder. "I don't want to talk about that. Don't spoil this lovely evening."

"You were one of her—hostesses?" he asked, trying to tame the anger in his voice. A picture rose unbidden of Bonnie with some other man, and his heart thudded angrily.

"No!"

"How, then? Are you her daughter?"

"Certainly not!" she said hotly.

"Why would she leave her money to you—especially if you didn't even work for her?"

"I did work for her. I worked in the kitchen first, then as a sort of housekeeper," she said. "I was never a hostess."

"People don't leave their fortune to a housekeeper."

"I said I don't want to talk about it!" Flora repeated. Her voice was becoming thin with annoyance.

"We must talk about it, my dear."

"Why must we?"

John nuzzled he ear with his nose. "Because I want to know all about you. Tell me. I'll understand. What about your husband? Was Belmont the sort of bounder I think he was?"

"The Mrs. is a courtesy title. I never had a husband."

John was relieved to hear it, yet immediately it occurred to him that she hadn't been escaping a loathsome marriage, as he often imagined. "I still don't understand how a gently bred girl ends up keeping house in a brothel. It doesn't make sense, Bonnie. Are you an orphan?"

"My father's dead," she prevaricated. "We were short of money when he died. I'm the oldest of a large family. I was sent to the city to work. I—I didn't realize what kind of a house I was entering."

He wanted to believe her, but since he was a rational man, doubts kept arising. "If Mrs. Hyde thought enough of you—made a sort of daughter of you—why didn't you take your inheritance and go back home?"

"She didn't mean for me to do that!" Flora said. "You don't understand, John. She left me the business. She wanted me to take care of the girls for her."

"The Aviary must have cost a fortune to set up. You could have given each of the girls some money and still—"

"No, no. That's what I wanted to do. Maggie said the girls would just squander the money and end up on the streets. And they would. They haven't a ha'pence of sense between them. They all wanted me to do it, John. I had to protect them. Don't you understand?" Her voice throbbed with sincerity. "It's the last thing I ever wanted to do. I hate it!" she said. A hiccoughing sob came from behind the mask. In the darkness of the park, he couldn't even see the mask.

He moved to slip it off, and, secure in the darkness, Flora let him. She buried her head in the crook of his neck and let the tears flow. John comforted her with soft, forgiving words as his hand stroked her back, the way she used to stroke the baby at home. She felt like a baby, safe, protected, with someone finally caring about her, and didn't think of herself as a degraded, vile woman.

"It's all right, Bonnie, my love. Don't cry. I'll take care of you." He was delighted to hear that she wanted to leave the Aviary.

"I hate every minute of it," she sniffled. "I never wanted to be there."

"I know, darling. Don't cry. Please, it kills me to see you cry."

John tilted her face up to him. He couldn't see her features clearly, but the oval of white showed in the darkness, giving an idea of her beauty. Tears sparkled in her eyes. He gently touched her wet cheeks with his finger, then lowered his head and kissed her tears. He felt her tremors subside, and in this tender mood, he gathered her into his arms for a kiss. His heart wrenched to feel the tears on her cheeks, but soon passion grew and the kiss deepened.

It happened so quickly, the surging tide of love that came swelling up in her. Flora wrapped her arms around his neck and pressed herself against him. His hand stole under her pelisse, and in one swift move he gathered her on to his lap and kissed her a fleeting touch on the lips. Her head drooped trustingly, their foreheads touching for a moment in the darkness of the carriage. John leaned her head back against the soft velvet squabs and she felt his hot lips burning a trail of embers along her throat, resting at the hollow of her neck, then inexorably down to where her breasts rose taut in inviting swells, pushing against her gown. He cradled her tightly against his swelling need, moving her by the hips in an insinuating, insistent rhythm as his moist tongue played over her breast in tantalizing strokes.

She drew a shuddering sigh and pulled his head up. In the shadows, he found her lips. Before he kissed her, he said, "We won't make it to the inn at this rate. I'm going to love you right here." His fingers began probing at the back of her gowns for fasteners.

Flora lifted her head. "What inn? We're going home."

"Are you afraid I won't pay the toll?" he asked, laughing in a lazy, drugged way. "I directed the driver to the George, on the Chelsea Road." His lips tasted her breasts again. He went back to them like a bee to honey, lured by their inviting warm smoothness. "No one will know me there," he murmured.

"But I have to go back to the Aviary. It's late."

"You're never going back there, my darling. You said you hated every minute of it. You can stay at the inn till I find a cottage for you."

Flora sat silent a moment, trying to sort

out what he was saying. He planned to make her mistress, then. The first spurt of joy was already tainted with anger. A mistress, to be hidden away in a cottage. But it would be nice . . . No, she was insane. "I have to go back, John," she said. "I can't desert the girls."

"That older woman—Maggie is it?—she can run the place."

"Oh, Maggie hasn't the wits for it!"

"Good God, Bonnie," he said impatiently, "most of the 'girls' are older than you. They can fend for themselves. You must see I can't have you running a brothel. I'd be the laughing stock of London."

"But I have to. It's—it's my duty!" she said, unhappy with the last word, but no better one occurred to her.

He sat back and jabbed at his cravat in a way that was becoming familiar to him. "Is it the loss of revenue that's troubling you?" he asked. His gentleness was rapidly dwindling. A sting of anger was present now.

"They can't live on nothing."

"Sell the house."

"I don't own it. It's only rented. I've spent a small fortune fixing it up. I can't just run away and lose all that investment."

"I won't have my mistress running a whorehouse on the side," he said. "There are limits, even to my lunacy."

"What lunacy?" she charged. "I see you weren't so besotted you forgot to tell your driver to take me to an inn. You said we were going dancing. That's all I agreed to! That's all I wanted."

"You agreed to be my mistress! The only thing we haven't settled is the terms."

"I did nothing of the sort!"

"What the hell do you think I was talking about back at the Pantheon? Picnics and parties? I wanted you to be my mistress. A man doesn't waste his time entertaining ladies of pleasure without enjoying the perquisite of their favors."

His words were like a whip to her heart. "I'm not a lady of pleasure! I told you how it happened!"

John drew a long breath before answering, and when he spoke, his voice was cold. "And I want to believe you, Bonnie. I really want to believe you're not what you so obviously appear to be. But innocent orphans aren't lured into places like Mother Hyde's to wash the dishes. They don't walk out with the madam's fortune in their pocket to open a more illustrious whore house. That isn't the behavior of a saintly orphan hot off the farm. You are an abbess, and a dozen masks aren't going to disguise that fact. I accept it, but I can't and won't even *try* to accept your continuing with this profession while under my protection. You either give it up, or you give me up."

"You didn't believe me!" she squealed.

"I'm willing to overlook a few slips on the garden path. I don't claim to be a saint."

"I should say not! If my place is so reprehensible, why do gentlemen come there? Maggie is right. Men want all women to be virgins, but they want to have their way with them for all that. You can't have it both ways, John."

"I don't care about other women! It's *you* we're discussing. And nothing was said about virginity." But there was a question in his voice. "You're not claiming to be a virgin?" he asked. She gave a snort of disgust, but didn't answer. "Then you *were* a hostess?" he asked, his voice stiff with disapproval.

"I never took a penny from any man for my favors. I never did, and I don't intend to start now, not for you or anybody else. Please take me home."

He didn't pull the checkstring. "How much do you make at the Aviary?" he asked. His voice was cold now, as cold as ice. "I'm rich. I'll reimburse you, but the place is either shut down or a new manager is hired. That's it. No more compromise."

"I can't desert the girls."

"Don't try to pull the saint act with me. No one in her right mind takes a fortune and turns it into a circus like that, with herself the ringmaster. There's something you're not telling me, Bonnie. You *like* it—that's the only answer I can think of. And you like more than sitting in that office. Who is he? Who is it you won't leave?"

Bonnie reached for the checkstring, but John's fingers bit into her arms and jerked them to her sides. Anger closed over him like the sea, robbing him of sense. "Answer me!" he growled. He was appalled at the uncontrollable temper that seized him, but he couldn't quell his harsh breaths and the blazing heat in his bowels. His heart pounded so furiously it frightened him. "Who is he? Who is your lover?" he rasped.

Her pale face and frightened gasp only served to fire his temper. "He must be a gentle wooer! We soldiers deal more harshly with our women."

"John, you're hurting me," she pleaded in a light voice.

"Hurting you? I should kill you!" But he took his anger out in a punishing kiss instead. He crushed her in his arms and attacked like a tiger, hands ripping at her bosoms, roughly grasping her breasts while she fought to free herself. He felt he could subdue her with his passion. It had always worked before, but in this temper he was too impatient. He forced her down on the banquette and began to remove his coat.

"John, don't! Don't! Please," she whimpered.

It was her desperately frightened voice that finally brought him to his senses. He was about to hurt this small, delicate woman he loved. By brute force he was going to force her to lie and say she loved him, either in words or actions. He was despicable. He must be mad. He pulled himself back up on the seat and pulled the checkstring, while Flora sat up and straightened her gown.

The carriage rumbled to a stop and she moved to the other banquette. "Tell him to take me home," she said primly. "This conversation is finished."

With gritted teeth, John opened the window and called, "Back to the whorehouse." Then he crossed his arms and scowled across to the other seat.

As they drew out of the park, he saw that the mask was in place again. Bonnie sat like a nun, her pelisse gathered tight around her neck, her lips clamped in a prissy line. Flora knew that if she didn't keep them rigid, she'd burst into tears. He hadn't believed a word of it. After ruining her, he dared to fling in her face that she wasn't a virgin. She hated him. She hated all men. She'd raise her rates through the roof and become the most infamous whoremaster in England. Let them talk. They weren't interested in the truth. They believed what they wanted to believe.

The carriage drew to a stop in front of her house and she opened the door herself, since John made no move to do it for her. As she began to climb out, he grabbed her arm. Anger with himself spilled over to its cause, this abbess who dared to look like a nun. "I can ruin you, Mrs. Belmont," he said in an arctic voice. But there was fire in his eyes. "I can have this den closed down with one stroke of my pen. Your investment will be lost, as well as your income. I'll hound you to the farthest corner of the country to see that you don't open shop somewhere else."

He was surprised to see her lips curl in a sneer. "From brute force to threats and everything in between! Your ingenuity knows no bounds, Lord Hywell. Having failed to attach me with the bribe of ducking for apples at Bartholomew Fair, you now think to do it with threats? I wish you luck of that, sir. The numerous dukes and marquesses who patronize my parlor might have something to say about it. I wish you luck of trying. You'll only make a flaming jackass of yourself. But then, that will hardly be a new experience for *you*. No doubt the polite drawing rooms will be buzzing with curiosity. Who is it at the Aviary who has got Hywell in such an uproar?"

On this taunting question, she pulled her arm free and strode into the Aviary without looking back. She nodded to a few departing guests before disappearing through the portals. Then she ran up to her room and cast aside the hated mask before flinging herself on the bed to cry.

15

Flora didn't think that evening could possibly hold any more sorrows for her, but just as she was drying her tears to go downstairs, there was a tap at the door and Jennie Whitehead came in. She was smiling tremulously.

"Flora, you'll never guess what!" she exclaimed. "Mr. Walbeck wants to take me under his protection."

"You mean you'll be leaving me!" Flora exclaimed. Jennie was one of her favorites. She thought of her as almost a sister. Flora had taught her to speak properly, had assisted in preparing lemon paste to cure Jennie's freckles, and had seen her through other small storms. "Oh, Jennie, Mr. Walbeck's so old! Are you sure—"

Jennie flopped unceremoniously on the side of Flora's bed. "He's very kind. He's hiring me a sweet little cottage in Camden Town. I'm to have a carriage and team of my very own, and a male and female servant, and two hundred a year for gowns. I know he's old, Flora, but he's nice. And he says when his wife dies, he'll marry me."

"She'll probably live longer than he will."

"She's not well, but even if she does—. The thing is, I'm preggers, Flora. Mr. Walbeck wants to acknowledge the baby—unofficially, I mean, while his wife's still alive. After, he'd adopt it legally. He doesn't have any children."

"Pregnant? Oh dear!"

"So I wouldn't be of any use to you soon anyhow."

"Anyway!" Flora smiled at her foolishness in correcting grammar at an important moment like this. "What makes Mr. Walbeck think the baby is his?"

"He's my regular. Of course he's not the only one, but he wants the baby. You'll have to come and visit me in Camden Town, and bring the girls. Mr. Walbeck would prefer me not to come back here," she added with an embarrassed smile.

Jennie rose and walked slowly toward the door. "Aren't you happy for me, Flora? I thought you'd be glad."

"If you're happy, Jennie, then so am I. But I'll miss you."

"We'll see each other all the time."

"When will you be leaving?"

"As soon as Arthur hires the cottage. He asked me to call him Arthur," she added proudly.

"I hope we'll have time for a farewell party."

"Oh, we're having that tomorrow. The girls are taking me to the Clarendon Hotel for lunch. I know there's no point asking you to join us. I must fly now."

The door opened, and Jennie whisked out. Flora stood alone, thinking. She should be happy for Jennie. Being under the protection of one kind, fatherly gentleman was surely better than the life Jennie had here. Yet it hurt that Jennie was so eager to leave her. Already Jennie was getting above this place. Her gentleman didn't want her coming to visit. Was the Aviary really that bad? Then she thought of the child. Being able to keep her baby was surely a strong inducement to Jennie. Sal cried for a month when she had had to give up her Johnnie. She still drove out to Ilford to see him every week. Johnnie was two years old now.

Flora's mind drifted to other matters. She'd have to do something for Jennie. Part of Mrs. Hyde's money was Jennie's by rights. She'd give her a dowry. It was one less girl to worry about, at any rate. If they'd all find protectors, she could close up the parlor. While Flora was considering Jennie's offer, there was another tap at the door and Maggie came in. "Jennie told me the news," Flora said. "What do you think of it?"

"I'm glad for her."

"I'd be happier if he were a bachelor and could marry her."

"Oh, Flora," Maggie laughed. "Gentlemen don't marry girls like Jennie. She's doing well to get the sort of offer she got."

I got an offer of that sort tonight too, Flora thought. I couldn't take it because of Jennie and the others, yet she's leaving me without blinking an eye. "He said he would when his wife dies."

Maggie hunched her shoulders. "He's getting on. Maybe when he retires and leaves London, he'll do it. He could never present her to his respectable friends. But that's not really why I came. I'm afraid I have bad news for you."

Flora's face blanched. John! surely he wasn't making trouble for her already! He hadn't had time to try to close her down. "What is it?" she asked.

"Dryden was here tonight."

"Mark Dryden! Good God, I'd forgotten all about him. What did he want?"

"He came in like the cock of the walk, strutting all around and adding up how much money you'd spent. I didn't want to cause a riot in front of our gentlemen. Willie let him in—of course he didn't know about Dryden. The man looks decent enough. When he asked to see Flora, I gave Willie and Tom the eye and they showed him the door."

"He used my name?" Flora asked. If John had been there—. She felt weak considering it.

"I told him Mrs. Belmont was the mistress here, not anyone else."

"I don't suppose he believed you?"

"He looked highly suspicous. I expect he'll be back. He was ugly when the lads threw him out. I told them not to let him in again."

"That's good."

Maggie noticed that Flora was more upset than a visit from Dryden should have made her. "How did it go with Hywell?" she asked.

"We went to the Pantheon and waltzed," Flora answered.

Now, why should that make her look as if she'd just lost her mother? Maggie wondered. "Will he be coming back?"

"No, he won't be coming back," Flora said. Her voice sounded half dead. "I'm very tired tonight, Maggie. Would you mind finishing up downstairs?"

"I intended to. I just wanted to let you know about Dryden. We'll have to do something for Jennie, eh?"

"Yes, we'll give her a dowry. I'll look at the books and decide tomorrow how much. Good night, Maggie."

"Get right into bed, Florie. You look worn to the socket."

"That's just the way I feel."

"You're not used to waltzing."

Flora's eyes looked haunted with sadness to Maggie. Going out with Hywell had seemed a good idea to Maggie at the time. It was unnatural for a pretty young girl like Flora never to have any fun. She never showed the least interest in any of her customers, but she obviously felt something for Hywell. And he must feel something too, or why did he keep turning up like a bad penny? Maybe Maggie should warn Willie and Tom to keep him out too.

The world was a strange place entirely, Maggie thought as she went back downstairs. She was now fifty years old, and very happy that her salad days were behind her. When young people fell in love, they lost the use of their reason. And in that state of insanity they made decisions that affected the rest of their lives. If she had it to do over again, she'd show young Jerry McMahon the door so fast his head would spin. Her mother had told her the man was no good, but she'd gone running off with him. Her father had no choice but to give her her dowry from Aunt Ada—only two thousand pounds, but still it could have bought her a decent man in Ireland in those days.

It only rented Jerry McMahon for a year. When the money was gone, he disappeared, leaving her stranded in London with ten guineas owing on the rent and winter coming on. She was too proud to go home in disgrace, and too lazy to work, so she did what women like herself had been doing since Eve gave Adam a taste of the apple. Yes, she was glad she was too old to put the gleam in any old gaffer's eye. Though if Colonel Cameron didn't have a sweet tooth for her, she was much mistaken. Old fool. Close to sixty-five years old and coming to a place like this to waste his money.

In her room, Flora undressed and lay on her pretty canopied bed. She left the lamps burning and gazed at what lay around her. If her mother could see her now, she'd think her daughter had landed in the honey pot. Flora had decorated her room with rose-sprigged wallpaper. Reflections from the lamps glowed with a rich chestnut light on the facade of a mahogany dresser and desk. In the clothes press hung an assortment of silk gowns that any fine lady might envy. The coiffeur came every week to arrange her hair. The brocade draperies added a note of luxury. On the carpet, invisible but well memorized, more roses were scattered. She had constructed a very beautiful prison for herself, and she was trapped in it as surely as Maggie's canary was trapped in its gilded cage. The Aviary—she had named her house well.

Where had she gone wrong? Each step, as she took it, had seemed the right one. Was her mistake stopping for toast and tea at Mother Hyde's Parlor? How could she have known what would follow from the simple act of seeking food when she was hungry? Was the mistake to return to the parlor the second night, when she was being chased by those two bucks at St. Martin's Lane? She could have been done with all this when Mother Hyde died. *That* was her mistake. She should have just divided the money and gone home. And would she be any happier at home, knowing she had abandoned the girls?

Last of all, she thought of the moment that had really ruined her. The moment John Beauchamp had stepped through the door and said, "Good evening, Flora," with his black eyes smiling at her. With Mother Hyde's Hellpot burning in her, she had mated with him like a wild animal. And she would have done the same tonight without the Hellpot, if things had gone a little differently.

Why couldn't he understand? She had spewed all her secrets out to him, all but one, and he had sat in judgment on her. Pretending to be a saint, he said. She never pretended to be a saint. She didn't have the luxury of living in heaven, but had to adjust to the real world. He was a fine one to call her a sinner! Her present position was all due to his lechery. And before she slept, she thought again how nice it would be to have a little cottage in the country, with John coming home at night, like a husband. Perhaps to Camden Town, with Jennie living nearby.

16

As Hywell drove home that night, he didn't know whether he was more angry with Bonnie Belmont or himself. The woman must take him for a moonling, thinking he'd swallow that story about Mother Hyde giving her money for no reason. And she trying to make it sound like a sacred duty to run a brothel. If he weren't so angry he'd laugh at it. But the battle wasn't over yet. A member of the House of Lords held considerable power, and if he chose to exert it . . .

But already his better nature was causing second thoughts about trying to close the Aviary. Did he want to win Bonnie by a show of force? Trying to buy her favors was bad enough.

There were plenty of distractions to keep Flora from harping on John over the next few days. She didn't go to the Clarendon with the girls for Jennie's farewell party, but she did arrange for the dowry. When Sal heard of it, she came storming into the office. "How come Jennie's getting money and the rest of us aren't?"

"Because she's leaving, Sal. I'm giving her her share of Mother Hyde's estate. If you leave, you'll get your share as well. But if you leave without having somewhere to go—well, you know what will happen. You'll squander it."

"I could've married Joe Sadler if I'd of known about this," Sal said accusingly.

"I don't recognize that name. He's not one of our gentlemen, is he?"

"He's not a gentleman exactly. It's his mum that takes care of Johnnie. He's sweet on me, I think. He has to take care of his mum, but if I'd known about the dowry, we could pay off the mortgage and the farm could support me as well."

Another of her girls eager to leave her! Fine, let them all go. "If you want to marry Joe, you can have your dowry. The business is doing well. We can afford it and still carry on here."

A light of pure joy sparkled in Sal's dark eyes and she threw her arms around Flora. "Oh, would you do it, Flora? Would you really? I won't leave you short-handed. I'll get a girl to replace me."

"No!" Flora shouted. "No, I don't want to

increase the size of my family. When the girls are all gone, I'll close the house."

"But if we go off one at a time, how will you pay the bills?"

"I don't know!" Flora said in exasperation. Things were changing too quickly. "I'll manage somehow."

Sal left. She could see that Flora was worried and didn't want to add to it. She'd have to get someone to take her place. It stood to reason you needed girls to run a place like this, and she knew just the girl that would jump at the chance. Marie Simpson, who worked for Johnson on Swallow Street, was always griping. Her beau had told her she should try to get in at the Aviary.

But soon Sal's thoughts turned to Joe, and her baby. Sunday she'd tell him. Joe knew all about her. He didn't like the sort of work she did, but he knew the value of a penny. He never tried to talk her out of it. He knew she had to pay her own way in the world. He was a good lad, a hard worker—and he'd make a fine father for Johnnie.

Sal came back from Ilford on Sunday evening to announce that everything was arranged with Joe, and she'd be leaving on Tuesday. "Monday I'll spend packing up and doing a bit of shopping for the wedding—and it'll give you time to arrange my dowry," she reminded Flora.

When Sal returned from her shopping, she had a pretty young friend in tow. "This is

Marie Simpson," she said. "This is Mrs. Belmont, Marie. She runs the house, and you won't find a better madam in London."

Marie was a black-eyed, black-haired, sharp-faced girl, pretty but sly looking. "Good day, Mrs. Belmont," she said. Her accent was not bad. "I'm to take Sal's place, if it's all right with you."

"I'm not looking for a replacement," Flora said, aghast.

"But, Mrs. Belmont, she's already left Johnson's," Sal said. "I told her you were short-handed, and she gave up her position. Marie has ever so many customers that'll follow her here. She'll be good for business."

"No, I'm not taking on any new girls."

"My room'll be standing empty. Look at the waste," Sal pointed out.

Marie drew out a handkerchief and began sniffling daintily into it. Maggie and Flora exchanged a defeated look. "She has nowhere to go now," Sal said.

"Oh, very well," Flora sighed. "You can come here for the time being, but start looking for another position, Marie."

A remarkably dry eye lifted from the handkerchief. "Oh, thank you, Mrs. Belmont. I'll have my trunks brought in." She and Sal darted off to see to the trunks.

As soon as she was installed, Marie Simpson wrote a note to Mark Dryden, announcing her success. Even before this, she had ascertained that Mrs. Belmont was in fact Flora Sommers, though why that mattered she couldn't imagine. Mark Dryden's schemes were nothing to her. She had much more important matters on her mind. Someone had been watching Johnson's place for two weeks now. Marie needed a new base of operations and a new errand boy. Mr. Dryden seemed the sort of gentleman who would do as he was told, without too many questions.

"Saucy piece," Maggie sniffed as Sal and Marie ran upstairs. "She's pretty, though. And coming from Johnson's place, her clients would be top drawer. They do a deal of business with gentlemen from Whitehall."

After the sudden spate of change, things returned to a new normalcy at the Aviary. Jennie's room remained empty, but Marie actually did bring a new raft of clients to the house, so the decrease in revenue was small. Financially the Aviary was doing fine, but Flora found her job more unpleasant than ever. She realized that while she had sacrificed herself to keep the girls safe, their aim in life was to get away. It was soon borne in on her that they felt no loyalty either. Jennie proved quite cool when some of the girls went out to Camden Town to see her one Sunday.

"The snooty manner of her!" Elsie complained. "You'd think she was Queen Charlotte to see her strutting around that little old cottage. It's Arthur this, and Arthur that. Calling herself Mrs. Walbeck and wearing a gold band on her finger. Of course her condition's showing already. She served us day-old cake, and she didn't even ask for you or Maggie, Flora. To the devil with her, say I. I'll not go back. Old Walbeck lifting his eyebrows as if he'd never seen us before, and he always merry as a grig when he came to the house. I expect it was the neighbor landing in on the middle of our visit that got him all stiff as starch. Jennie was ashamed of us—that's what it was."

"If she's trying to pass as a respectable married woman, she wouldn't want the likes of you girls there to give the show away," Maggie explained. "It might be best if we forgot Jennie."

"I've already forgotten her," Elsie declared. "I never had such a boring visit since the vicar used to call at the orphanage and make us recite scriptures."

Flora tried not to be angry with Jennie. Jennie had no idea that Flora had considered her a replacement for her sister. Every new occurrence bore in on Flora how reprehensible her position was. She determined to close down the house, and with that in mind, she began urging her girls to look around for a protector.

"What will you do, Flora?" Maggie asked as they sat together that Sunday evening, the one day the Aviary was closed to customers.

"I'll hire a little flat somewhere and just

rest," Flora said. "Perhaps we can live together, Maggie."

"I plan to go home—to Ireland, I mean."

"Ireland? That might be nice—"

"Why don't you go back to Bradbury?" Maggie asked. Flora was a little hurt that Maggie didn't encourage the idea of their sharing a flat.

"I don't think I could go back. I've changed too much. And Mama would expect me to be looking for a husband, you know."

"That might not be such a bad idea. Why you're only twenty years old."

"The gentlemen in Bradbury would expect to marry a virgin," Flora said bluntly. "I'd be stoned if anyone there ever knew what I'd been doing. And they might find out—you never know."

"That's true. But in the city, they're more broad-minded. You might arrange a marriage of convenience with some cit."

There was a sound outside the window and Flora jumped up, her face white. "What was that?" she exclaimed. "It's Mark Dryden, trying to get a look inside to see if I'm here."

"You're becoming loony on that subject. What difference does it make if he does know? Nobody cares who you really are. It's probably just Tom taking out the trash."

Somebody cared! John had asked her a dozen times to take off her mask. "Tom and Willie are out. They went to Kew Gardens this afternoon and aren't back yet."

"Maybe they're coming in the back way."

They waited a moment, but there was no sound at the back door. "It must have been a dog or cat knocking over a dust bin," Maggie decided. "You're jumpy tonight. What's the matter?"

"I just have a feeling—I don't know. This house is getting on my nerves."

They went to the window and looked out, but there was nothing to be seen. Outside, Mark Dryden smiled softly to himself in the shadows. Mrs. Belmont, was it? It was Flora Sommers, as Marie said. But why the devil was she making a secret of it? He was sorry he'd gone ranting to Bow Street when they kicked him out like a dog, demanding that the Aviary be closed down. Not that Bow Street would do it on his say-so. They'd take their silence money and leave it at that. And that suited him fine. It gave him time to learn more.

There was someone Flora wanted to hide her identity from, and the only person Mark could think of was Lord Hywell. He'd watched her come back in his carriage that night they'd kicked him out. She'd pay to keep her little secret. Then he opened the note Marie had flung out the window and read it. Tomorrow he'd have to walk along Bond street and hand it over to Dupuis. A pretty good business deal he'd worked out with Marie Simpson.

Flora drew the drapes. Although it was

early, she soon retired. She felt listless lately,
fatigued. And it was worse in her room. The
image of a bird in a gilded cage had taken
root. She was coming to hate her pretty
room. She couldn't sleep, knowing those
rose-spangled walls were there, staring at
her. She had the feeling they'd close in on her
one night and smother her. That's how she
felt, smothered. She'd lie in bed for hours,
just staring at the canopied roof of her bed,
wishing she were somewhere else.

Somewhere else. How she longed to get
away—anywhere, just away from the Aviary,
where everything reminded her of John. He
hadn't come back. No doubt he had found
some other ladybird to set up in the country,
till he decided to take a wife. At least he
hadn't managed to get her house shut down.
Sometimes she even wished he had tried and
succeeded, to take the responsibility from
her. She wondered if he'd tried—or was he
even that interested?

Getting away from the Aviary became an
obsession. All Flora wanted was a little room
somewhere, the more spartan the better,
where she could go and be alone, away from
all the luxury—the reminders of who, and
what, she had become. She seldom left the
Aviary, and when she did she still wore her
widow's veil and went in the carriage,
usually at twilight. "You behave like an
escaped criminal," Maggie scolded one
evening as they were driving out. "If you're

that squeamish, you should get out of this business, Flora. I thought you had more gumption.''

"So did I," Flora admitted, "but I was wrong." Her energy was sapped, spent on useless pining for what could never be. If she didn't get a good night's sleep soon, she feared she'd become ill.

The carriage turned off Oxford Street on to Swallow. "Look! There's a 'Room to Let' sign!" Flora exclaimed, pointing to a red brick house. It was in that transitional state between faded elegance and mere respectability.

"Yes," Maggie said with very little interest.

"I wonder how much they charge for rooms."

"It's only one room—the sort that clerks or milliners hire, with a bed and a grate to make tea. Probably a guinea a month, something like that."

"It's third from the corner," Flora said.

"Yes, the backyard must touch ours. We're third on the next street over, Riddel Street."

"That's handy," Flora said pensively.

Maggie shook her head. "Good Lord, you're not thinking of moving there after you close down the house?"

"No, before," Flora said, and laughed.

Maggie thought she was joking, but the next day Flora went to look at the room. It was exactly as Maggie had described: a once-elegant bedchamber turned into a bed-sitting room, with a grate where an ingenious and poor person could do some elementary cooking over the hob. The house reeked of cabbage and dust, and the staircase Flora was shown up had no carpet. But the room was clean and bright. It had a view of her own backyard.

"I'll take it," she said without even asking the price.

The proprietress, Mrs. Fellows, looked at her silk gown and the fancy hat above the veil. "I don't allow any carrying on here," she said firmly.

"I am happy to hear it," Flora replied.

"Why would a lady like yourself be wanting to live here?" the woman asked suspiciously.

"I don't plan to live here. I live in Devonshire. I have some business to conduct regarding my husband's death, and only need somewhere to sleep from time to time." Yes, she thought she might actually be able to sleep on that little cot, so similar to her cot at home.

Mrs. Fellows settled down. "I see. Hotels are awful dear. That'll be three months in advance, Mrs.—"

Not Belmont! The name might be known. "Mrs. Banyon," she said, once again appropriating Mother Hyde's real name. She paid three guineas, her landlady left, and Flora sat down on the cot, looking all around to see what she would need to be completely comfortable here.

A feeling of peace descended on her for the first time in months. It was strange she should feel so peaceful, so free in this little room, when she was stifled in the larger house on Riddel Street. It was a haven, a place where her troubles couldn't find her. Mark Dryden wouldn't know she was here. John wouldn't know. Nobody knew. She could curl up and die on that cot and nobody would ever know. What a peaceful thought.

17

It was while Flora was arranging her little haven on Swallow Street the next afternoon that Officer Townshend of Bow Street visited the Aviary. Maggie McMahon had to deal with the corpulent gentleman in his blue coat and broad-brimmed white hat, and an awful experience it was to be visited by the law. Not only the law, but an officer so important that he was chosen to protect royalty when they felt the need. Maggie had no way of knowing that Townshend had personally undertaken the chore with his noble patrons in mind. The Aviary was coming into prominence. One of the royal dukes would certainly show up sooner or later, and he wanted to know that the house was suitable for royal patrons. There had been only one complaint, and that from a nobody called Dryden. Still, it made an excuse to come in and look about.

Flora didn't hear of it till she returned at

four o'clock, feeling rejuvenated after her visit to her new room. Maggie met her in the hallway, her eyes large with fear.

"You'll never guess what, Flora! We've had a visit from the authorities, threatening to shut us down! Townshend himself came storming in like Attila the Hun. This is Dryden's doings, mark my words."

Flora felt it was her other Nemesis, Lord Hywell, who had begun to stir up trouble. Her heart beat heavily, and a crimson stain touched her cheeks. If he couldn't have her, he'd drive her out of town—or try to. "Dryden couldn't get Townshend to come here in person. What did he have to say?" she asked coolly.

"He went over the place with a fine tooth comb, complaining of dirty kitchens and slovenly housekeeping, calling us a menace to public health. Why, you could eat off cook's floors. This never happened at Mother Hyde's, and you know what a shambles that was before you came. He said if we don't clean up, he'll have to shut us down."

"He didn't complain that I'm running a common bawdy house? That's odd!"

"Willie says that if they closed us up, it would set a precedent. The authorities don't really want girls walking the streets. They'd prefer to have them decently housed. It's spite, pure and simple."

"It certainly looks like it," Flora agreed, but she kept her opinion as to who the perpetrator was to herself.

"You thought it was Dryden sneaking around the yard last Sunday. He was trying to find something he could report," Maggie decided.

"What exactly do we have to do to prevent being closed down?"

"Hah," Maggie scowled. "The magic key is money. I paid Townshend a guinea and he said he'd be back next month for another look. We'll have to pay him a guinea a month is what it amounts to."

"I daresay we can afford it to be insured against closing down," Flora said. She was surprised that John had not been more resourceful.

But Lord Hywell had a far different matter on his mind. His fascination with Bonnie Belmont must take a back burner while he attended to business. His investigations were beginning to point to a certain Mr. Addison as the leak in security. Addison had been followed, and a change in his routine had occurred. His twice-weekly visits to Johnson's on Swallow Street had been discontinued. John racked his mind for a bright fellow to put on the case, and came up with Nigel Taylor, a friend from the Army. He'd get him moved into Bathurst's office and have him strike up a friendship with Addison. Bathurst didn't want John's own involvement to be known.

When this was decided, he allowed his thoughts to turn once more to Bonnie. He'd write a note—not overly friendly, but giving her an opening if she was too proud to approach him.

Flora went upstairs to prepare for the evening, and as she slid her gold taffeta gown over her head, it occurred to her that John wasn't finished with her yet. He was waging a slow campaign. Townshend's visit—surely John had sent him—was only the beginning. When she received a note from John that evening, she was certain she was right.

She opened it and read, "Mrs. Belmont: My offer still stands. If you change your mind, I can be reached by a note to my house in Berkeley Square. Regards, Hywell."

Flora's blood boiled as she read his curt instructions. A note to his house! Did he think she was so gauche she'd arrive on his doorstep with her trunks? Did he actually think she'd ever change her mind when he had as well as called her a liar? When he had set out to harass her? She strode angrily down to her office. Later, she went to the peephole and noticed with satisfaction that no less than three peers were present, two of them higher in the scale of nobility than John. A duke and a marquess were enjoying the comforts she provided.

As she stood watching, every person in the saloon turned and stared toward the doorway, which was invisible to Flora. A spasm of fear gripped her—John! He had come with some new weapon to fight her. What could it be? A team of Bow Street Runners to turn out her patrons and haul them off to the roundhouse? Her guests rose as one body to their feet. The frozen faces eased into polite smiles as the gentlemen bowed and the women curtsied.

Flora stood transfixed, consumed with curiosity to know what was happening. Suddenly a gentleman stepped into her line of view. She had never seen him before, and had no idea who he could be. He was middle-aged, with white hair and a portly build. His jacket was extremely elegant, and on his chest he wore many medals and ribbons. His head, she noticed, was oddly shaped, rather like a pineapple. He behaved most graciously, smiling at all the gentlemen and chucking Elsié under the chin in a condescending manner. Maggie showed him to a seat, where he sat as though he were a king on his throne, being gracious to everyone. After enduring their attention for a moment, he lifted a sausage finger and waved them away. It was Elsie that he chose to partner him in a game of cards.

Tom ran for a new deck. The brandy decanter was brought and set on the table beside the couple. Flora could no longer endure her suspense. She ran to her door and beckoned to Willie.

"What is it? Who has come?" she demanded.

Willie smiled a rollicking smile. "We're entertaining royalty tonight, Mrs. Belmont. That there's a prince, one of the king's sons.

Him what was a sailor before they pulled him home to keep the seas safe."

"A royal prince!" Flora gasped. Her hand flew to her lips in astonishment. She trembled from head to toe to consider the incredible thing that was happening. A member of the royal family was sitting in her saloon. She was dying to go out and meet him. What a thing to tell her children! Then her heart cooled to normal. What children?

"He's the one who was a sailor, then?"

"That's him, Willie the Tar. It's all off with him and Mrs. Jordan, after depositing ten or a dozen kiddies on her. He's out to marry himself a fortune, they say. He'll not find it here. Heh heh."

"Good gracious! See he gets whatever he wants, Willie—the best in the house."

"Would that be Elsie or Marie?"

"That will be up to him—it seems to be Elsie. Send Maggie to me."

Maggie came panting into the office. "The Duke of Clarence, Florie!" she exclaimed. "Was there anything like it? Sitting there playing Pope Joan with Elsie for shilling stakes, and she, the gudgeon, is winning."

Together they ran to the peephole to observe this bizarre phenomenon. For an hour the royal duke played at cards, drank brandy, and ate half a plate of lobster pastries. Then he rose, kissed Elsie's hand, bowed all around, and walked away.

"I'll dart out to say good evening," Maggie

said, and ran to the door.

Flora stood trembling with excitement, wishing in spite of it all that she could meet him. Within a minute there was a tap at the door and Maggie came in with the royal duke by her side.

"Your grace, pray allow me to present Mrs. Belmont," she said.

Flora gulped and performed a graceful curtsey. The duke stumbled forward and took her hand in a merciless grip. She noticed that his nose was red and his eyes bleary. "By God, you captain a very snug little frigate here, madam," he said in a loud voice. "They have poured brandy down me till I am quite droll."

"Thank you, your majesty," Flora said, worrying whether she used the wrong term.

"Yes, I fear I am up in the world, as folks say, but I ain't too overhauled to know you have a very pretty little frigate here. All ship-shape. I shall recommend it to my friends. Why are you wearing that mask?" was his next blunt question.

"I—I always wear it, sir," she answered, so nervous that she hardly knew what to say.

"Hah, the Masked Lady, a nice touch of mystery. I shouldn't mind having one of those to hide my own ugly phiz. Perhaps then I could convince some rich deb to take me aboard. I am quite run aground, you know. It fell through with Lady de Crespigny, I regret to say. The lovely little angel led me a merry chase. However, I keep a weather eye on all the pretty lassies. Carry on, Mrs. Belmont."

On that nautical remark, he turned on his heel and swayed out the door, followed by Maggie McMahon, who curtsied two or three times before running back to Flora. "What do you make of that?" she asked.

"I like it very much," Flora smiled. "We'll see about being closed down now, Maggie! If the duke sends any of his royal friends around, show them every courtesy, and don't present them a bill."

"I didn't!" Maggie said.

"Good. Do you think he'll really bring us into fashion?"

Within a few days, Flora knew it was so. Other royal dukes came to view the Aviary, and in their wake came the cream of London society. The great attraction appeared to be Flora's mask, as that was the item the Duke of Clarence remembered when he spoke of the Aviary. Cartoons appeared in store windows showing the Masked Lady greeting royal princes. It was de rigueur for the more important gentlemen to be brought to the office to meet Mrs. Belmont, but despite their urgings, she refused to remove her mask.

One foolish nobleman offered her a thousand pounds to see her face, but Flora feared he wanted to see rather more than that, and graciously declined.

"You should wear a mask too, Elsie," Marie said, with one of her sly smiles. "It would help to hide the wrinkles. Why, you could probably carry on for another year or two if you took up a mask."

"What you need is a muzzle," Elsie retorted, and stomped to her room to examine her face for aging. She was twenty-seven years old. This hard life aged a girl—woman. Older woman? Damn Marie Simpson!

Several of the girls got masks made up as a sort of joke. Business was booming. Everyone was in a happy mood, and Flora relaxed a little too. John appeared to have called off his campaign.

At Whitehall, John turned white as paper and stared at Nigel Taylor's impassive, stolid face. Taylor wasn't a man of much imagination, but he was a good, solid, dependable worker. "The Aviary? Are you positive?"

"That's where Addison's taken his business since leaving Johnson's place. It was a Marie Simpson he visited. She told the girls there that Mrs. Belmont particularly wanted her. She sent one of her girls over asking for her. This Mrs. Belmont is a bit of an enigma. Why does she wear that mask? She might be someone who's wanted by the law."

John considered it silently a moment. "Possibly. Have you met this Marie Simpson?"

"I've visited her—in her professional capacity," he added. "She plays a close hand."

"Addison was under suspicion before he began visiting the Aviary," John pointed out.

"But why did Mrs. Belmont solicit Miss Simpson's services? She must have discovered what the girl's up to, and decided to cut herself in. I think we really must discover who this Mrs. Belmont is, John. This is too important to leave any stone unturned. Shall I have Mrs. Belmont arrested on suspicion? We could interrogate her—"

"I'll handle it," John said.

He had a reason to close the Aviary now. Yet he was strangely loath to take action. After Taylor left, John's mind roved back to his last meeting with Bonnie, at the Pantheon. She had made a point of asking about his work—pressed a little to confirm that he wasn't involved in the war effort. And once she was sure it was the Luddite question that occupied him, she had turned him down flat. There was nothing she could learn from him. That was the only reason she went out with him that night, to see if he was fool enough to betray any secrets. The woman was a spy.

18

Though life at the Aviary was more interesting with royal clients, Flora still used her haven on Swallow Street when time permitted. Her hours for visiting it were irregular, but when that old feeling of suffocation came over her, she would slip away for an hour or two. After the business was closed down at night, she often put on a plain pelisse and her veiled bonnet and went out the back way, through the gate and in at the other back door, up the stairs to her little room. She went quietly as a mouse, to prevent disturbing the other tenants.

"A widow," the landlady explained to inquisitive neighbors in the same hallway. "Poor thing, she puts on a good show, but she's seeing hard times, I believe, having to stay in a place like this."

Though Flora's hard times were not as imagined by the landlady, the new girl, Marie

Simpson, was giving her some problems. She was sly, as Flora had thought when she first laid eyes on her. Marie's special target was Elsie, who was more beautiful, and therefore more hated, than the others. Marie never hesitated to remind Elsie that she was getting older. Marie had demanded the best and biggest room for herself, and bribed Elsie to give it up. She made free with the other girls' belongings, taking a ribbon or even a gown that appealed to her, and very saucy she was when anyone reprimanded her.

"I pull my weight here, Mrs. Belmont," she said boldly. "I've brought you a dozen new customers."

"And kept every one of them yourself," Elsie threw in. "You entertained three gentlemen last night, one after the other, while two of the girls sat idle, waiting."

Marie tossed her impertinent shoulders. "Is it my fault Mr. Addison would rather wait for me than make do with an older woman like yourself, Elsie?"

"I was busy! It's Hester that was idle."

"You're just jealous," Marie snipped. "Mr. Addison wants to take me under his protection."

"Please accept!" Flora urged.

"I'm happy just as I am, Mrs. Belmont. I'll do better than a plain Mr. Anyone when I settle on a patron. Oh, and by the by, I'll need the carriage this afternoon."

"I already reserved the carriage!" Elsie said."We're going for a ride in the park."

"You can all go together," Flora pointed out.

"Oh, Marie doesn't go the park," Elsie said, with the air of telling a secret. "She goes shopping. It seems to me she's got more money than the rest of us put together."

"Yes, tips from my gentlemen," Marie replied. "I give satisfaction, Elsie. Of course, I'm not so long in the tooth as some. Do you not have an age limit, Mrs. Belmont?" With a deprecating look at Elsie and a bold toss of her black curls, Marie strode from the room.

"I wouldn't be a bit surprised if she's emptying her clients' pockets," Elsie said when Marie had left. "She has a bankbook in her reticule. What would the likes of her be doing with a bankbook? There's plenty of money deposited too. I took a look when we were changing rooms."

"You shouldn't snoop," Flora said, but she couldn't suppress her curiosity. Good gracious, if Marie was stealing from the guests!

"Over a thousand pounds," Elsie said, nodding her head wisely.

"Well, she was at Johnson's before, you know. He pays well."

"She deposited a thousand since she's been here."

"That's impossible! She's only been here a month."

"It's not impossible if she's rifling the gents' pockets," Elsie insisted.

Later, Flora mentioned her fears to

Maggie. "Have you heard any complaints from the guests about money missing?" she asked.

"No, it's just spite on Elsie's part. Her nose is out of joint, with Marie being so popular."

"Perhaps Mr. Addison is trying to bribe her to go with him. I wish she would do it," Flora said.

"Addison can't be the one. He isn't that well-to-do." Maggie looked as if she would like to say more, but hesitated. Finally, she spoke. "If you really believe she's stealing, you could watch her, Flora—you remember that peephole in the secret corridor. Marie's in that room now."

"Mrs. McMahon!" Flora exclaimed, shocked. "Maggie—I would never do such a thing."

"It seems low, but really—if I hear any complaints about missing wallets, I'll spy on her myself."

"Oh, I wish Marie would leave. The girls are always fighting among themselves since she came. Let us hope she accepts an offer from someone soon."

That night Flora was in her office as usual. With the business running smoothly, she often spent an evening reading. She had just bought Miss Austen's *Pride and Prejudice*, and was pitching herself into the role of Elizabeth Bennet, with John filling Darcy's shoes. She wished with all her heart that she could enjoy the innocent problems of these two lovers. The mask was cast aside to make reading easier.

At eleven o'clock, tea time, Willie came tapping at the door. "Just put it on my desk," she said, glancing up from her book.

"I've got bad new for you, lass," Willie warned. He wasn't carrying the tea tray.

"If someone's intoxicated, throw him out," Flora said, without even asking for details. Elizabeth Bennet was just reading Darcy's letter, and Flora didn't want to be interrupted.

"I'd like to, I would. The trouble is, he has a search warrant."

"What!" The book fell to the floor. "Who is it?"

"It's young Hywell."

Fear clutched Flora's heart. So he had succeeded after all. It had taken him a little time to do it, but John had finally made his next move to close her down. He couldn't know about the new clients she had recently attracted. Surely royal dukes could save her. Clutching at this shred of hope, she said, "Show him in."

"Yer mask," Willie reminded her.

Flora picked it up and slipped it over her head. She hardly cared now whether John knew who she was. No doubt the story of her disgrace would soon be in all the journals. "Show him in," she repeated. Willie had never seen such a look on her face before, nor heard such a rasping voice from his beloved mistress.

Without waiting for permission, John pushed the door open and strode in. His mood was evident at a glance. A scowl darkened his face, etching angry lines from his nose to his lips, which were pulled in a thin line. His eyes wore a dangerous glitter, and the whole posture of his body was one of rigid, proud arrogance. Flora opened her lips in an effort to speak, but no sound came out.

John took a step forward and handed her the search warrant. "You will have the bull set on me at danger of incurring the courts' wrath, Mrs. Belmont," he said scornfully, glancing at Willie. At closer range, Flora saw that he was enjoying her disgrace. There was an edge of triumph in his voice.

" 'ere, who you calling a bull?" Willie demanded.

"You can go, Willie," Flora said. To show her defiance she added blandly, "I can handle Lord Hywell."

"I won't be far away," Willie warned, and glared at Hywell before leaving.

When they were alone, Flora tilted her chin high and spoke with a boldness she was far from feeling. "What is it you're looking for? Shall I ask the various royal dukes and cabinet members littering my rooms to depart before you make your search? I'm sure that you honorable gentlemen stick together. You wouldn't want to embarrass your government by catching so many of its members *in flagrante delicto*."

"It's not the gentlemen I'm interested in, Mrs. Belmont. You can ask questions at your trial," he said, and handed her another letter. "I've come to arrest you."

Trial! Flora's cheeks blanched and the room began to spin. She backed against the desk to keep from falling over. It had come to that, then. She was to be tried, sent to Bridewell. She wouldn't go. She'd sooner drink a cup of hemlock and have this wretched life ended. There were dozens of brothels in London—why was hers singled out? Oh it might be illegal, but if no worse vices were perpetrated than prostitution, the law looked the other way. Hers was chosen because she refused to become Lord Hywell's mistress.

John watched as the blood drained from her face, and felt his moment of triumph blurred by a weakening stab of pity. Was it possible she didn't know what was going on here? He had found it suspicious that the Simpson woman was involved with Adisson before coming to the Aviary. It was that damned mask that aroused curiosity and suspicion. Soon he'd see what was beneath it.

"What exactly is the charge?" she asked in a hollow voice.

"Treason."

"*Treason?*" Her voice was a whisper of incredulity. Not satisfied with having her thrown in jail, he meant to see her hanged. He had invented some scheme to tar her with a crime worse than running a brothel. The room began to spin, and as Flora grabbed the desk to steady herself, the door was thrown open and Willie rushed in.

"If you've hurt her, you won't leave this room alive," he growled, with blood in his eye.

She watched as one in a trance while Willie pitched the full weight of his body at John. John moved aside and Willie plunged against a chair. When Willie recovered his feet, John lifted his fists and drove a punch at Willie's solar plexus. Again, it was obvious that he was enjoying it. A thin smile curved his lips till he looked like a demon. Willie grunted, but soon recovered to come at John again. This time, John rammed a blow against Willie's chin. Flora winced, and tried to come between them.

"It's all right, Willie," Flora said, and turned to Hywell. "I'll go. My lawyer will handle this." Willie left with one last, murderous glare at Hywell.

"A wise decision," John sneered.

Frustration and fear warred within her. "Do you have a carriage waiting, or am I to be led to prison at the cart's tail?" she asked stiffly.

"Considering the nature of your new paramour, a little discretion is being used, but don't expect the Duke of Clarence to rescue you. There's no love lost between him and the prince regent. Royal princes have come to trial before. The Duke of York didn't escape unscathed for allowing his mistress to sell Army commissions."

A hot denial rose to Flora's lips, but she suppressed it. She would not grovel for mercy for a crime she hadn't committed. She put on her wrap and asked, "Where are you taking me? To the Tower?"

John lifted an ironic brow. "The Tower of London is reserved for more exalted prisoners than a whoremonger."

A flame of anger leapt in Flora's breast, and without counting the cost, she lashed out at him. "It's where innocent women are usually locked up, isn't it? Anne Boleyn and Catherine Howard—those dastardly victims of Henry VIII, who committed the crime of being alive when he wanted a new wife to mistreat. My crime, sir, and you are very well aware of it, is not treason but having the good taste to refuse to be your mistress. That's why you've trumped up this charge of treason. Having failed to starve me out by closing my doors, you resort to the coward's trick of lying. I am a whoremonger, and proud of it. I come to see I've been too nice in my ideas of what constitutes indecent behavior. I don't steal, or lie, or cheat. I provide a service at a fair price. And if I have the opportunity to take the stand, that is what I shall shout to the world. I'm here because I wouldn't sell my body to Lord Hywell!"

John stared, fascinated at what he was seeing. Shy Bonnie, turned to a lioness, speaking like a queen. Her voice was full and rich, her head held high. She had never looked more magnificent. Her tirade sounded so sincere that he was nearly convinced she was innocent of treason. As the words sorted themselves out, he said with a puzzled frown, "Starve you out—close your doors?"

"I received a call from Bow Street, as you threatened."

"Not at my behest. You must have other enemies."

Dryden? Maggie had always thought so. There was no reason John should deny it. But it was only a fleeting thought. Her present worry was much more pressing. "Where are yo taking me, if not to the Tower?" she asked disdainfully.

"Just come along with me. I have some questions to ask before turning you over to the authorities."

John's carriage was waiting outside. He opened the door and Flora climbed in unassisted. Then he turned his head aside and stared out the window as the carriage sped through the city, turning north. Not another word was exchanged as they left the lights of the city behind, traveling now over a country road. John's face might have been a mask carved from ice. He looked inhuman.

At length the carriage turned onto a side road and continued another mile. Eventually it stopped in front of a cottage that was completely isolated. One light glowed downstairs. He could murder her here, and no one would ever know. This wasn't an arrest; it was a kidnapping! Flora's heart pounded in her throat and her face grew hot with fear. But he had had those official papers, bearing a governmental seal. And they knew at the Aviary that he had taken her away. He couldn't plan to murder her.

John opened the door and got out. "Stable the rig," he said to his groom, still in that icy voice that sent shivers up her spine. He didn't assist her from the carriage, but stood watching warily as she clambered down. He put a restraining hand on her elbow as he led her to the cottage doorway. "A screaming attack will do you no good," he warned. "There's no one for miles around to hear you." On this menacing speech, he opened the door and she went inside.

19

One lamp glowed in a small parlor. The room had a horsehair sofa, a few tables, and dimity curtains at the windows. Flora had no idea why he had brought her here. Lord Hywell looked as out of place in this simple cottage as a marble statue in a stable. The chill of the room was unrelieved by the cold ashes in the grate. When they were alone, John crossed his arms and stood staring at her. His body was rigid, his face impassive—she would have thought he was bored if it weren't for the fiery glow in his eyes. "Take off the mask," he ordered.

Flora wanted to refuse, but in this isolated spot, she dared not. What would he say when he realized who she was? With trembling fingers, she removed the feathered half-mask and stared at him from fear-darkened eyes. She still held her head proudly erect. She watched with disbelief as his gaze flickered with apparent indifference over her features. He didn't recognize her!

Much time had passed since John had seen her that one night when he was half drunk with brandy. He was too preoccupied now at finally seeing her full face to be thinking of ancient history. The long hair arranged high on her head bore no resemblance to how she used to look. Time, and more especially her emotional troubles, had carved vulnerable hollows at the back of her cheeks. The loss of weight highlighted the structure of her bones —the delicate nose, the firm little chin. He could see she was a very beautiful woman, but failed to recognize in her the near-child of yore. He only knew he still wanted this woman as he had never wanted anything or anyone in his life.

Flora looked at him, not believing he wouldn't eventually recognize her. It was obvious he didn't, and that angered her further. A man shouldn't forget a girl whose life he had ruined. He had no right to stand staring at her from his lofty height, with contempt gleaming in his black eyes. Eyes that used to smile on her. He hated her. It showed in the stiff set of his face, the cruel, twisted line of lips, and that awful mocking expression.

And still he went on staring, as though mesmerized. God, she's beautiful, he thought. Why has she hidden that face? She might have had any man in London—why did she choose to waste herself on the old, debauched, penniless Duke of Clarence? Awful images darted through his head. Dry old hands caressing those white velvet breasts that heaved in fear, her hot lips opening in a kiss. He swallowed convulsively. "Take off your wrap," he ordered. His voice was thick with rising passion.

It was impossible to pinpoint the precise moment when Flora realized that murder wasn't what John had in mind. He meant to wreak his revenge in a different manner. Her arms remained by her sides.

"Take it off!" The words lashed the silence like a whip.

Flora slowly removed her wrap and let it fall to the floor. Her eyes slid to the sofa against the far wall. Is that where he meant to shame her? He advanced the two steps that brought them together. Their eyes were locked in a frozen stare. He lifted one graceful hand and touched her breast. "Why did you choose him?" he asked.

Flora felt the fingers tighten convulsively. She swallowed and answered in a small but rebellious voice. "I'll answer questions at the trial, milord."

"You will answer me *now*, madam!" His voice was a silken menace, soft and low, and very angry.

"I didn't realize Wellington's heroes were so brave—threatening ladies—when they're sure no one can interfere. This is what your boasting amounts to then, Lord Hywell?"

"You used to call me John," he reminded

her, still in that hateful, mocking voice. His other hand rose now, touching the nape of her neck, soft as a bird's wing, but twitching, ready to tighten. Already she felt his finger-nails grazing her flesh, and an involuntary tremor shook her. She felt like a helpless animal, caught in the hands of a marauding predator. Why didn't he just do it? Why this game of cat and mouse?

John felt her light, panting breaths, saw the fear in her eyes and wanted to assauge it. "Remember?" he asked softly as his lips lowered to hers. The breath caught in her throat, and her lips quivered. She noticed that John's lips were trembling too, when they touched hers. Trembling and fevered. Almost as soon as he touched her, his lips firmed and he pulled her into his arms, crushing her against him in a wild fury. There was no love, no tenderness, but only a frightening violence that spoke of his inten-tions. Flora placed her hands on his chest and tried to push him away. He only crushed her more tightly, pinioning her arms between them while he continued with that punishing kiss. She was a hot-blooded woman—he thought he could overcome her resistance. She wasn't this cold with her royal lover!

His lips hardened along with his resolve as the brutal kiss continued. There—she wasn't fighting now. There was a stirring of response, beginning with the lips. John immediately moved his tongue to stroke moistly against them, not roughly but with a

sensuous, caressing touch that excited the
nerve endings and finally eased her reluctant
lips open.

Flora felt her resolve weaken. It was the
moaning, inchoate sigh from deep in his
throat that had undone her. Her treacherous
body was warming to his ardent embrace. His
tongue moved with sensuous mastery around
the perimeters of her mouth, grazing against
the roof, plunging deeper, curling to mate
with her tongue in an agonizing ecstasy that
caused a melting glow deep within her. One
arm released her and cupped her shoulder,
kneading it with warm fingers. The hand
glided possessively down over her bosom, the
fingers inching inside her bodice to stroke
her velvet breast, flicking at the nipple now
till it puckered to erection under his
commanding touch. And the ruthless kiss
continued. His other hand was at the small of
her back, arching her against him while her
head spun with a cyclone of conflicting
emotions.

His lips left hers, and the raw silk of his
hair tickled her flesh as his head lowered to
her breast. She felt the moist abrasion of his
tongue on her skin, licking a path to her
breast, his mouth devouring her, his teeth
grazing her nipple. Her whole body was alive
with tumultuous sensations, vaguely
remembered, newly experienced. Every
sense seemed newly born, acutely sensitive.
Her skin was cool where the moisture trail
evaporated, hot and tingling with delicious

prickles where his tongue performed its magic, his hands gathering her buttocks to pull her against his swelling need now as she looked down on his black head against the curve of her white breast.

She could feel his need grow against her and pressed to encourage it, pulling him more tightly to her. Her breath came in quick, light gasps, trying to draw air against the suffocation in her lungs. She felt light-headed, intoxicated with desire. How could she desire this man who was bent on destroying her? A sob of frustration caught in her throat, and John looked up. The harsh determination had faded, leaving him open, vulnerable.

"I might be able to save your life, Bonnie, if you'll—"

Flora lifted her chin and twitched away. She would not sell herself, not even for freedom. "I'd rather hang. Do what you obviously brought me here to do, but don't expect cooperation from me. I am not for sale, at any price. Not a guinea, not a house in the country, not my life. It would be too dearly bought."

She watched curiously as the light faded from his eyes and the harsh features hardened again in mockery. He followed her moving eyes to the sofa. "What sordid minds you lightskirts have," he said. "And what an inordinate value you place on your shopworn charms. You think I brought you here to take my pleasure?"

"Why else? Prisoners aren't taken alone to a cottage in the woods for questioning. I would like to hear the charge, if you please."

"You've already heard it. Treason. And it is punishable by death."

"What have you trumped up against me? You know perfectly well I haven't committed treason. I wouldn't know how if I wanted to." She desperately sought in her mind for any small wrong that might have been magnified. "Maggie said someone called the prince regent the Prince of Whales, but that was weeks ago."

John made a batting sign of dismissal. "If that were treason, there wouldn't be room in the prisons to hold us all. It's obviously more serious than that."

"But what is it? You don't seriously believe I'm trying to overthrow the government?"

"There's more than one way to go about it." He walked stiffly to the sofa and sat down. Flora stayed standing where she was, and he continued, lifting a satirical eyebrow. "Certainly I believe it, or you wouldn't be here. Do you deny quizzing me about my involvement in the Luddite riots—you seemed surprised that I wasn't involved in the war in some manner."

Flora frowned, wondering what this had to do with treason. "Only because you had been in Spain," she said.

John studied her closely, trying to gauge whether she told the truth. If Bonnie wasn't lying, she was in an exceptional position to help him. That was why he had taken her away for private questioning. And she had convinced him she was innocent.

"I am working with the War Office, but in a secret capacity. I've been helping Wellington get the supplies he needs in the Peninsula. Weapons, ammunition, more men, medicine, in some cases money. They have to be shipped to Spain, of course."

"But what has that got to do with me?" Flora asked.

"Nothing, I hope, though I did notice you asked me quite a few questions about my government work."

"And for that you're having me arrested?"

"Of course not. It merely alerted me to your interest, and possible involvement. We've lost two ships of desperately needed supplies. In theory, England rules the waves, but there have been piracies, and in both cases it was Englishmen who led the attack. One occurred not far off the coast of England. In the other case, a ship was plundered in the Bay of Biscay, quite close to Spain. The pirate ships were waiting for us, disguised as fishing boats, but armed and with extra masts they put up at the last minute. It's a well-organized operation. Someone told them the supplies were on the way. We have a few gentlemen under suspicion whom we've been following. After a process of elimination, Mr. Addison has become our chief suspect."

"Mr. Addison!"

"I see you recognize the name. He's a clerk in my office. A man of no real importance, but he copies documents and has access to some important information. He visits your establishment frequently. Of course he goes to other places too, but our investigations haven't turned up anything at his clubs. In a place like yours—in an intimate atmosphere where a man is relaxed, takes wine, he might let slip things he shouldn't. What girls does he visit?" he asked. If she lied . . .

"Marie Simpson. She's the only one he sees."

John breathed a sigh of relief. "What do you know about the girl?"

"She's new. I don't know her as well as the others. She's always been troublesome—she takes things that don't belong to her—but I can't believe she's a spy." Flora frowned and caught her lower lip between her teeth. John looked, and shook away the rising urge to kiss his suspect.

"Why did you go after her to invite her to join you?"

"Go after her? I didn't! One of my girls who was leaving brought her in. She'd already quit her other position or I wouldn't have hired her." John was happy to hear it.

"Are you going to arrest her?" Flora asked.

"Eventually, but first I must get evidence. When does Addison come? What night?" He also knew these answers.

"He comes twice a week. Usually on Wednesday and Saturday." John nodded, satisfied that Bonnie wasn't trying to fool him.

"Tomorrow night, then. I'll have to listen to them and see if she uses her wiles to learn his secrets."

"You don't mean watch them while they're —together?"

"I'm afraid I do. I don't relish it, but she won't do her digging while they're actually making love. It will be before, or after. This is too important to let squeamishness stand in the way."

"Why do you assume Marie's guilty? Maybe Addison sells the secrets himself."

"No, we know virtually every move he makes. He doesn't have any large sums of money sequestered away. He just goes from work to home or a club—and to your place. I have to do it, and I'll need your help."

Flora considered it reluctantly, and saw one ray of hope. "Does this mean I can go home?" she asked fearfully.

"Yes, if you'll agree to help me." Flora gave a doubtful look. "Let me rephrase that," he added. "You will either help me or I shall have to place you incommunicado. I can't have you telling tales back at the house."

"What do I have to do?"

"The first item is not to mention a word of this visit to any of your girls."

"Marie knows you were there, that we left together," she pointed out. "She'll probably tell Addison."

A gleam of mocking amusement flashed in

his eyes. "They know I've been there, trying my charms on you before. We have been out together before. That won't cause them any undue worry. And Addison has no idea I'm involved in anything but the Luddite problem. Our leaving together, coming here —if we were followed—should convince them of my purpose in visiting you. Mind you, they may have to be given the notion I've met with some success. I shall be spending rather a lot of time with you. You'll have to turn off your duke."

Flora gazed up at him, rebuke in her eyes. "I suppose it won't be quite as bad as going to prison," she said. "And as to the duke, when he comes, he plays cards—with Elsie."

"What does he do with Mrs. Belmont?" he asked, a satirical grin distorting his face.

"He drinks her brandy and eats her lobster, and leaves without paying."

A snort of amusement erupted from John. That testy answer fell like rain on a wilted flower, reviving his hopes. "Then Clarence isn't the chosen one? Who then is your lover?" The last word had an angry sting, and revealed more than he knew.

Flora just stared. "You came with a warrant for search and arrest, Lord Hywell. Not for prying questions that don't concern you."

"Let me make clear, Mrs. Belmont, that my sole interest in whom you see has to do with the secrecy required in this matter of treason. Till it is settled, you won't see anyone but myself, and whatever of your staff is necessary to the running of your business. That can't be interrupted at this critical juncture or Addison might become suspicious."

"Then may I go home? Addison won't be coming tonight. He never comes on Tuesday," she said, and looked to see if he had anything else to say.

"That's good. It gives us time to make our plans. Put on your pelisse. I'll take you back now."

Flora picked he pelisse up from the floor and put it on. John extinguished the lamp and called for the groom. They went together to the carriage and drove home. When the carriage arrived at Riddel Street, Flora put on her mask and John accompanied her into the house. Willie's eyes, one with a black ring beneath it, turned suspiciously to John, then back to Flora. "Are you all right, lass?" he asked.

"Yes, Willie. I'll be in my office."

"I'll be right outside," he said, with a measuring look at Hywell.

They went into the office and Flora sat on the sofa, still in her pelisse. She felt as if a herd of horses had run over her. They talked about how to handle the matter for a few moments, then Flora lifted the wine decanter and poured herself a glass. John sat on the closest chair. "May I join you in a glass of wine? I see that Willie, your superb butler, brought only one glass."

"I'll get another," Willie called through the door.

John opened his eyes in consternation. "The secrecy here leaves something to be desired!"

"He warned you he'd be listening."

Willie came in with another glass, not on a tray, but just handed it to John. "It don't surprise me, what I heard you saying," Willie said. "I never thought much of that Simpson trollop. A baggage if ever there was one. I'd like to offer my services, Lord Hywell."

"In what capacity? Not that of waiter, obviously," John remarked and poured himself a glass of wine.

"Whatever you need," Willie replied. "I'll take on Addison for you, if you like. Or I could follow the wench and see who it is she runs to with our secrets. Pirates, did I hear you say? I thought we'd seen the last of that breed."

"If I think of anything, I'll let you know," John told him.

"Better think fast," Willie warned with a fiercely gleaming eye. "I have a lad in Spain. How can he beat the Frenchies if he don't get his guns? You was there yourself, was you?"

"Yes, for two years."

"Then you might know my young lad—Bill Tranter. He's with the second brigade of the Light Division."

"I was with the Dragoons myself, but we were with the second brigade at Badajos. A brave regiment."

"Aye, they're good lads," Willie smiled.

Flora looked at her footman, who stood with his arms folded over his chest in a posture that said he intended to stay put. "That will be all for now, Willie. Thank you," she said.

"We'll have a word on your way out," Willie told John, and finally left.

"You were right about him," John said. "A diamond masquerading as a rock." He scrutinized Flora closely. Again he caught a trace of familiarity in her, not recognizable, but naggingly familiar. "Why did you take up the mask, Mrs. Belmont?" he asked. "I don't see any crowsfeet, nothing to hide."

"I had my reasons," she said vaguely. Her composure was beginning to shred at this sudden turn toward personal matters. "About Marie, I wonder who she sells the information to. Do you think it's someone she meets here?"

"She'll be followed when she leaves. I'll have to get a list of all her clients as well, and listen when she's with them, or have one of my assistants do it. I can't spend hours with my ear to the keyhole."

The future sounded extremely troublesome. Flora frowned in vexation. "It will all be done discreetly," he told her. "I'll try not to interrupt your business. I know how dear it is to your heart," he added snidely.

She sniffed. "Do you?" She stared at him from darkly accusing eyes. Fatigue from the night's troubles left her exhausted. Flora was overcome with a deep wish to leave the Aviary, to escape to her little room for an hour.

John regarded her closely. "What is it, Bonnie?" he asked. All mockery and snideness were gone. His voice was warmly sympathetic.

"Do you really have to ask that? You come storming in here with arrest warrants and search warrants, kidnap me and practically rape me! You calmly announce you will be battening yourself and your assistants on me to catch a spy operating in my house, and then ask me what is the matter? The matter, Lord Hywell, is you! I've never had a moment's peace since I first laid eyes on you! I wish to God I never had to see you again. Just go! Please go and leave me alone."

John looked abashed at her violent outburst. He set his glass down and rose reluctantly. "Very well. A gentleman knows when he is being hinted away, but I must remind you, I'll be back tomorrow evening."

Then he left, and Flora sat thinking about the future, and the past.

20

Lord Hywell was thoroughly ashamed of himself when he left the Aviary. His behavior that night had been despicable. Not quite so bad as Bonnie thought—he really had no intention of raping her—but that private cottage in the country had been chosen with some hope of winning her over. For a moment there, it had seemed he might succeed too. Why did she always flare up in anger just when it seemed he was about to win her?

The night he took her to the Pantheon she had turned bitter when he suggested that she become his mistress. Tonight he had made the error of saying he could save her from prison. Her interpretation was that she must pay with her body, though in fact it was her help in catching the spy he meant. She didn't want *any* payment, that's what it amounted to. How should he have guessed that a woman in the business of selling bodies wouldn't take any payment for herself? A smile tugged at his lips at this quixotic behavior.

Both times, her first reaction to his love-making had been warmly spontaneous and positive. It was what he said that set her off. Next time, he'd keep his tongue between his teeth and let her do the talking. If there was a next time . . . He could spend as much time as he chose with her now. He'd go slowly, set her fears at rest, and let the strong physical attraction between them set the pace. Of that, at least, there was no doubt. Bonnie Belmont might hate him, but she wanted him as badly as he wanted her. When they touched, it was like a spark to tinder.

Why should she despise him? She'd never had a moment's peace since she first laid eyes on him, she said. And neither had he. Since he set foot in Mother Hyde's Parlor and saw that bewitching woman hiding behind her feathered mask, he had been enthralled. Of all the women in London, why did he have to choose the one woman who despised him? Yet he couldn't forget her. His work, and he'd been doing a great deal of it, working most nights, didn't succeed in putting her out of his mind. A vision of her white shoulders kept rearing up between his eyes and the page. That bewitching chin, with the little dimples at the corners of her lips. Now he'd have her whole face to distract him.

By rights, he should be the one who did the

despising. An abbess was bad enough, but a hypocrite into the bargain—claiming a sacred duty to run a brothel! Was there no end to woman's folly? And man's—his own was as bad. In spite of it all, he still wanted her.

There was no necessity to go to the Aviary before eight the next evening. Still, Hywell went at four in the afternoon and was shown into Flora's office. He found her at her desk, working at her account books. For afternoon wear she had on a modest blue Indian cotton gown with a lace fichu rising high at the neck, decorated with a modest cameo pin. Her hair wasn't formally dressed, but gathered behind in a basket of curls. Flora looked younger, more innocent than before, and even more adorable. She had looked up from her work when Willie knocked, expecting only Maggie or one of the girls. Her first instinctive reaction at the sight of John was a smile. He watched as she schooled her features to a scowl.

"You've come very early, Lord Hywell," she said.

"I'm sorry if I'm interrupting your work. There are a few points I want to clear up about tonight."

She indicated the chair by her desk and waited for him to continue. She had seen John many times now, but this was the first time she had seen him in anything but evening clothes. A blue jacket of Bath cloth clung to his broad shoulders. Beneath, she caught a glimpse of a thinly striped waist-coat. Faun trousers revealed the outline of well-muscled legs as he advanced and sat down. Then she saw only his head and shoulders. He wore an expression of polite reserve, but his eyes revealed a trace of his former interest.

That glint in his eye made her uncomfortable, and she spoke brusquely. "Well, what is it?" she asked.

"Addison didn't show up at work today."

"Oh!" she exclaimed, and frowned swiftly. "Do you think he realizes you're on to him? He's run away?" It occurred to her at once that if this were the case, John wouldn't have to come to the Aviary. She should be glad, but the heaviness in her heart was disappointment.

John gave a deprecating smile. "Sorry to disappoint you, Bonnie. He hasn't given us the bag, he's ill. He sent a note around to his office this morning."

Flora heard that "Bonnie" with mixed feelings. He had called her Mrs. Belmont last night. "It could be a ruse," she pointed out.

"It isn't. I had a clerk go over to his house, ostensibly to check on a few letters, but the reason was to make sure Addison was home. He is, with a bout of flu."

"Then he won't be coming tonight."

"I shouldn't think so."

"Then I expect you won't come till Saturday evening?" she asked.

His smile broaded to a grin. "Why do I get

the feeling that comes as a relief to you?"

"I can't imagine. I haven't known you to be so sensitive to my feelings in the past."

"A lack of sensitivity! That's a new charge against me. I must become more closely attuned to what you would like, now that we'll be seeing a good deal of each other," he replied mischievously.

"I believe I made quite clear last night what I would like from you."

"I was less successful in making *my* desires kown," he said. John wasn't smiling, he looked eager and sincere. "I didn't take you to the cottage for the reason you imagine. I had to speak to you away from this house, and thought you would prefer the anonymity of a private cottage to a jail cell. I'm sorry I got carried away. That seems to happen between us," he added.

Flora's cheeks grew hot at the memory of last night. "You didn't try to barter my favors for my freedom either, I suppose?"

"The barter I had in mind was your *help* for your freedom. Nothing more."

She sniffed indignantly. John wanted to overcome that misunderstanding. He knew that if he failed, he would never succeed in his ultimate goal. "If I had intended what you think, there was nothing to prevent my over-powering you, was there?"

She grudgingly admitted it, not in words, but with a hunch of her shoulders. "Is there anything else we have to discuss? As you can see, I'm rather busy."

"Settling-up day, eh?" he asked. "The bane of bookkeepers. Are you having trouble with your accounts?"

Flora had been juggling columns for an hour. She sighed wearily. "I can't believe we paid five guineas for green peas," she said. "And that's not the worst of it. I only have fifty pounds in cash, yet according to my books, I ought to have nearly a hundred. I've lost fifty pounds somewhere between the books and the cash box."

"Does Marie have access to the box?" he asked.

"No one but myself and Maggie, and we're both above stealing, I hope."

"I'm considered an excellent cipherer," John said. "Would you like me to a crack at it?" He was curious to see how much money Bonnie made.

"I'm sure you have more important things to do," she said, with a rather pointed look. "I wouldn't want to detain you, Lord Hywell."

"It won't take me five minutes," he insisted, and reached to turn the book toward him. His eyes flew up and down the columns. He reached for a pen and began rearranging the figures. In slightly less than five minutes, he returned the book to her. With a small smile of triumph he said, "In future, I suggest you keep the pounds and shillings and pence in straighter columns. There were a few sly shillings puffing themselves off as pounds."

Flora took the book and examined it. "I've

had that problem before. I enter the figures every night, and sometimes I'm so tired I can hardly see straight, but I like to keep on top of it, you know."

"I have another suggestion," he added reluctantly. Flora looked a question at him. "You should either provide less elaborate dinners and wines or charge your customers more. Fifty pounds' profit on an establishment of this sort is ridiculous."

"Oh, but that's with everybody paid and all the overhead accounted for. The rent and heat and everything."

"But still, if you're working so hard you can hardly see straight, it's not much profit," he said.

"It's those royal dukes," Flora scowled.

John smiled at her fretful scowl, which was half proud to be able to boast of such customers. "The royal brothers are a sad drain on all our purses," he admitted. "We must support them, one way or another. If they're asked to pay their way, they'll only demand a higher income, and that will come out of our pockets in taxes. Wellington calls them 'the damnedest millstones about the neck of any government that can be imagined.'"

"That is Lord Wellington you're talking about?" Flora asked. She had often thought of John fighting in the Peninsula, and was eager to learn something of his experiences. By feigning an interest in Wellington, she

could find about John himself. "What is
Wellington like?"

"He's a hard man, but fair, and probably
the greatest military genius of the century—
certainly right up there with Bonaparte. I
wasn't with him at Talavera, but I was with
him at Lisbon when he outfought Massena's
massive army."

"How did he outmaneuver him?" Flora
asked.

John gave her a brightly curious smile. "I
can show you exactly how it was done, if
you've got a sheet of paper."

Flora gave him a sheet and he began
drawing an outline of Portugal and Spain. "If
you move over here, I'll explain," he said
blandly. Flora hesitated a moment, but if she
didn't want to see the map upside-down, she
had no alternative but to move beside him.

"This is Portugal," he said, and drew a line
toward the left side of his map. "And this is
the Tagus River. Here's Libson." As he spoke,
he quickly sketched in these features. "This
is the Torres Vedras, right across the
Peninsula between the ocean and the Tagus.
Wellington was in retreat then, with Massena
following hot on his heels."

John spoke on about the campaign,
retreating and burning as they retreated to
force the French out of the Peninsula. "It
sounds hard, but we had to take the
fortresses guarding the route into Spain," he
explained.

It was all a jumble in Flora's head. The excitement of sitting beside John, listening to him, being near him without the imminent danger of lovemaking was what she had often imagined. She had never really had an opportunity to know him as a person, only as a lover. She watched his hand sketch in retreats and advances, her head alive with images of guns firing and shoulders dropping.

He brought alive the heat and hunger, the squalor and deprivation, the danger, the loneliness, and somewhere along the way, the reality that he cared very much for his country. Not only his country, but the poor peasants he'd met in the Peninsula too. He talked about coursing hares and shooting birds. "Some of the peasants were reduced to skin and bones. It would tear your heart out to see them, almost kissing your boots for giving them a piece of meat."

After a while, he turned to her. His eyes were sad with memory. "And that's why we have to stop whoever is passing information about our shipping plans," he said. "I know you hate having me here, Bonnie. I shan't say I hate being here—I enjoy it—and you must endure it."

"It's all right, John."

"I don't look forward to eavesdropping on Addison's rendezvous with Marie. One thing we must arrange is where I can go to overhear them. I'm afraid we're going to have to bore a hole in the wall of the adjoining room. I could hide in the clothespress, but Marie might take into her head to go there for a peignoir, and really I'd like to be free to leave when I've heard what I must."

The timing could hardly have been worse. Just when John's heroism was established, she must admit that her room had a voyeur's hole. He'd think she used it! "Yes," she said, and moistened her lips.

21

The confession must be made. She squared her shoulders and said, "There's a corridor with a—a place for watching." Her gray eyes flickered toward John, then quickly away.

"What do you mean?"

She blushed and fidgeted with her fingers. "A corridor—I keep it locked up!" she assured him. "But before I came here, there was another—house like this," she said. Every word she was forced to speak made her ashamed. "There's a little trellis in Marie's room, covered with silk vines and flowers. Behind it, a portion of the wall is cut away so someone in the corridor can—watch," she said.

John looked, noticing that her hands were balled into fists. "A voyeur's peephole," he nodded. "I've heard of them." To lessen her embarrassment, he added, "Those who can, do. Those who can't, watch."

"John, it was here when I came. I never use it! I hope you don't think—" She looked at him beseechingly. Why did he smile like that? John—she had called him John in her distress.

He took her hand and pulled the fingers loose, one by one. "I understand, Bonnie."

"If I owned the house, I'd get rid of it. Truly I would."

"It's all right, my dear. It will certainly be useful. How do I get to this peephole?"

"You have to go upstairs. From the main hall, you can't even see the corridor. It's walled across."

"How do you get into it, then?"

"From my bedchamber," she said, blushing.

"Does Marie know about it?"

"No one knows but Maggie and I. I nailed the door shut. I took that room on purpose so that no one would know about the peephole. It's horrible," she said.

John listened, his face a mask. "I'll have to use the entrance from your bedroom then," he said matter-of-factly. "We'll wait till Addison and Marie have left the saloon, then we'll go up to your room."

"Why do I have to go?"

"Because it will look rather bizarre if I go upstairs by myself. You don't have to listen. You can stay in your own bedchamber."

Flora frowned and drew her bottom lip between her teeth. "It's not pleasant, but it has to be done, Bonnie," he said gently. "Too much is at stake to let scruples stand in the way. We'll go up there tonight and you can show me the route. We'll have to get the nails out before Saturday night, without anyone knowing. If you'll bring up a hammer, I'll do it while Marie's downstairs."

"All right."

There was really no excuse for remaining longer, but John felt he was making some advance in overcoming Bonnie's aversion. As a good officer, he knew you didn't retreat when you were gaining ground, you forged ahead. He gritted his teeth when there was a knock at the door and Willie's grizzled head peeped in.

"Do youse want some tea?" he asked.

The look on Bonnie's face, John noticed, was not entirely unhappy. "Am I invited?" he asked his hostess.

She nodded to Willie, and returned to her own side of the desk. John took the sheet with the map and began to tear it.

"Don't!" Bonnie exclaimed, then felt foolish at the surprise in his eyes. She only wanted to keep it because he had drawn it for her. It was foolish, but she didn't want to lose it. "I'd like to look at it again. It's very interesting—about the Tagus, and Torres Vedras and—everything." John handed her the sheet and she put it in her ledger.

Willie brought the tea tray and Flora served John. "You will want to try my Chantilly creams," she said. "You could stand a few more pounds, John. You lost weight in the Peninsula, I think.''

John accepted the plate, but he gave her another of those curious looks. ''You never saw me before I left, did you, Bonnie?''

''Oh no!''

By God, she was lying! And very badly too. Where had he seen this woman before? This wasn't a face a man forgot.

''Are you from Sussex?'' he asked.

''No, why do you ask?''

''That's where my home is. On the Sussex Downs, facing the sea. I think we might have met—''

''No, I've never been to Sussex. What is it like?'' she asked, trying to quickly divert his mind from more dangerous things. How had she let that slip out? ''What is your estate called?''

''Heron Hall. It's an old Restoration building—a sprawling heap of brick and stone. Drafty, expensive, pretentious—I adore it,'' he laughed. ''I grew up there with my uncle. My own father was a younger son. He was with the Army in India, where he died. Uncle Charles adopted me. I grew up at Heron Hall, not with the expectation that I'd ever be the heir. There was another brother older than my father, who had a son. George drowned in a boating accident.''

Flora listened eagerly to these meager gleanings. ''What did you do at Heron Hall?''

''What any youngster does. Rode, sailed,

chased the pretty milkmaids. I loved riding over the downs. They're England's front door. Celts, Romans, Anglo-Saxons—they all came calling, leaving churches and roads and history behind. You've never visted that area at all?"

"No, never," she said wistfully.

"It's not far. You should go there for a holiday sometime."

"Yes," she said, but in the politely vague way that showed she wasn't serious.

"What part of the country are you from, Bonnie?"

There didn't seem any particular point in disclaiming Devonshire. It was so far away, and John didn't even know her real name. "I'm from Devonshire. It's rather bleak—the moors, you know, but I liked it."

"You're an orphan, I think you said?"

"Yes," she said, as she had already made this claim. "My father was a schoolteacher."

"That would account for your accent. Did he have his own school?"

"No, he taught at the village school, but we didn't attend it. Papa gave us private lessons, my brothers and sisters and me."

"I didn't realize you had brothers and sisters."

"An orphan can have brothers and sisters," she pointed out hastily.

"You never mentioned them before. Are any of them in London?"

"No, I'm the oldest. The others are still at home."

"Who looks after them, if your parents are dead?"

"An aunt," Flora invented, and seeing that this was dangerous ground, she immediately switched the topic. "If you think Addison is the one betraying secrets, why don't you just get rid of him?"

"It's my feeling that Addison is a dupe, no more. He's being used. Who I really want to catch are the people using him. If they escape, they'll just cultivate some new source at the Foreign Office and continue their work."

John noticed the quick change of topic, but he was determined to be obliging today, to do or say nothing to make Bonnie flare up again. He had already learned more in this one afternoon than she was ever willing to reveal before. They discussed Addison a few moments, then there was another tap at the door and Elsie came in.

She stared to see Flora entertaining a gentleman, and without her mask. "I'm sorry to interrupt you, Mrs. Belmont," she said, "but Nel burnt a hole in my best blue silk. That gown cost me five pounds—how can Nel pay that out of her wages? And why should I lose it?"

"It's all right, Elsie. I'll replace it. And tell Nel not to use the iron so hot. She scorched the hem of my green muslin too."

"You should turn her off, Mrs. Belmont. She's got two left hands, that Nel."

"Yes, and two sick parents, Elsie. You

must be a little considerate toward Nel. She has a lot on her mind at the moment."

"So have I," Elsie said, and stood looking important.

"What has Marie done?" Flora asked, with a sinking feeling that something unpleasant was going to arise in front of her guest.

"Nothing."

Elsie's expression, Flora noticed, wasn't that of complaining about Marie. Actually she looked rather smug. "What is it?" Flora asked eagerly.

"You'll hear soon enough," Elsie said. "But I'll just warn you, you'd best start preparing my dowry."

"Elsie! Chalmers hasn't made you an offer after all these years!"

"That old malkin. I should say not. Mr. Carter's being shipped off to his uncle's plantation in Jamaica, and wants to take me with him—as his wife."

"His *wife*! Good gracious!" Flora exclaimed, and broke into a wreath of smiles. "But that's marvelous, Elsie! When did it happen?"

"Just two minutes ago. We're going out tonight, Mrs. Belmont. Imagine, I'm going to get married." She laughed and spun out of the room.

Flora was so excited she couldn't keep her pleasure to herself. "I confess Elsie is my favorite of all the girls," she said to John, who listened pensively. "So pretty, and very popular. What a stroke of luck—actually getting a proper offer. What can have possessed Mr. Carter to do it, I wonder?"

"How much is this dowry you mentioned?"

"Four thousand pounds. Elsie was with Mother Hyde for many years. She deserves it."

"Eligible ladies can't be plentiful in Jamaica, and no doubt society there isn't as critical as in London. She seems a nice girl. I think she'll do well in Jamaica, but won't her customers miss her here?"

"You can't think I'd begrudge her this chance?" Flora asked, amazed at his remark. "We'll all be very happy for her."

All this struck John as a very peculiar way to run a brothel. Happily turning one of your best employees out the door, handing her four thousand pounds, replacing a gown that got destroyed, and asking consideration for the servant who had burned it. Almost as though the girls were Flora's family. Was it possible she really *did* feel she had a duty to look after them? He was eager to learn more, but Flora soon let him know it was time to leave.

"I must go and talk to Mrs. McMahon about Elsie's offer," she said. "We'll have so much to do. Elsie must have a trousseau. Oh, I'm so happy for her. She isn't as young as most of the girls, you know. Elsie's twenty-seven. She feared that her work days were numbered, and now to get an offer of marriage! The best she hoped for was a mistress-ship from old Chalmers, and that isn't what anyone could really want.''

It came as a shock to John that romance still blossomed in the hearts of women from a brothel. No doubt that was what Bonnie would like for herself too, marriage. That was impossible for him to offer, but he feared that nothing less would be accepted. He left in a troubled mood. He knew that Bonnie liked him, and he knew he loved her. But he also knew that a man in his position didn't marry an abbess.

22

John returned to the Aviary that evening at ten o'clock, telling himself there were important details to arrange, matters that couldn't wait till tomorrow, but he knew that what couldn't wait was his eagerness to see Bonnie again. If Addison showed up at some time other than his usual Wednesday and Saturday night, Willie was to send a note off to Hywell's house to let him know. Removing the nails from the door into the secret passage could be done by a servant. He didn't have to be there in person, but the officer in him wanted to follow up the afternoon's success.

At ten o'clock there was a tap on Flora's office door and John stepped in. He had won Willie over—an escort and a threat were no longer necessary. When Bonnie saw who it was, she removed her mask, revealing a shyly smiling welcome. "Lord Hywell! I didn't expect you till tomorrow," she exclaimed.

John schooled his features to mere politeness and answered, "I had to discuss a few matters with Willie, and decided to stop in to see you while I was here." It was true he had gone over Willie's instructions again, and offered the services of a footman, which were quickly rejected. "I thought we might unblock the door to the corridor and have a look at the secret panel."

Taking him at his word, Flora said, "Marie's not in her room at the moment. We could go now, if you like."

She went to the office peephole to confirm that Marie was in the saloon. "Oh dear, her Mr. Taylor has just arrived. I fear they may go upstairs."

John walked behind her to see Mr. Taylor. It brought him within touching distance of Flora. He felt a compulsion to reach out and touch her, but kept himself under tight control.

Flora turned around, her face just inches from his. From his superior height, he had a stunning view of her breasts. "Do you know anything of this Taylor? Is it possible he's her contact?"

"No, he's my man. I had him come here following Addison to see how he behaves. I know him from the Army. Taylor's completely trustworthy. He's acting the clown, but you may be sure he's attending to business. He was to strike up an acquaintance with Addison's woman to see what he could learn. Marie hasn't revealed anything, but he knows she's greedy, the sort of woman who wouldn't balk at selling her country."

Flora nodded and turned back to observe the saloon. John noticed a stray curl resting on the ivory nape of her neck. His fingers wanted to touch it. "They're starting a game of cards," she mentioned.

"I doubt they'll do more than that tonight. Taylor knows he'll be watched."

"You told him about the secret panel?" Flora asked, annoyed to hear it.

"He's the soul of discretion. You needn't fear that Taylor will give your secrets away. Shall we go upstairs while Marie is occupied?" he asked blandly, but excitement curled in his breast. He wanted to see where Bonnie spent her private moments.

"Very well," she agreed, and put on her feather mask.

She called Willie and asked him to slip her a hammer, without being seen. With this under her shawl, she and John went into the hallway, up the broad, curving staircase. It was upsetting, passing those closed doors, knowing that behind them people were making love. It occurred to Flora that anyone watching would think that she and John were bent on the same business. A stab of regret pierced her heart. She was relieved when she turned the corner to the relative privacy of her room and Maggie's, situated across from each other in a shorter hallway.

She opened the door and took off the mask, then struck a flint to light the lamps. Knowing the luxury of the rest of the house,

John expected to see chandeliers and silk and the fashionable appointments of the ton. He stood gazing at her rose-sprigged bower—a pretty room, but not in the style of the saloon. It was the room of a gently bred young girl. On a mahogany desk there was a letter half-written. He glanced at it while Flora busied herself lighting another lamp. "Dear Mama:" he read. An odd letter for an orphan to be writing!

Flora turned around and saw with horror what John was looking at. "I write letters home for some of my girls," she said. "They aren't too steady on their grammar. This is the door to the secret panel." She handed John the hammer, reading the doubt in his eyes, the disbelief.

He took the hammer and went to the doorway that was behind a bookcase. "We'll have to move this," Flora said, and went to take up one end.

A lady wouldn't have done that. Her instinct would be to send for a footman. What a curious mixture this Bonnie Belmont was! They slid the bookcase over the carpet quietly and John busied himself prying out the nails. He noticed that the door had indeed never been used by Flora. It was not only nailed shut but the nails had been painted over.

When the door was free, he went into the narrow, airless hallway and peered through the vine-covered trellis. Flora remained behind. Marie had left two lamps burning low. The chamber he gazed at was what he had expected Flora's room to be. It as the master bedroom of the house, large, ornate, with an embossed ceiling. The drapes and canopy had been chosen by Elsie, in blue to match her eyes. On the dresser an array of crystal pots and a silver dresser set twinkled. Flora's room had no such cosmetic table. Vision from the secret panel was excellent. He should be able to hear the voices as well.

John returned to Flora's room, where he found her straightening the books that had become jarred out of place by their move. He leaned down to help her, reading titles as he pushed them back into line. History, a little philosophy, books of travel and religion, all well-thumbed, some novels of the less sensational sort. She had books by Walter Scott and Frances Burney.

"I see you're an avid reader," he mentioned.

"My schooling was interrupted when my father died. I've tried to continue the curriculum he set up for us. Papa used to say I was ignorant as a swan." She smiled sadly.

He had to look away or he'd kiss Bonnie right there as they knelt on the floor. He looked at the books and saw one entitled *The Iberian Peninsula.* It was more worn than most.

Flora saw what he was reading. "I bought that to follow the Peninsular War," she said matter-of-factly. He couldn't know why that war had interested her in particular.

Everyone was interested in the war.

John rose and offered his hand to help her up. "A new book will have to be written after the war. Things have changed drastically there the last few years. Invaders always leave something behind—new customs—death. The more fashionable Spanish ladies were becoming quite British in the matter of gowns, I noticed. A few of them even adopted the turban."

"Shall we go downstairs now?" Flora suggested. She was acutely aware of the bed. Other than her desk chair, it provided the only seating in the room.

"It will look more natural if we stay an hour or so. If I was seen coming upstairs, I don't want anyone suspecting the visit was unorthodox. Just make yourself comfortable, Bonnie. I'll sit by the desk, you can have the bed. Shall we ask for some wine to pass the time?"

"No!" Her answer came very emphatically. She didn't want her mind fuzzed with wine, not when she was alone in a bedroom with John. She didn't particularly want him at her desk either, reading things she wished to keep private. "I'll order tea," she said more mildly.

When Willie came to the door, she asked for another chair as well. "I didn't want the servants running up here to see what was going on," Willie said, to explain why he had answered the bell. "Or what *ain't* going on," he added with a laugh, but there was a warning note in the glance he shot at Hywell.

John smiled. "Your caveat is unnecessary, Willie. As you see, I'm being a perfect model of propriety."

"See that it stays that way. Do you want yer sewing box, lass?"

"That's a good idea, Willie. Please bring it up."

"If 'un gets fresh, you can stab him with your needle," he suggested playfully.

Flora sat at the desk and closed up her writing pad. She scanned the surface to see that no other telltale items were on display before she could relax. When she glanced at John, he was studying her closely. What was it about that face that he seemed to remember?

"Were you ever on the stage, Bonnie?" he asked.

Flora had begun to suspect why John asked these question, and was determined to thwart him. "Why yes! How odd you should ask." She smiled mischievously. "I played a shepherd in our church Nativity play one Christmas. I had to carry a lamb. It bit me. I don't know where lambs get their reputation for meekness."

The feeling of familiarity faded as he watched her. That other face he couldn't quite recall had not shown any liveliness. "I too seem to have picked up a reputation I don't deserve—well, don't totally deserve," he amended, when she tossed him a sapient look.

"If Willie really mistrusted you, he would have supplied me with a more formidable weapon than a needle."

"Yet a needle is suffient to deflate my hopes," he smiled.

"What hope is that, sir?"

"The hope that you're beginning to trust me. I plan to be on my best behavior, Mrs. Belmont. Bonnie—don't worry," he added, more seriously. "I have no intention of taking advantage of this enforced intimacy. At the cottage I—"

"Oh, let us forget the cottage," she said irritably. It was enjoyable having these few hours with John, coming to know him a little. She wanted to forget all their rocky past.

"Amen."

A new feeling entered the room as their eyes met. It was more than forgetting the past. It held an intimation of the future as well. A future that might hold friendship, if love was impossible between them.

23

"If we aren't going to apologize or argue, what shall we do to pass the time?" John asked. "Cards?"

Flora shook her head. "I despise cards. I can't afford to gamble, and what's the point of shuffling bits of cardboard around a table if you don't have the incentive of greed?"

"Are you interested in acrostics? We might give Willie another chance to run up and down stairs for us, bringing the *Morning Observer*. I'm sure he'd be delighted. It had a rather good acrostic this morning."

"I don't want to reveal my ignorance. Besides, it seems you've already looked at the acrostic."

"I was hoping to impress you with my quick intelligence."

"You forget I've asked for my sewing box. Idle hands are a lure for the devil," she quoted primly.

There was a noise in the hallway. "That's either a bull loose in the corridor or Willie with our tea," John said.

He opened the door and Willie came in carrying the silver tray, laden with food and drink and a cane sewing box. "Good gracious, Willie!" Flora laughed. "We can't eat all that."

"I had cook put on a wee drop of your favorite steak and kidney pie, lass. And a bit of lobster tart for the gentleman."

"That sounds like favoritism to me," John objected jokingly. "Does your mistress not merit lobster tart?"

"She don't care for eating sea parasites," Willie said firmly. Flora's lips quivered in amusement. "Not since she saw cook put them wiggling into the pot. No man with the blood of human kindness in him could eat them. Enjoy your meal," Willie ordered, and left to bring a hall chair into the room.

John placed the chair at Flora's desk and smelled the lobster tart. "With that appetizing reminder of cruelty to dumb animals, I shall now enjoy my lobster," he said. "Smells delicious."

"Cook puts white wine in the sauce, and a bouquet garni. Also some haddock to eke out the lobster," she admitted with a smile. "An old housewife's trick I learned at home. No one ever seems to notice. In fact, the Duke of Clarence is so fond of this dish that cook is thinking of renaming it Clarence pie."

"In which case it's brandy she should use,

not wine. I think that in spite of Clarence's tendency to live on tick, you enjoy his visits."

Flora looked into the distance, a musing smile on her lips. "I would never in my wildest dreams have imagined entertaining a royal duke—or that he'd be such an ordinary sort of man. I thought they would be more—more—" More like you, is what she meant but did not want to say.

"Less like commoners?" he suggested. "Actually you've attracted one of the less polished royal gems. I daresay it's Clarence's stint in the Navy that destroyed his conversation. Prinney is very gentlemanly. A wretched spendthrift, of course, but knowledgeable about art and things. You should see Carlton House."

"What's it like?" she asked eagerly.

While they ate, John described some of the grander features of the prince's London residence, then moved on to describe his Brighton Pavilion, in understated terms that still sounded too incredible to be real. Lotus flowers in marble, sofas shaped like dragons, porphyry columns, gilt and magnificence everywhere. "And on top of it all, he keeps it so hot you feel parboiled," John said.

"I'm going to drive to Brighton and see the Pavilion one day," Flora decided.

"I'll take you," he offered at once. "After this unsavory business is over, we'll drive to Brighton."

Flora sat silent, thinking how pleasant that would be, and thinking too that a person probably didn't go to Brighton and return the same day.

As if reading her mind, John continued. "Prinney claims to have made the trip in under four hours. If my grays can't outrun his, I'm a yahoo. We'll leave early in the morning, to get you back to your post by evening. We'll have to drive the curricle. You won't mind forgoing a closed carriage in this fine weather?"

"It sounds lovely," she said uncertainly.

John set down his fork and gazed at her. Her copper hair glinted in the lamplight, but it was at her eyes that he looked. Those stormy, dark eyes that bore traces of a hard life. A pretty young woman's eyes should sparkle with joy. "Will you come?" he asked.

Flora answered hesitantly. "I have it on the best authority that a gentleman doesn't entertain a woman like me without expecting the return of her favors," she reminded him.

How he rued those hasty words, uttered in anger. "You've earned the outing by helping me in this matter of catching the spies. No further payment will be expected, Bonnie," he answered mildly, but it cost him something to restrain his temper. He was a jackass to have said that to a sweet girl like Bonnie.

John acknowledged that she wasn't what he had taken her for. There was no getting over the fact that she was an abbess, but an abbess like no other in the country. She was more like a mother to her girls than anything else. Even as these thoughts darted through his mind, Flora opened her sewing basket and took out a pair of silk stockings. He had expected to see some elegant embroidery, and was shocked again at the homey nature of her sewing.

"Am I being too farouche to mend my stockings in front of a gentleman?" she asked upon seeing his surprise. "I usually do it in the privacy of my bedroom, but as that's where we're taking tea . . . Silk stockings are very dear," she scolded. "And the toe is always the first bit to go."

She moistened the end of thread between her lips and threaded the needle. While she was concentrating on this job, John stole a glance at her profile. She looked like a fashionable lady of the ton, but behind that facade there beat the heart of a housewife, and the knowledge cheered him insensibly. A million questions battered in his head, and he couldn't pose one of them without hurting her feelings. "How did a sweet girl like you come to be here, in this place?" he wanted to ask. He was coming to believe her story about coming to London to work and joining Mother Hyde without knowing what she was getting into. But it really was impossible to believe that. There had to be more to it, something she didn't want him to know.

The mystery intrigued him. "I believe there's something of the thrifty housewife in you, Bonnie," he said to fill the silence. "Eking out your lobster patties with haddock, and mending your stockings yourself."

"A schoolteacher's family has to be thrifty. They don't have money to burn. At home I was the fortunate one. I was the eldest. My sisters had to wear my reach-me-downs. And Lily's coloring was different from mine too. She took after Papa, with dark hair."

"You resemble your mother?" he asked, hoping to hear more.

"Yes, but Mama's eyes are green," she answered.

Not were, *are*, John noticed. So the mother was alive. Perhaps the great secret was that Flora didn't want her mother to learn what she was doing. This seemed probable, and he wanted to follow it up, but it must be done with the utmost caution.

"Do you keep in touch with your family?" he asked.

"Of course. We write every month. At first we could only afford one frank a month, but now that I could afford more frequent letters, I find I don't have much to tell."

"I should think Clarence could fill a few pages," he mentioned.

"Oh, I don't tell them anything about this place!" she exclaimed, shocked. "They think I'm a governess. Ma—my sisters would be shocked," she said, and bit her lip at the near slip. Mama would be shocked, she had nearly said.

"You've never seen them since leaving home?"

"How could I go back?" she asked simply, and sat looking at her mending. The tears no longer boiled behind her eyes when she thought of home. It had been so long. Too long. She had accepted that she was cut off from her family forever, except for the monthly letters.

"Is there no danger of their coming here, to London?"

"I should like to invite Lily," she answered. The room on Swallow Street was where she would invite her, if she ever took such a daring step. It would mean putting Maggie in charge of the Aviary for the duration of the visit. But then, how to explain that she was free of her job as governess? Lily would want to meet her employer. "No, I don't think it can be done," she said matter-of-factly, but her jaws worked with the effort of hiding her feelings.

John watched, helpless. More than anything, he wanted to comfort her. But he knew that a word would be enough to stop her confidences. Thinking how he could make himself useful, he said hesitantly, "I have a house in Brighton, on the Marine Parade. You could invite Lily there—say it's your employer's summer home, and they're on vacation."

Flora frowned, considering this possibility. "We'd have to let the servants know the truth, of course," he added.

Flora turned a disillusioned little face toward him. It was close to tears, and his heart wrenched to see it. "Lily wouldn't be comfortable there, in a house with servants. And how could she come, all alone?"

"You came to London alone," he pointed out.

Flora drew a finger across her lips to conceal their quivering. "Yes, and see what happened to me," she said. "My sisters are better off where they are. Lily has a beau— the man who replaced Papa. She'll be marrying him soon. Let her live her own life. I wouldn't wish this one on my worst enemy."

Then she shook her head and smiled ruefully. "Dear me, how did we fall into this lugubrious subject, and just when we were having such a nice visit too. Tell me about Carlton House again, John. Does he really have a Gothic conservatory with marble floors?"

It seemed best to follow this line of talk for the time being. "My dear girl, it's nearly as fine as his stables at Brighton, which always remind me of a cathedral, with their carved woodwork and gothic arches. I'll try to arrange a tour when we go to Brighton."

Flora had no intention of going to Brighton, but she liked to hear all about it, and this was their topic of conversation till John left.

He had gleaned more information about Flora than he was happy with. If she was what she appeared to be, it was unconscionable of him to try to seduce her, to make her his mistress. Yet if he saw much more of her, that's exactly what he would do. He wrestled with his conscience as he drove home. A woman in her position could hardly expect to marry. She'd become someone's mistress eventually. Why not his? At least he loved her. He'd never mistreat her, or abandon her in her later years.

Flora sat in her office, thinking about that visit. It hadn't gone as she expected at all. She had been dreading it, but John had behaved so nicely, chatting like an old friend. Perhaps she had told him too much about herself . . . It was very kind of him to offer his Brighton house for Lily's visit. That whole undertaking presented so many difficulties that she didn't plan to go through with it. And very likely John wouldn't repeat the offer anyway, once he had caught his spies. He was serious about the drive to Brighton, though. He had mentioned it more than once. Could she hazard that one outing? He would drive his curricle, he said. An open carriage without a veil or mask—not that anyone would recognize her. Perhaps she would go . . .

24

On Thursday evening Lord Hywell returned
again to the house on Riddel Street. His
excuse on that occasion was to tell Bonnie
that Addison was back at work, though his
true reason was to enjoy the company of the
woman he loved. He didn't know exactly
when an overpowering physical attraction
had turned to love, but he was in no doubt
that it had happened. Was it when she had
pulled out her silk stockings to mend? He
found that thrifty, domestic side of her
enchanting. Or was it when she flirted with
him, in her shyly mischievous way? Perhaps
it was that wistful droop of her lips when she
said, "How could I go back?"

He rather thought it was a combination of
all these enchanting facets that had left him
sitting idle half the day, staring out a window
and seeing in the bushes a Titian-haired

woman. His heart pounded with eagerness as he entered the Aviary and handed Willie his hat and cane. No greatcoat was necessary. That brief lessening in the chill that Englishmen called summer was in the air.

Flora had been warning herself he wouldn't come. Why was she bothering to primp and preen in front of the mirror? Why did she place that modest gazue shawl over her shoulders, trying to lessen the immodesty of her fashionable gown? She didn't want John to see a "hostess" when he looked at her. And when at last he did come, she tried in vain to keep the glow from her eyes.

"Addison was back at work today. He might decide to visit Marie tonight, as he missed last night," John explained. He knew, but didn't say, that Thursday was Addison's evening for cards at Brook's Club. The man was a creature of habit, and the investigations had shown that Brook's was Mr. Addison's favorite night out.

On this occasion they visited in Flora's office, where they would be informed by Willie if Mr. Addison came. Flora had a novel open before her. She was just finishing *Pride and Prejudice*, and was imagining herself and John sharing the final explanations and apologies that would smooth the way to a bright future.

"Don't let me interrupt what you're doing," John said politely. "I'll just sit here quietly and write a few letters.''

"Then you'll need the desk," Flora said at once, hopping up to vacate it. "I'm just reading. I don't need it."

"No, really! I don't want to put you out."

"I'll be more comfortable on the sofa," she insisted.

But when she arranged herself on the sofa, John went and sat beside her. She smiled shyly and said, "Don't let me keep you from your work, John."

"That's *my* line," he replied archly. "You must find some other excuse to escape my attentions." His eyes examined her, noticing the flush of pleasure, the sparkling eyes that revealed her interest, and noticing too the demure shawl that pleased him in some indefinable way.

"I'm happy for your company, if you can spare the time," she replied, and gracefully put aside her book.

They sat self-consciously a moment in silence, then John asked, "No mending tonight? Take care or old Nick will find some occupation for those idle hands. Perhaps pouring a drink for that sad rattle, Lord Hywell," he suggested.

Flora took the hint and poured two glasses. She didn't hesitate to have one herself in her office, where she felt less vulnerable than in her bedroom.

"How is the bride-to-be's trousseau coming along?" he asked. "Elsie, is it, who's nabbed herself a groom?"

"Yes, Elsie Pringle. She shopped all morning. She'll be leaving us in a week's time. All my girls are desperately searching for a gentleman about to leave for Jamaica, in hopes of getting an offer from him. This afternoon Elsie had the exquisite pleasure of visiting an old competitor who is only living under a gentleman's protection, and boasting of her conquest. She said Rose is jealous as a green cow," Flora smiled. "I'm very happy for Elsie. We had begun to worry about her— because of her age, you know."

"How old are you, Bonnie?" he asked nonchalantly, hoping to steer the conversation to personal topics.

She tilted her head and gave him a knowing smile. John decided it was the flirt in her that he loved best. "Considerably younger, sir. And I'm sure it is not at all nice of you to ask a lady's age."

"But if I don't ask I'll never learn anything about you. You're as silent as a jug about yourself."

"There's nothing interesting to say about me. You know what I do, and before I did this, I lived in the country. My life has been as dull as dishwater," she said, a little bitterly. The only exciting events were so unhappy she wanted to conceal them. John gazed, and thought perhaps it was the lips drooping in pique that were most enchanting. "Let us talk about you instead," she suggested.

"And that from a young lady who was bitten by a lamb!" he teased. "Come now, did you never fall down a well, accidentally let the pig into the home garden, get chased by a bull, or get drunk trying your mother's peach cordial when you were young?''

"No, but I fell out of my brother's tree house and split my head open.''

"And you say you've had a dull life! Your Miss Austen could make something of that experience." He smiled, picking up the novel to flip through it. "I didn't realize you had a brother. You mentioned your sisters yesterday."

"I have two younger brothers. Roger is going to attend university," she announced proudly. It would sound like boasting to say it was her financial help that would make this possible, but John surmised that would be the case. "He's very clever. He's studying Latin and Greek and everything."

"How old is Roger?"

"He's fifteen. Richard is only nine—or—no, he'd be ten now," she said, shaking her head ruefully. She had lost track of her own family. Her lips pursed a moment. "I probably wouldn't recognize Dick if he walked through that door," she added.

"You would certainly recognize him a minor, I hope, and send him home with a flea in his ear."

"There's no danger of his landing in on me. Dick lives in the local stable. He plans to win the cup at Ascot when he grows up. Oh, I did have one other adventure," she remembered.

"Talking about Dick reminded me of it. I had a ride on Sir John's hunter at a picnic one day."

"Sir John?" he asked, trying not to reveal his interest in this name, which might be a clue to Flora's origins.

"Sir John Osborne, he's the local squire who owns everything where I live, including a vicious brute of a hunter. Dick dared me to mount it, and I, like a perfect greenhorn, did it. I managed to stay in the saddle too. I was never so frightened in my life. It felt as though I were sitting on top of a galloping mountain. I was sure Sir John would have my hide, but he only lifted me down, laughing, and said I had a very good seat."

"Sir John, is he a knight?"

"You would offend him if you suggested it! He's a baronet, sir. His family was one of the first to be honored by King James, or whoever it was who invented the baronetcy."

John just smiled, but he would look Sir John Osborne up in the Baronetage when he returned home that evening. "Do you do any riding now, Bonnie?"

"Good gracious, no. It would cost a fortune. I can scarcely afford the two monsters for the carriage. They spend their days eating expensive oats and hay, and growing fat. I expect you are a bruising rider, John?"

"Like you, I manage to stay in the saddle," he replied. He noted that Bonnie wasn't making any fortune from her establishment. She really wasn't doing this for the money.

"I'm too old to take up riding, but I should like to have a phaeton. I think I could master the reins."

"We'll try your fiddling skills when we go to Brighton."

"Indeed we will not! You've already boasted of your grays—or something about making the trip in less than four hours. That would be a sixteen-mile-an-hour team, I expect?"

"Of course, any Corinthian worth his salt has a sixteen-mile-an-hour team. Odd it takes them five or six hours to complete a drive of under fifty miles, *n'est-ce pas?* That attempt at a joke eludes you. It has to do with arithmetic," he explained.

"I know that! It has nothing to do with shillings and pence. It's the crooked columns that confuse me."

They chatted for nearly two hours, the time flying by till Willie came to the door with the silver tray.

"Here's yer lobster tarts," he said to John as he placed the tray on the table.

"I'm beginning to feel like that royal leach, Clarence," John said. "I shall pay for this dinner, Willie."

"That you will not, sir," Flora announced firmly. "We don't charge the King's men for pursuing their duty."

John wished Willie would leave, but he remained with his ear cocked, rattling the cutlery. "I don't consider this strictly a business visit," is all John said. He noticed Bonnie blush and divert her eyes to the table, under the pretense of arranging the dishes.

He stayed for another hour, and still hated to leave when the time came.

25

On Friday John returned, carrying a box of bonbons and flowers like a suitor. "As I've come to cadge more lobster tarts, the least I can do is bring a gift for my hostess," he said when he presented them.

It was the first time Flora had ever received a gift from a man, and she blushed furiously. It would be difficult to say whether she felt more embarrassed or pleased. "That wasn't necessary," she said in confusion.

John examined her with a searching gaze. He had fully accepted that Flora's owning this establishment was some freak of circumstance. She was no more an abbess at heart than he was. Less! She looked as pleased as a child with a new doll when she sniffed the flowers and touched their petals, looking at him with a little question. "I—I must get a vase," she said, and in her confusion she fled to the door to call Willie rather than pull the bell cord. When he came, she handed him the bonbons by mistake.

"They're for you, lass, not me," Willie said in confusion.

"Would you please bring a vase and water," she asked, trying to recapture her dignity. "The nice crystal one, Willie, with the pattern cut into it."

She arranged the flowers with care, her white hands hovering over the blossoms, moving them this way and that till the composition pleased her. She wondered how long they'd last, and knew that she would keep not one pressed in a book, but the two dozen of them. When they were arranged, she spent another few minutes trying the vase in various positions in the room.

John was overwhelmed at the fuss she made over this simple gift. He had given diamond bracelets that were received more cavalierly. He wanted to shower diamonds on Bonnie, to buy her the phaeton she wished for, to carry her off and set her up like a queen, but he knew this wouldn't really make her happy. What she wanted was the one thing he couldn't give. She wanted her reputation back, to be able to go home. To see Lily and her brothers and mother again.

He had checked the Baronetage and there discovered Sir John Osborne of Osborne Hall, county of Devon. The fifth person he asked, his Aunt Mathilda, had been able to tell him that Sir John was a country rustic who lived near Bradbury in Devon. She had never been there, and couldn't tell him who the schoolmaster might have been a few years before.

"Why do you want to know that, John? Has it something to do with your work at Whitehall?" she asked.

"Indirectly," he replied evasively. Now he had the name of a town at least. Pity it was so far away. His duties prevented his going to Devonshire at the present. What good would it do in any case? It would be mere prying to satisfy his curiosity. What stuck in his craw was that a gently bred girl should have been sent off to London alone. That wasn't the behavior of genteel parents. They must have sent her to relatives or friends. What had happened along the way?

Was there, perhaps, someone in London who might help rescue her from the Aviary? Was that why she was at such extraordinary pains to conceal her identity—because she had relatives in town that she wanted to protect? It occurred to him that with his help, these relatives might be able to establish her, if not in society, at least in respectability. Very few people knew her. It also occurred to him that she wouldn't use her real name if she was that determined to remain incognito. She called herself Mrs. Belmont, but she wasn't married, and she probably wasn't Miss Belmont either.

These thoughts flitted through his mind as he watched Bonnie set the flowers down on her desk, where she apparently had decided to leave them. Next she turned her attention to the bonbons, carefully removing the gold foil wrapping and peeping inside. "Sugared cherries! These were Mama's favorite!" she exclaimed. How odd that John should choose this treat. But the box was different—John wasn't on the lid. She reached for one, then like a little girl remembered her manners and passed him the box first.

John popped a sugared cherry into his mouth and continued watching Bonnie. His eyes wore a sad, longing look. Why did he torture himself by coming here? He was in the prime of life. He should be choosing a bride, setting up his nursery, not hanging on the skirts of Bonnie Belmont, upsetting her and himself. He sensed that she shared his growing love. It glowed in her eyes, betrayed itself in a hundred small ways. The lingering looks, the brief touch of fingers over the teacups, the spontaneous smile when he appeared, the lengthy departures, both of them seeking an excuse to prolong the visit.

In the end, nothing could come of it. He couldn't marry her; she didn't want to be a mistress, and really he was coming to agree with her. A man shouldn't be madly in love with his mistress. She should be someone you could visit when necessary, and turn off when it was time to marry.

But he stayed later than ever that evening. To pass the time he introduced her to the game of hazard, as she disliked cards, and found her quick to pick up the arbitrary rules. She was clever, no denying, but it wasn't the challenge of a clever partner that made the game so enjoyable. It was her tense, eager little face across from him, the sudden smile when she made a point, the exaggerated frowns when she lost—you would think her life depended on the throw of the dice, and they were only playing for pennies.

It didn't escape notice at the Aviary that Mrs. Belmont had a beau, and she was subjected to awful teasing. She couldn't tell the girls why John really came. Marie had to believe that his calls were personal, and all the girls believed the same thing. Only Maggie, Willie, and Tom knew the truth. The teasing remarks were an exquisite form of torture.

"My, he is hot for you!" Elsie smiled. "Roses and bonbons. Be careful, girls, or Lord Hywell will carry her off, and then where will you be?"

"Don't be foolish, Elsie," Flora scolded, but in some secret corner of her heart she was proud of her conquest. At least it was a sort of conquest. John didn't have to come so often and stay so late, when Addison wasn't due to call till Saturday.

Flora hadn't been to her room on Swallow Street since the visits began. On Saturday morning she slipped over and sat alone, looking out the window to the back of the Aviary and thinking. It was kind of John to offer the Brighton house for Lily's visit. He had mentioned it again the night before. Much as she wanted to see Lily, she didn't believe it was a good idea. Lily would have too many questions, and she would know that her own stylish appearance wasn't that of a governess. Something was bound to go wrong. She couldn't face her family, carrying this dreadful burden of guilt on her shoulders. She would grow old alone, that was her inevitable fate.

She thought of Mother Hyde buying companionship, dying alone in that room, asking for Mark Dryden, who refused to come. She remembered Sal and her Johnnie —both of them safe with Joe in Ilford now. If Sal hadn't been pregnant with Johnnie, she would never have stayed at Mother Hyde's. Life was strange. All these people that passed through your life, changing it irrevocably, then disappearing—as John would disappear after this business was over. But Sal wrote occasionally, and even spoke of stopping by at the Aviary if she ever came to London.

Flora didn't want to grow old alone. Elsie was the lucky one—running away to a strange country, married, respectable. But Elsie's was a uniquely fortunate case. There would be no forgiving husband for Flora. She didn't want just any husband. She wanted John. Her heart was heavy as she sat dry-eyed at the window, too sad for tears.

Images of a halcyon future that would never be more than a dream floated through her head. She and John at Heron Hall—she

tried to imagine it, and had to make do with
Sir John's stolid brick house. She was sure
that Heron Hall was much finer. John would
teach her to drive his curricle, even buy her a
phaeton. They would go to Brighton in the
summer and visit the seashore. Perhaps
they'd take their children there one day. She
imagined a dark-haired baby John playing in
the foam, running to her and throwing his
arms around her neck when the waves came
in. She hugged herself to ease the lonely ache.

Later, Flora tried to remember just when
the idea occurred to her. Why couldn't she
have John's child, even if she couldn't have
John? It had happened to plenty of girls
before. The babies were raised in the country
with a wet nurse, the mothers visiting or not,
as their nature decreed. In a few years, when
she'd saved enough money, she'd close the
Aviary and retire to some county town far
away from London and raise the child
herself.

She would claim to be a widow. No one
ever questioned the existence of a Mr.
Belmont. But she wouldn't be Mrs. Belmont
—that name had too many unhappy associa-
tions. She couldn't call herself Mrs. Sommers
either. Her late husband would be an officer
like John, except that he would have been
killed in the Peninsula. John had mentioned a
Lieutenant Stack, who died at Badajos. She
would be Mrs. Stack, and if at some future
date anyone investigated, they would learn

that Lieutenant Stack had indeed existed, and had died as she would claim.

The only thing to decide was how to convince John to go along with her notion. She knew him well enough now to know he wouldn't willingly saddle her with an illegitimate child. He had become gentle, tender in his dealings with her. He knew her aversion to being a mistress—that hadn't changed. She couldn't live in the shadows, spurned by decent society, seeing him only when his real life allowed an hour.

She remembered the reaction of Jennie's neighbors to her girls' visit. She wouldn't raise her child in such an atmosphere. She'd rather not see John at all. Her child would grow up proud and strong, like his father. She would have a part of John, without his being aware of it. And if the child was a girl, that would be all right too. She'd see that her daughter was reared differently from herself.

An uneasy peace descended on Flora, and she felt strong enough to return to her duties. As she went through the fence to her own yard, she noticed that the delphiniums by the side of the house were beginning to bloom. Mama had delphiniums when they lived in the schoolmaster's house. She went closer to examine them, and saw a cigar butt tossed between the plants.

That was odd! Neither Willie nor Tom smoked cigars. She picked it up, and noticed it was quite fresh. It hadn't been rained on, and wasn't covered in dust either. She noticed that a few of the delphiniums were bent over as though they'd been stepped on, and examined them. There was another cigar butt on the ground, also fresh. The only person she could remember who smoked cigars was Mark Dryden. She had thought it was Dryden the night she and Maggie heard some noise outside. He was spying on her, trying to discover some way to make mischief! He must have seen John enter the house. He could tell John all about her, if he decided to do it.

Flora ran in and told Maggie what she had found. "You don't think it would have anything to do with Marie and Addison?" Maggie asked.

"No, I'm sure it's Dryden. He means to tell John about me."

"What he'll do is demand money to keep quiet," Maggie said. "Not that it matters, as far as I can see. I wouldn't give him a sou, Flora. Tell John who you are. He must know everything but your real name by now."

"No, I shan't tell him," Flora replied.

"He still hasn't recognized you? He doesn't know he's the one who—"

"I don't want him to know!" Flora said fiercely. "What's the point of burdening him with that story? He never meant me any harm. What did he know about me, finding me in Mother Hyde's Parlor? He thought I was just one of the girls."

"Oh, Flora, I wish you'd tell him. It doesn't seem right, you suffering all these years and him getting off scot-free."

"He didn't get off free, Maggie. He went to fight the war in Spain. He's paid for his sins."

"You've paid too, and you didn't have any sins," Maggie pointed out.

"It's all right," Flora said. "I'm used to it. Tell Tom to keep an eye on the back yard tonight, will you? Tell him that if he sees Dryden to put a good scare into the jackanapes."

"He'll do more than scare him if I know Tom. A taste of the home-brewed is what he'll give Dryden."

"I hope that's enough to get rid of him. We'll make sure all the drapes are drawn too. If Dryden's peeking in windows, he won't see anything."

Discovering the signs of a trespasser was upsetting, but Flora soon forgot that minor incident. Her mind was on the night, when John would come. They'd be in her bedroom tonight, waiting for Addison to visit Marie. Should she wear a peignoir to let him know she was susceptible to his persuasions? Not that there had been any persuasions since the night he arrested her. Her cheeks flamed at the memory of that night. It wouldn't take much to push John into indiscretion. A word, a glance of the right sort would do it. Even that would be hard, but she had made up her mind, and was determined to do it.

26

Flora was too excited to go downstairs that evening. After she had dressed with care in her emerald green silk gown, she stood at the mirror, brushing her hair the hundred strokes that were to make it full and rich and loosen the curl. She thought it was the weight of hair rather than the brushing that had done it, but it had lost its tight curl. It hung in loose, luxuriant waves like a mantle about her white shoulders, beautifully set off by the richly colored gown. John had never seen her with her hair down. Perhaps he'd loosen the pins tonight when he made love. She had a premonition that he would like her hair out loose, to let his fingers play through its silken strands.

A warmth crept up her throat at the thoughts that whirled in her head, tingeing her cheeks a delicate pink. She lifted the single perfume bottle, a parting gift from

Sally, and touched the stopper on her wrists, behind her ears, then between her breasts as she had seen the other girls do. Her eyes burned with a feverish fire. She couldn't go downstairs. Not tonight. Anyone who looked at her would know she was desperately in love. Passion beat like a caged bird in her chest, and John wasn't even here yet.

Flora looked in the mirror and despised the woman there. She was behaving like a harlot, planning to seduce John. She'd bind up her hair, wash off the perfume and greet him in her office, as he expected her to. She picked up the brush, and as she held it above her head, there was a knock at the door. It was only eight-thirty. It couldn't be John yet. It would be Maggie, trying to persuade her again to tell John the truth.

"Come in," she called impatiently.

The porcelain knob turned, the door opened slowly and John stood framed in the doorway, staring. "I'm sorry, Bonnie. You're not finished your toilette. I'll wait downstairs." But he didn't retire from the door. He just stood, gazing at her. The lamplight danced like a million flickering candles in the tumble of tresses around her face and shoulders. She looked like a fairy child, her face so small and pale and beautiful.

Bonnie stood motionless, trying to decide what to say. Caught unawares, she realized she was happy that he had come early and taken the decision out of her hands. Coward, she chided herself. But her decison was only

strengthened to see him there, even more
handsome than she remembered. He wore a
deep burgundy velvet jacket tonight, setting
off the spotless white ruffle at his throat. He
usually dressed more severely, but in this
elegant outfit John looked every inch the
lord. It wasn't fair that he grew more
irresistible every time she saw him.

"Shall I go?" he asked uncertainly.

"You might as well come in. I'm only
dressing my hair."

He walked slowly toward her, his eyes
never leaving her face. When he was beside
her, he reached out and took a lock in his
fingers, fondling it. "Leave it like that," he
said. His voice was unsteady, a little thick.

The breath caught in Flora's throat,
rendering her mute. Her eyes flew to the
mirror, and she found herself staring at the
two of them, together. What a handsome
couple they made! John's head towered
above her, his body inclined toward her. As
she looked at the image, she saw his hand
move to his pocket. The silence stretched,
grew tense, till she could no longer bear it.

"You must be planning to attend a ball
tonight," she said, and allowed herself to
turn from the mirror and examine him in
person.

His eyes were like glittering jewels. "No,
I've been to dinner with Bathurst, the
minister. I left early."

"Oh. I can't go downstairs like this. I'll put
my hair up," she said nervously.

John took the brush from her fingers and put it aside. "We don't have to go downstairs. I don't want you to make a great fuss, Bonnie, but I've brought you a small present. I would be honored if you'd accept this as a token of my appreciation for your help." His artistic fingers fumbled nervously with the catch on the box. It was blue velvet, long and slender. He opened it and lifted out a string of delicate pearls. He had wanted to give her diamonds, but instinct led him to select this perfectly matched set instead. Their very modesty reminded him of Bonnie.

"Oh, John!" she gasped. Her hands fluttered like doves. "No, I couldn't! They're too valuable." She actually stepped away, to remove herself from the temptation.

He smiled ruefully. "I knew you'd say that. Stand still, woman, and let me put them on you. I won't take no for an answer. You've earned them."

Shyly, hesitantly, she took a step nearer. It seemed fitting that he should bring a gift tonight. She almost felt this was her wedding night. Flora found herself wishing he had brought a ring instead, a pearl ring. She turned around and lifted her hair to allow him to place the cool necklace around her throat. That one wayward curl clung resolutely against the nape of her ivory neck again. John gently pushed it aside to fasten the clasp. The scent of flowers rose from her, so light he didn't realize it was perfume. Then he took her hair in his hands and lowered it.

Flora looked over her shoulder and caught the yearning look in his eyes. "Thank you," she murmured softly.

She examined the pearls in the mirror, smiling proudly. "They're beautiful, John. I shall always treasure them."

"It should be emeralds," he said. But the pearls suited her. Their creamy opalescence looked beautiful against her white skin.

If he didn't move away from her now, he'd sweep her into his arms and kiss her. "We have a little while till Addison comes. Shall it be hazard or do you have your sewing box?" he asked. His voice sounded too loud in the still chamber.

Flora knew he was ill at ease, and suspected the cause. She gathered up her courage and said, "Whatever you want, John." Her gray gaze met his and held it. There was no mistaking the invitation in her voice. "I had some wine brought up. Would you care for some?"

"That would be nice. Thank you." He spoke stiffly, trying to fathom this change in her attitude. She almost seemed to expect him to kiss her. What was that enigmatic look in her eyes?

The ruby wine picked up the lamplight and reflected it as it swirled in the glasses. Flora held his glass out, waiting for him to come to her. He felt he was walking into a dream. "Thank you," he said more stiffly than before.

Flora noticed his lack of ease and tried

another bit of encouragement. "I really shouldn't have this," she smiled. "Wine makes me giddy, I fear."

John sipped and put his glass down. His throat felt dryer than before. If she didn't stop this wanton encouragement . . . "Why don't you sit down, Bonnie?" he asked.

Her gaze turned to the bed. She had had the extra chair removed, John noticed. He put his hand on the desk chair, indicating that it was waiting for her. She went and sat down. She didn't think he would make love to her before he had finished with his business. First let him hear what he must from Addison, then he would come to her.

"I'll get the other chair," he said, and fled out the door.

When he returned, he wore a new air of excitement. "I met Willie. Addison's here. I'd best take up my position. I don't want them to hear me moving about after they're in her room."

The news put everything else out of Flora's mind. "Yes, go on," she urged.

John quietly opened the door into the secret corridor and went to the slatted opening just as Marie's door opened. For a few moments, she and Addison embraced passionately. Soon Marie began removing her gown. She made a seductive performance of it, slowly lowering one shoulder while casting provocative glances at her aged lover. Before she had finished, Addison went to her and she put her arms round his neck. John felt degraded, watching them move their hands over each other, and watching Addison finish the undressing. He wished that Marie would get on with her subtle queries at once, but she only murmured soft endearments. She didn't wait long, however. When she wore only a black lace gown, she curled up on Addison's knee and began to run her hands through his gray hair.

"I've missed you, Addie," she crooned. "Were you very sick?"

"Just a little cold," he assured her, as his hands slipped under her peignoir and palmed her breasts. The motion stirred echoes in John's memory. In his mind, it was himself holding Bonnie's breasts in the palms of his hands. He felt a throb of passion and tried to quell it down.

"I bet they missed you at the office," she said leadingly.

Addison, the old fool, immediately began bleating out his secrets, trying to make himself sound important. "I'll get Wellington's guns to him, never fear."

Marie leaned over and kissed him full on the lips. There was a moment of lovemaking, then she spoke again. "How will you send them to make sure they're safe, Addie? You told me the last time some horrid pirates stole them off the ship. You must be very careful."

"Not real pirates, my pet. It was some wretched French scoundrels that did it. But I

fooled them this time. I'm sending the goods
in a trio of fishing trawlers."

"Oh, you're so clever, my darling Addie,"
she praised, and rewarded him by placing his
age-spotted hand on her breast. "How I
should love to go down to the dock and see
them leaving. Can I?"

"Heh, heh, you would have to travel all the
way to Portland. I'm slipping them out of a
different port this time."

John listened, torn between annoyance and
triumph. The false plans that had been fed to
Addison were safe enough. Even if Marie
slipped through the hands of the men who
were watching her, it would do no harm. The
triumph was that he had discovered the
disastrous leak in his department. Addison,
he thought, was only a harmless fool. He
would be moved to some less strategic post,
where he could copy letters of no
importance.

"When will they be leaving?" she asked. "I
like to know everything you're doing," she
smiled. "When you don't come to see me, I sit
wondering all day what my Addie is doing."

"I'll have the ships out on Sunday night,"
he said, trusting old goat. "No more loading
or shipping in daylight. I must play a closer
game than that. Now, mind you don't tell
anyone, minx," he remembered to warn her,
after he'd told the whole story.

"Oh, Addie. kiss me. I've missed you so
much."

Marie twined her white arms around his neck. Her peignoir fell away, revealing the curve of a pretty spine and buttocks, with Addison's hands massaging her body. John found that the scene acted like an aphrodisiac on his senses, which were already aroused by Bonnie. He wanted to go back to her, but was afraid of making a noise. And he didn't want to go to her like this, throbbing with passion.

Marie suddenly jumped off Addison's lap. "Shall we have some champagne, Addie?" she suggested. It must take a great deal of champagne to endure this old man's fondling.

"Whatever you like, my little darling," he agreed.

John took advantage of their moving around the room to slip out of the corridor and back into Bonnie's room.

"Well, is it what we thought?" she asked eagerly.

He nodded. "Yes, she manipulates him like a puppet on a string. He'll have to be replaced at once."

"Thank God it's over. What will happen to Marie?"

"The law will probably deal leniently with a young woman. I wouldn't worry about Marie. Her sort land on their feet. More importantly, we must discover who she works for. She's being followed night and day. I shouldn't think she'll deliver her message before morning. Not for a while, in any case. They've just ordered champagne. They haven't—haven't made love yet," he said.

"Then we have a little while before you must leave," Flora said. Her dark eyes looked frightened, but she was more determined than ever to have John's child. He might not return after tonight, now that he had learned about Marie and Addison. It had to be tonight.

She walked to the table and filled her glass, which she had emptied while he was away. John's was still full. He lifted it and followed her with his eyes, imagining her arms around him, caressing him as Marie had embraced her elderly lover.

She lifted the glass. "Shouldn't we make a toast to your victory?" she asked. "You propose a toast." She cast a long look at him and smiled. "This is your night, John." Her voice was husky with invitation.

John swallowed convulsively. "Why are you doing this to me? I've just watched two people making love, Bonnie. I'm—don't play with me," he said harshly.

"I'm not playing," she answered evenly. Then she lifted her glass, "To us, John." He lifted his glass in unsteady fingers and drained it. While they drank, their eyes held together, unwavering.

A dozen questions were asked and answered in that look. When their glasses were empty, he went to Flora and pulled her into his arms. "Are you sure, darling? You know I'm not offering marriage."

She saw the passion burning in his eyes, and saw too the underlay of fear that she'd change her mind. "I know. Why should I be lonesome, just because I'm not eligible for marriage?" she asked.

"I love you, Bonnie," he said. "I've never loved any woman so before. I'd marry you if I could."

"I don't expect marriage. I just want you," she answered simply.

His lips seized hers in a fiery kiss. She tasted the wine, and felt its effects in the spinning of her head. Was she mad to do this? It felt like madness, and like a wild, delerious joy, to be crushed against John's solid, warm body. This man she had hated, and grown to love so desperately she would die for him, or kill. The frenzied kisses were interrupted by even more frenzied declarations of love.

"Oh, Bonnie, you can't know how much I love you. How I want you. I'll never let you go. We'll be together forever." These tempestuous whispers tore through her, melting away any last trace of reserve. To hear he loved her, what else mattered?

Best not to think of the future. She only had tonight. That's all that was certain. His fingers were in her hair, gripping its waves. "Like an ocean of fire," he said, and buried his face in its perfumed mane while she luxuriated in his ardor. Better one night with John than a lifetime with some dull, respectable husband. She would have tonight forever.

"I'll lock the door before we undress," she said.

John looked surprised at her cool speech, but he was intoxicated with passion. She blew out one lamp and lowered the other, till the room was washed in dim shadows. John unfastened the front of her gown and gazed a long moment before burying his face in her breasts. He reveled in the creamy coolness of her flesh against his heated face. That's how he felt, like Devon cream, smooth and soft and sweet.

"We haven't much time," she said, and pulled away to remove her gown while John hastily undressed, feeling he was in a dream.

It pleased him that Bonnie removed her gown modestly, with no trace of coyness or provocativeness. After the performance he had just witnessed, her natural movements had a cleansing effect. And she was so beautiful. That hair, like a flame, inflamed his ardor. Her body in the dim lamplight had the dull sheen of ivory, smooth and sharp in outline. But when he came to her and touched her, the flesh moved with feminine compliance beneath his fingers.

He buried his face in the crook of her neck. "What made you change your mind?" he asked, still unable to believe this was happening, and just when he had given up hope.

"You," is all she said.

A warm glow suffused John as he tenderly

folded her in his arms to love her. He had never felt so moved, so protective and loving of a woman before. Their bodies touched, hesitantly at first, in a silken embrace. He felt the melting softness of her breasts against his chest, arms drawing him nearer. Small hands fluttering over his back, the disturbing brush of flesh as his legs grazed hers. Then he crushed her to him in a fiery kiss that unleased the building passion in a wild, instantaneous explosion. He felt himself swelling uncontrollably and swooped her into his arms to carry her to the bed, before he released himself while still standing.

When they were lying together, John's head hovered over hers resting on the pillows, her pale face surrounded by that flaming river. Something in the drugged glow of her dark eyes pulled at the cords of his memory. Flora put her arms around his neck and smiled, such a sad, sweet smile it tore at his heart.

"Say you love me, John, as I love you," she asked. Her voice sounded so young, as though she were a child.

"Love you? I adore you," he said. His voice was a husky rumble deep in his throat, and totally sincere. She knew it by the glow in his eyes, and the quivering of his lips in anticipation. She gazed a moment, memorizing this crucial image to cherish for the rest of her life. He loved her. That's all that really mattered. A ring and a wedding were only the icing on the cake. In a better sort of world, they could be together always.

Then he rose and gently eased his body on top of her, while their lips clung in a heady kiss. The irrevocability of what she was doing washed over Flora as she felt his weight descend on her, remembered from the other time. It felt like the weight of the world, yet she welcomed it. She welcomed this new world she was purposely creating for herself. She had to conceive, to save a part of John to cherish forever.

This time she acted with the full knowledge of her faculties. She knew what was happening when his fingers stroked her belly, clinging to the damp flesh. They gradually moved over her hips, pulling her more closely against him, grazing her thighs, and causing such a swell of desire that her whole body shuddered. His stroking fingers moved between her legs, inching higher, squeezing gently, lovingly, and all the time his lips possessed hers, and his tongue created another chaos in her mouth. His head moved, he was breathing insane words of love in her ears. Words like "forever."

Her heart pounded, it swelled till it filled her chest, her whole body throbbing with love for John. It was an unbearable excitement, so strong she almost felt sick. Her breath came in light, rapid gasps that didn't ease the suffocation of her lungs. She felt a vast, infinite ache of longing. It was like the lonesomeness of leaving home, but more immediate and demanding. Even while John loved her, she thought of the desolate future without him. But the present exigency pressed around her, obliterating thought. She was awash in a whirlwind of feelings and sensations.

She felt a warm moisture at the core of her being, and John's fingers, moving, feeling, increasing the ache till she could hardly stand it, then guiding himself to possess her. It stung like before when he plunged in—one short, sharp stab of welcome pain that eased the ache of longing. Then his hands gathered her buttocks and he began moving in a regular, increasing rhythm that carried her on a tide. She arched herself against him, gasping to relieve the unbearable tension that was part paradise, part hell.

The wave of sensation swelled higher, pulling her toward rapture, every atom of her being alive and singing. John was around her and in her, possessing and possessed in a perfect union, urging her toward bliss. "Now . . . now," he begged, and she found her body heaving spontaneously to keep pace with the frenzied imperative of passion. There was a brief, dizzying climax of shuddering perfection, then they fell limp and gasping against the pillows.

John rolled over and gathered her against him. He nuzzled her neck with warm kisses, whose gentle sweetness pierced her to the quick. He hadn't done that before. She lay, smiling contendedly in his arms.

27

John had to leave early that night, but Flora was reluctant to let him go.

"Why must you leave? Marie might plan to pass along the information to one of her other lovers," she pointed out. "You should wait and listen at the secret panel again, John."

"All Marie's gentlemen have been vetted," he explained. "She sees Sir Humphrey Waddell. With a son in the Dragoons, he's not likely to undermine the boy's safety. The others are also known and watched, though we don't consider them likely conspirators. But tonight Taylor's waiting for her. I should think tomorrow's the earliest she'll move, but I have a man watching the house twenty-four hours a day."

"Where are you going?" she asked.

"Bathurst's waiting to hear what I learned tonight. I told him I'd report back. I'll come tomorrow, Flora. I'm flattered at your eagerness." He smiled softly as he arranged his cravat at her mirror. Then he gave her quick kiss on the lips and left.

When she was alone, Flora sat thinking of the future. From his conversation, she knew John assumed she was giving up her work here to move to a cottage in Chelsea. She hadn't disillusioned him—not yet. She wanted to be sure she was carrying his child, and once might not do it. She wanted to make love with him again. It had been an experience beyond her wildest imagining. One or two times more—that was all. But she wouldn't become his formal mistress. What would he say when he learned she had fooled him?

These thoughts were so troublesome that Flora wanted to escape them. She dressed and was about to go downstairs when there was a tap at her door and Maggie came bustling in, big with news.

"They've caught him!" she exclaimed. "Caught the fellow Marie was passing her messages to."

"Already? Good God, it wasn't *Taylor*!" Flora exclaimed.

"Devil a bit of it. She threw a note out her window to a man who was skulking outside. Hywell's man was watching and arrested him on the spot. He took him down to be locked up and questioned."

"Who was it?" Flora asked.

"They didn't recognize him. It happened just as Hywell was leaving. The man refused to give his name, but they'll know soon enough. I couldn't be happier that it's over."

"What about Marie?"

"They took her along as well. Oh, it was all done very discreetly. None of our clients knew there was a thing going on. She was arrested and taken down the back stairs, claiming she was innocent, of course. Willie was speaking to Hywell's assistant—he says he won't let the journals find out about it. They found a box holding over a thousand pounds in Marie's room—that on top of what she has in the bank. She was willing to sell her country for money. It would only be fair if they hang her."

Flora frowned, remembering those cigar butts in the garden. "You don't think it could have been Dryden that was waiting for Marie's note?" she asked.

"I doubt he'd have the wits to be involved in anything this big. Petty conniving and cadging off women is more in his line. It can't have been Dryden who left the cigar ends if that's what you're thinking, Flora. It was the spy. Hywell will tell us all about it tomorrow."

"We'll just have to wait and see, then," Flora replied pensively. But after Maggie left, she wondered if it had been Dryden. If it had, and if he knew she was seeing John . . . Would there be any point in his telling John who she was? And did it really matter anyway? John knew she had been at Mother Hyde's. Even if he learned her real name, John would never tell her family, and that was a major consideration.

She didn't want him to know he was the one who had set her on the road to ruin, but that was the worst that could happen—that he hear the real truth about her and himself. Maybe people should know the truth. She had acted like a wild animal, but it was the draft that caused it. The John she knew and loved now would understand.

She went down to her office and paced to and fro, her mind ranging into the past and future. What could she do? Nothing, so she might as well sit down and try to be calm. Too much had happened that night for any calmness. At midnight she put on her mask and beckoned to Willie.

"Tell Maggie I'm going over to Swallow Street," she said.

"Nay, lass, not alone at this hour of night."

"I'll just slip through the backyard. I have a key for the door."

"I'll go with ye, to see nothing happens," Willie insisted. "You're lucky you weren't attacked before now, with spies loitering in the garden."

She was happy for the company that night, with her nerves all on edge. Had she passed right by the lurking spy on other nights, and never seen him? He might know about her secret room—but there was no danger now. Whoever the man was, he had been arrested.

Willie went to the back door of the house with her and waited till she had gone in and locked it behind her. A strange lass entirely, he thought as he hastened back home. Living in a fine mansion and running to hide herself in a shabby room. Folks were queer, when all was said and done.

Flora went quietly to her room, unlocked the door and felt again that sensation of welcome peace she always felt here, away from the troubles of her life. She knew she wouldn't have slept a wink in her own room that night, with the bed holding such memories of John. Here she felt almost as if she were home at Bradbury, amongst the simple furnishings. Yes, she thought she could sleep forever in that little cot. She undressed hastily, for the air was cool. The cot was cool too, till she had been in it for a minute to warm it. She made a conscious effort to forget the night, forget John and Marie and the spy—was it Dryden?

She forced her mind to think of more peaceful days. Sometimes if she thought hard enough about home, she dreamed about it. Sharp, vivid dreams. Papa dressed in his severe black jacket, going to the schoolhouse. Mama in the kitchen—with cook in those good old days, before her father died. The smell of gingerbread hot from the oven. Dick's favorite treat. She thought of Roger too, and the other girls and of Lily. Often of Lily.

Lily would be eighteen now—older than she'd been when she left home. No, don't think of leaving home. Think of the garden,

Mama's pride and joy. The yellow primroses and pink tea roses so pretty, with the delphiniums pushing up between the bushes. The delphiniums must have been trampled by the spy. You'd think a spy would be more careful. Dryden always smoked cigars, rank-smelling things.

Mother Hyde's face reared up, to be subdued by a fleeting memory of the church at Bradbury. The family going together to their seat, the children ranged in file behind their parents, looking like a parade of ducks on their way to the pond. Reverend Kelso's sermons, so long and so tedious, and never giving any practical guidance. She couldn't think of a single bit of advice from Reverend Kelso that had helped her decide what ought to be done with her life.

The tension began easing from her muscles. She dozed fitfully, then twitched back to consciousness. A feeling of peace was on her. Yes, it was all right to sleep now. She was safe at home. Her eyelids fluttered closed, and her body grew soft in slumber.

She awakened a few hours later and lay still, wondering what had disturbed her. Her body clock told her that some hours had passed, but it wasn't morning. Yet through her closed lids, an orange mist gave the sensation of daylight. Still foggy with sleep, she opened her eyes. Had she left the lamp burning? The light seemed to be right in her eyes. She sat up in alarm and stared at the lamp that was held right over her head. It took a few seconds for her eyes to adjust. She shook her head, trying to wake up and dispel the image that loomed behind the lamp.

That long face, thin sliver of nose, quivering in disgust, those pale blue eyes. Dryden! Her heart clenched in fear.

When John left Bonnie's room, he turned his mind purposefully to business. He was sorry for Addison and the disgrace that faced him. It could be wrapped up in clean linen so far as the public was concerned, but Addison must be told, and he would face the shame of his superiors' knowing. Worst of all, he must live with his own folly and the harm it had done. What fools we men are for love, he thought. And inevitably he thought of Bonnie. What had made her change her mind? She had been so loving tonight—almost as though she were determined from the moment he arrived that they should make love.

His man, Mr. Harkens, appeared from the bushes just as John was about to enter his carriage. He had someone with him, and John was annoyed that Harkens wasn't attending to business. He didn't realize at first that Harkens had the muzzle of a pistol against the other man's back.

"We've got our man! I caught him red-handed!" Harkens exclaimed. "The woman tossed him a note out the window. I was there when he arrived an hour ago and had been waiting for him to make his move. It was the

dark-haired wench you suspected all along—
the Simpson woman."

John studied the arrested man carefully. A
conning rogue if ever he saw one, but
wearing the outer shell of a gentleman. Tall
and lean, with blue eyes and a long nose. He
was sure he'd never seen him before. "Did
Simpson see you?"

"I don't think so. She must have known he
was there. She just tossed the note out and
closed the window again."

"Good work, Nigel. I'll take this fellow to
Bathurst for questioning, and you arrest
Miss Simpson. Do it discreetly."

"Where will I take her?"

"We're using the abandoned roundhouse
on Poland Street for spies now. Take her
there."

Harkens examined the spy and handed
John his gun. "You'd best take this. I won't
need it with a woman."

John reached into his carriage and slid a
pistol and manacles from the pocket. "Keep
it. You might need it with that hellion," he
said as he slid the handcuffs on Mark Dryden.
"Better give me the note," he added.

"I didn't get it. He stuffed it in his pocket."

John held out his hand. "Give it to me," he
ordered.

Dryden gave a sly look. "Take it," he
laughed.

A couple of gentlemen were coming toward
them. John didn't want to create a
disturbance on Bonnie's doorstep and

hustled Dryden into his carriage. It would be easy enough to get the note from his pocket after they were out of the carriage. He pulled the check string and the horses lunged forward.

John stared across the carriage, wondering how anyone who called himself an Englishman could be as low as this creature. He hated being in the same carriage with him. "What's your name?" he asked.

"John Smith," Dryden answered in an ironic voice. "And you won't learn anything different when you search me."

"That's all right. John Smith will hang as high as anyone else."

"Not without evidence," Dryden said. He had a gloating sound in his voice.

"We'll get that soon enough."

"Will you, Lord Hywell? The note I got from Miss Simpson was a billet doux, and you won't prove anything else."

"We'll see."

"You won't, you know," Dryden said, and laughed again, a gloating laugh. "I ate it."

A fierce stab of anger jolted through John. It couldn't be true! But he knew it could. That's why this revolting piece of humanity was smiling. And without the note, they hadn't a shred of evidence against him. He lunged forward and grasped Dryden by the throat. "I'll cut your gizzard open, you son of a bitch."

"You won't find much. I chewed it up well while you and your friend played with your guns."

Hywell's fingers twitched with the urge to kill. He hadn't felt such a blood-lust since leaving the Army. In Spain, he had learned the survival tactic of keeping a cool head in the face of disaster. He willed himself to calmness and resumed his seat. How did this change things—and what benefit might be rescued from nearly total failure?

His mind seethed with schemes, and when he herded his prisoner into the roundhouse on Poland Street, he searched him thoroughly to confirm that there was no note. When this was done, he locked the man in his room and waited for Lord Bathurst to arrive. Disappointment gnawed at him—he had come so close to success, only to be bested by this traitor. He had to think of something.

28

The bulky Secretary of State for War came smiling into the room, rubbing his hands gleefully. "Well done, Hywell! I knew we might count on you. Got the traitor by the toe already, what? Leave me at him."

"I'm afraid there's been a hitch, sir," John told him. "He ate the evidence."

"Ate it? *Ate* it?" Bathurst asked, dumbfounded. "Good God, this beats all. Any chance of cutting him open? No, I suppose not," he said. "I've heard of scoundrels bribing their way, but this is the first time I've heard of one eating a path to safety."

"All may not be lost."

"We'll have him followed, of course, but he knows we're on to him now. He won't do a thing but go to church and visit maiden aunts for a month."

"Here's what I think we should do," John

said, and outlined the plan he had come up with.

Bathurst asked a few questions, then nodded. "It might work—it's worth a try at least. What is the prisoner's name?"

"I haven't heard it yet. I didn't want to manhandle him in the public streets."

"A good point. Let's hope your plan works and he'll do something indiscreet."

"Preferably lead us to the rest of the gang. This operation of waylaying our ships isn't done by one person. There has to be a group of them, with a few Frenchies at the bottom of it, providing the money."

"Yes, quite. Well, let's get on with it then. My wife wasn't too happy at my walking out on her soiree. You brought the girl too, did you?"

"Harkens is taking her to a separate room. I don't want them comparing stories. We'll quiz her later."

Bathurst and Hywell went to the locked room where Dryden was sitting at ease on a plain wooden chair. Even with his hands in manacles, he had managed to light a cigar. Its rank fumes filled the room with a blue cloud. "Ah, Hywell, you have returned to molest an innocent citizen, have you? My lawyer will have your hide for this. False arrest is illegal in England."

"This is the traitor," John said grimly to Lord Bathurst. "My man caught him red-handed receiving secret information from his cohort."

"Let me see this information," Bathurst ordered, and held a peremptory hand out to Hywell.

John glared at Dryden. "He chewed it up and swallowed it, sir. But I swear he had it. Mr. Harkens saw him receive it."

Bathurst frowned his dissatisfaction at Hywell. "In what manner did he receive it, and from whom? Where is the other prisoner?" He spoke impatiently, showing irritability with his assistant.

"The other prisoner is on her way."

"*Her* way? Good God, you mean a *lady* is involved?"

"No, sir, a lightskirt," John replied. "She works at an establishment on Riddel Street."

"She's my bit of muslin," Dryden smirked. "The evidence, milord, was a note making an assignation to meet the female at Kew Gardens tomorrow."

Bathurst ground his teeth and turned on Hywell. "What is the meaning of this farce, sir? You draw me away from an important meeting to have me deal with lightskirts and their beaux? Good God, I knew I was surrounded by incompetents, but this goes beyond anything."

John clenched his hands into fists. "Let me have five minutes alone with him. I'll beat the truth out of him."

"The truth, sir," Bathurst charged, "is that you have arrested an innocent gentleman, and wish to compound the offense by assaulting him. A whore out of a common bawdy house has no secrets to sell. Get out of my sight, and don't let me see your grinning face again. And leave me the key for these handcuffs before you go."

John handed over the keys and turned one last fulminating stare at Dryden, to keep up the pretense, then turned and marched from the office. Marie Simpson was just being led in by Harkens.

The arrest had caught Marie totally unprepared. As she was being delivered to the roundhouse, she sat worrying about the money they had confiscated, and figuring out how this had happened. It couldn't have been done without Mrs. Belmont's connivance. That prim and proper little bitch had never liked her, and now she'd gone scheming behind her back. Marie knew all about Mrs. Belmont from Mark Dryden. It was Lord Hywell she saw slinking up the stairs with Mrs. Belmont, and now he was here. They'd plotted this together. She put on such airs, and Mark said she was nobody. A country wench that stole Mark's inheritance, then changed her name so he couldn't find her. Flora Sommers, that's who she was.

When she saw Hywell, a fit of spite seized her. Him thinking he was so high and mighty. "Run back to Mrs. Belmont and tell her I know all about her," she said, in a knowing way. "You think she cares for you? Hah! She'll only steal your money, as she stole Dryden's. Steal it and run off with a new name and a new beau. She's Flora Sommers,

that's who she is, out of Mother Hyde's
whorehouse. You think she loves you? She
hates you for what you did to her."

"Shut your mouth," John growled.

"Dryden is the other prisoner's name,"
Harkens told John. "Have you ever heard of
him?"

"No."

"Ask Mrs. Belmont," Marie sniped.

Harkens tried to pull her away. She opened
her mouth and spat at John. He realized the
woman was talking from spite, but the name
Flora Sommers wasn't quite forgotten. The
name soon conjured up a face, and as he
compared it with Bonnie's, he realized they
could be one and the same woman. She was
that girl he had known only once but never
quite forgotten. She had changed almost
beyond recognition. Actually he had been so
intoxicated that night the memory was dim,
but the eyes—they were the same large,
somber gray eyes. How young she had looked
then. He caught a glimmer of recognition
floating at the edge of consciousness from
time to time. It always unsettled him.

But what did Marie mean—what he *did* to
her? Their meeting that night had been
memorable. He hadn't been drunk enough to
forget her passion. It still haunted him, after
all these years. But afterwards—she had
been trembling, and behaved oddly. He had
thought she had too much wine. And there
had been a few drops of blood on the sheets.
It had occurred to him at the time that she

might be a virgin. "I didn't know what kind of a house it was I went to," she had said a while ago. Why hadn't she told him the truth?

He stood alone in the corridor, looking after Marie's retreating form. When he had gone back the day after he met her, just before his frigate left, Mother Hyde said the girl was out shopping. That didn't sound as if she had been overcome by what happened between them. The Simpson chit was lying. She just wanted some revenge because he had caught her.

He mustn't let this monopolize him now. He had to hurry and be prepared to follow Dryden. Bathurst had done a superb job of acting. You would swear he had meant every word he said. John darted at once out to the street to look for a passing hansom cab. Dryden wouldn't walk all the way back to civilization.

In a few minutes he heard the sound of wheels and hooves, and ran into the street. By good fortune, the hansom was empty of passengers. "I'll give you ten golden boys for the loan of your coat and hat and rig," Hywell said, looking toward the door to make sure Dryden wasn't coming out yet. He'd told Bathurst to keep him ten minutes if possible.

"Eh?" the driver asked in astonishment.

"I need your rig. I want to borrow it for tonight. I'll bring it back to you tomorrow. Where do you stable it?"

"Newmans."

Even as he spoke, the driver hopped down.

It was a queer request, to be sure, but the lad had the blunt in his hand. He wasn't disguised and he didn't look like a thief. A man would drive many a weary mile for that kind of gold. He watched with interest as John divested himself of his curled beaver and put on the other hat. He pulled it low over his eyes. With the shabby coat over his jacket, and in the dark, he looked like an anonymous driver. Dryden wouldn't give him a second look.

Inside the roundhouse, Bathurst turned a softer expression to the prisoner. "I'm sorry for your inconvenience, sir. I have been saddled with some officers returned from the Peninsula—that gentleman is one of them. A good enough soldier, but an abominable administrator. They think they may treat honest citizens as they treat enemy soldiers. I don't believe I caught your name, sir?"

Dryden saw no need to conceal it. He assumed an injured countenance. "Mr. Dryden."

"A thousand apologies. I hope you won't feel it necessary to broadcast this little contretemps."

"I'm not sure it ought to be kept quiet. Doing it a bit brown, hauling a fellow through the streets in manacles."

"Dryden—not one of the Surrey Drydens? Are you related to Maxwell Dryden?"

Dryden had often claimed kinship with this respectable stranger before, and allowed he was a cousin to Maxwell. "I couldn't be sorrier, Mr. Dryden. But all's well that ends well, eh? No point in making a brouhaha against the government. We have enough problems. There's a good lad. We'll have a glass of wine before you run along and forget this happened. I'll have a word with Lord Hywell."

"Well," Dryden said nobly. "I daresay there's no point making a to do over it. An accident, after all."

"Exactly."

Bathurst discovered there was no wine at the roundhouse, but he kept the man chatting for five minutes more before releasing him. They shook hands and Dryden went whistling into the street.

29

Dryden's air of offended dignity fell away when he was alone on the street in front of the roundhouse. He may have convinced Bathurst he was innocent—fancy a minister of the Crown being such a dimwit—but he knew that Hywell wasn't fooled. He'd be lurking around somewhere, following him. Or perhaps he'd be questioning Marie for the next hour. Better get away from here while he had the chance. He looked over his shoulder, all around, then struck out at a brisk pace, southwards toward civilization.

Would the stupid girl break down under questioning? He thought not. Marie was experienced in double dealing. It was Marie who had approached him in this business when she'd learned about him from Maggie McMahon. What was it old McMahon told her? He'd sell his bloody body—or soul— for money. How was a fellow supposed to keep body and soul together when all the cards were against him? Fine for those rich nobles to preach patriotism and duty, he rationalized. They didn't have to scrounge for every penny.

Marie had hit on Addison by mere luck, but with her French connections, she knew where to make gain on what she learned. The woman was likely a Frenchie herself, if the truth were known. She had a sharp French look about her, with those flashing eyes and pointy nose.

All he did was pass her notes to Alphonse Dupuis in the middle of Bond Street, at five guineas a trip. Pretty good pay! They couldn't hang a man for delivering a letter. Was that what English justice amounted to? If they caught him, he'd swear on a stack of Bibles he'd never read the notes. He was just delivering love letters for Miss Simpson. By God, it had been nearly worth arrest to see the look on Hywell's face when he told him he'd swallowed the note. That was one good trick he'd learned from Marie Simpson, or whatever her name was.

Dryden heard the clip-clop of a cab approaching and lifted an arm to stop it. The faster he got away from this cutthroat neighborhood, the better. At least he wasn't being followed. There wasn't a soul on the street but himself. Now where should he go? Best get to his flat and move out in case they went looking for him. "The corner of Glasshouse and Great Windmill Street," he called to the driver, hardly glancing at him. He hopped in and continued fretting and scheming.

Where could he go, with only a pound and a few shillings in his pocket? He'd have to get out of town for a spell, in case Marie gave him away. He couldn't risk meeting Dupuis tomorrow and demanding money. Bloody Frenchies, they'd put a bullet through him if he tried a threat. Flora Sommers—he still had that ace in the hole. She was ripe for blackmail. Why the little nobody made such a great and mighty secret of her identity was a mystery to him. Probably wanted by the law, if the truth were known. But he didn't like to go back to the Aviary. Hywell would likely go hotfooting it back there. Where could he go? A man couldn't drive around in a hackney cab all night.

The cab pulled in at a shabby rooming house on the corner of Glasshouse and Great Windmill. Dryden hopped out, looking up and down the street like a haunted man. "Wait for me. I won't be a minute," he called to the driver, and darted into the house to fling a few shirts and linen into a bag. And his pistol. He should have carried it tonight and he could have shot that bastard who grabbed him outside Marie's window. He stuffed it into the pocket of his jacket, looked all around, and left.

In the driver's seat, John sat tense. Should he follow now? Maybe the man intended to bolt out the back door. But he surely didn't suspect anything. It would be best to wait a few minutes. This was obviously where he lived—he was packing a bag to make a run to safety. Where else would he go but to his colleagues? John couldn't quite suppress a thought of Bonnie too, as he sat waiting. Bonnie and Dryden? Had he been her lover? No, the Simpson girl was just trying to make trouble. Bonnie always said the girl was a troublemaker. First catch Dryden, then think of Bonnie.

John's heart hammered with the thrill of the chase. He might have the lot of them rounded up before this night was over. He really should have another man with him. Too late for that now. He patted his pistol, then took it out to make sure it was loaded. He hoped he wouldn't have to kill anyone. He'd spilled enough blood in Spain, but if it came to that . . .

The door opened and Dryden came out, carrying a little case. So he was planning to make a run for it. "Drive up Glasshouse to the corner of Swallow Street," Dryden ordered, and climbed into the carriage.

On the perch, John called, "Aye, aye, sir," and gave the whip a crack. Where the hell was Dryden going? The corner of Swallow Street was perilously close to the Aviary.

He tried to keep all thoughts of Bonnie at bay. In his mind, John still thought of Flora as Bonnie, the name he had known her by for most of their acquaintance. He needed his wits about him, but Marie's words echoed in his head. "She hates you for what you did to her." "She'll only steal your money, as she stole Dryden's." "I know all about her." What was there to know? He couldn't believe that Bonnie had stolen money from Dryden. Yet he found it hard to believe that Mrs. Hyde had left her the money. Marie worked for Bonnie, and Dryden was working with Marie. The connection was there, try as he might to wish it away. The spying occurred at Bonnie's establishment.

He was being ridiculous—that innocent child couldn't have anything to do with this. Why, she'd helped him. She didn't have to tell him about the secret panel into Marie's room. Of course he had already made it perfectly clear he meant to listen in. In the course of choosing a spot, he would have come across the panel himself. It would look more innocent if Bonnie pointed it out to him. He remembered her shocked exclamations when she heard he planned to watch. Why hadn't she warned Marie not to ask any questions that night?

Were they such bold conspirators that they had decided to go ahead with their plan, right under his nose? Bonnie had asked a lot of questions—had asked if he meant to follow Marie. He hadn't told her the window was being watched. The thought inevitably followed that Bonnie had tried to distract him that night. She had all but flung herself on him. Did she count on her charms, withheld till now, to distract him from business? She had very nearly succeeded. While Marie was dropping her note, he had lain with Bonnie, enjoying her treacherous love. She had urged him to linger. "Do you have to go, John?" How the question had thrilled him.

He felt a sick wrenching inside at what he was thinking. It couldn't be true. Bonnie was so sweet, so incredibly innocent. Mending her stockings and complaining about the Duke of Clarence not paying his bill. Nobody could be that innocent. He hadn't believed her story himself when she first told him. Not till she had weaseled her way into his heart had he been fool enough to believe her.

He thought of that mask, which had always intrigued him. Why would a beautiful woman want to hide her face? Was it because she had stolen from Dryden, and didn't want him to find her? But he *had* found her—and forced her to work with him? That was mere white-washing of Bonnie. He knew there were stronger motives. Money for one—she talked about money a lot. It had been a bonus that she could pull the stunt on him, to repay him for "what he did to her." Part of her story was true. She had wandered into Mother Hyde's without knowing what sort of a place it was. And Mother Hyde had gotten her drunk before handing her over to a man.

The blood boiled in his veins at the wretchedness of the world, which had transmogrified an innocent child into a monster of vengeance. He wished he could turn back time and undo the wrongs of the past, but events were set in motion now. They were unrolling as irrevocably as fate. The carriage clip-clopped toward the corner of Glasshouse and Swallow Streets. Dryden pulled the checkstring, the horses were drawn to a stop, and Dryden got out.

"How much do I owe you?"

"That'll be two shillings, sir," John muttered, hoping he had chosen a reasonable sum.

With a grumble, Dryden handed him up the money. John kept his head low. In the darkness, his white, gentleman's hand went undetected. "Thank ye, sir," he said in a gruff voice and bobbed his head. He had to continue on with the carriage to keep Dryden from suspecting anything unusual, but as soon as he was around the corner, he threw out the weight to hold the horses and abandoned the rig.

Dryden was still standing uncertainly on the corner, looking all around to be sure he wasn't followed. John stood just out of sight at the corner. He took occasional looks to see which route Dryden chose. If he turned right and went up Riddel to the Aviary, John felt his worst fears would be confirmed. Perspiration formed around the band of his hat, though the evening was cool. He felt his shirt sticking to his back. "Turn around," he prayed silently. "Go to the Haymarket, or to your club. Go to hell, but don't go to Riddel Street."

And still Dryden stood, undecided. He daren't risk going to the Aviary tonight, but he needed money. And he needed someplace to spend the night. There was that room Flora had hired on Swallow Street. Curiosity had impelled him to investigate it when he'd seen her go there twice. What the woman wanted with a shabby bed-sitter was a mystery to him. Probably met a lover there, he decided. He must be some down-at-the-heels clerk, if that was all he could afford. No matter, it was some place to lay his head till morning. He'd send her a note telling her to meet him there.

His decision taken, Dryden struck up Swallow Street, and John's tension eased slightly. But Dryden was still perilously close to Riddel Street. John crossed the street and followed at a distance, noticing when Dryden turned in at one of the houses. Did the man have a string of rooms around town to escape the bailiff? He'd heard of men being put to such shifts. No, he wasn't going in at the front door. He was slipping through an alleyway to the back. This must be about opposite the Aviary. He was going to Bonnie! He planned to go in the back way!

He was going to meet his lover and

colleague, and John felt so frozen he didn't think he could move his limbs to follow. He didn't want to know any more. He didn't want to have to see them, and kill them.

30

By an act of sheer will power, John crossed
the street and quickened his pace. The alley
was empty. He entered and drew his pistol.
The blood beat slowly, steadily in his ears. He
had the strange feeling he was back in Spain,
following his quarry. Walk quietly. Don't
panic. But if Dryden meets Bonnie, I'll shoot
him dead. If they embraced, he feared he'd
shoot them both. He peered around the
corner of the house just as Dryden was
jimmying the lock of the back door. Dryden
was the sort of man who could break into a
house with the ease of long practice, John
noticed. He didn't have a key—what could he
be doing here? Maybe he wasn't meeting
Bonnie . . .

John waited a moment before going to the
door. He opened it quietly and slipped into a
dark corridor. The sound of secretive

footfalls on the stairs was heard. Dryden
must have a friend living here. It was the sort
of house where a man down on his luck might
take refuge.

From the bottom of the stairs, John heard
the telltale click of metal moving furtively on
metal. He was breaking into someone's room.
Was it a fellow spy? There couldn't be more
than one or two men there, along with
Dryden. Probably no one but Dryden. John
removed his shoes and mounted the stairs
silently, his pistol cocked in his right hand.

On the floor above John, Dryden still wore
his shoes, but they were soft-soled evening
shoes. He looked around the room, feeling
carefully for a table. There—that was it. Now
a tinder box. He struck the flint and lit a
lamp. Holding it high, he scanned the room.
He saw the mat of copper hair on the pillow,
saw it was a single cot holding only Flora
Sommers, and went forward, wearing a
gloating smile. The woman was deranged!
What the hell was she doing here? No matter,
she was alone, and before she left, he'd put
the fear of God into her. What was the wisest
course? She must be worth thousands by
now. He could kidnap her, and make
McMahon pay a handsome ransom.

He went to the cot and held the lamp to
examine her. By God, she was a good-looking
wench. He had always wanted to give her a
tumble, but old Hyde would have kicked him
out if he had. He saw her eyelids flicker, saw

her head stir on the pillow. Then she opened her eyes and stared at him. He watched in amusement as confusion turned to shock, then to horror.

"Dryden!" she whispered. As her eyes focused, she saw the black circle of his pistol pointing at her. Steady, unwavering. My God, he's going to kill me! Her throat went dry. She couldn't have shouted if she wanted to. If she opened her lips, if she breathed, he'd shoot. The man was a maniac. Why did he wear that awful, gloating smile?

"At long last, Flora, you and I are going to come to terms."

So that was it! It wasn't murder he had in mind after all, but something worse. Her fingers convulsed on the bedclothes. She pulled a sheet up under her chin. Her mind went blank. She should be thinking furiously, but what occurred to her was that if she did have a child, she wouldn't be sure it was John's. After all her misery, even that consolation was being snatched from her.

"Now, now, my pretty. I don't want to see less of you. I want to see more," Dryden said. As he spoke, he smiled triumphantly. He had half a mind to rape her, but common sense cautioned him against that course.

Her blood turned to ice in her veins. "Go away or I'll scream," she said in a voice so light he hardly heard it. "There are people next door."

He lunged at her, one hand covering her

mouth, the pistol in his other hand pressed against her ribs. "We don't want to disturb the neighbors," he said.

When John silently pushed the door open, he saw Dryden sprawled on top of Bonnie. All he could see of her was that flame on the pillow, but it was enough. There weren't two manes like that in all of London. The blood pounded in his ears, it seemed to blind him with a red curtain. Bonnie and Dryden, lovers! She had set him up, made a fool of him. "Say you love me, John, as I love you." She loved him with a white-hot hatred, as he loved her. When he spoke, his voice was not unsteady. It cut into the room hard and sharp, like a pistol shot.

"Well done, Mr. Dryden. I hoped you'd lead me to the rest of your colleagues. Mrs. Belmont—or should I say Flora Sommers?"

They hadn't heard John's stealthy advance. At the first sound of John's voice, Dryden sat up and stared at him. The pistol was out of sight, covered by a sheet, but Flora felt it move, take aim at John. She was pinned behind Dryden on the bed, unable to move fast enough.

"John, he has a gun!" she shouted, and tried to wrestle it from Dryden.

John saw the gun just as Dryden lifted it from the sheet. Even as she spoke, John took aim and a leap of fire came from his pistol. He meant to shoot the gun from Dryden's hand. He'd often made that shot before. He hadn't counted on Bonnie to pitch herself forward, trying to deflect Dryden's shot. John stared in horror as she was thrown back against the pillow. He saw her white gown ooze with crimson blood as she gave a low moan. The wound seemed to be right at her heart.

Dryden stared in confusion. "You've killed her, you bloody fool."

Hywell looked as though he'd turned to stone. His black eyes glowed like obsidian in his pale face and he stood perfectly motionless. It came as a shock when he spoke. "Get a doctor. And you'd better come back, Dryden, or I'll carve your heart out of your body and feed it to the carrion crows."

What a cold bastard he was, Dryden thought. Kill a helpless woman and act as though he hadn't a nerve in his body. Still, he'd best go for the sawbones. "I'm going, but I saw you shoot her. You won't lay this in my dish."

"Go!" The icy voice turned to fire and thunder.

Dryden darted out the door, and in three steps John was at the cot, gathering Bonnie into his arms. Her head fell back as though she were dead when he tried to lift her. Her face was deathly pale. He placed her gently back on the pillows. A dry sob was torn from his throat as he grasped her limp, white hand and buried his head in her tangled hair.

"Bonnie, Bonnie, my darling! Forgive me.

It wasn't meant for you. Whatever you've done to me, I deserved it and more."

For a moment, he was overcome with the enormity of what he had done—killed the only woman he ever loved. First ruined the innocent child, then murdered the woman. His body shook with uncontrollable grief and tears gathered unashamed in his eyes as he gathered her in his arms to gaze at her face, still as sweet and innocent as that child he had destroyed.

There was a timid tap at the door and a gray-haired woman looked in, her eyes big with curiosity. "I'm Mrs. Fellows, the landlady. We all heard the noise. What happened to Mrs. Banyon?"

"There's been an accident. The doctor's on his way. You might boil some water. Close the door, and don't let anyone else come to bother us."

"Oh, dear! It sounded like a shot."

"Start boiling water," John ordered, and she left.

The interruption proved useful. Years of training surfaced through John's grief. He should be trying to help Bonnie. Perhaps she wasn't dead yet. He returned her to the pillow and took her pulse. There was a faint fluttering beat at her wrist. The bullet couldn't have gone right into her heart. Oh, but she looked so dead. There wasn't a flicker of her long eyelashes, which lay motionless against her pallid face. He couldn't see any signs of breath. His fingers trembled slightly as he took the bodice of her gown in his hands and ripped it to reveal the wound.

Impossible to tell whether the bullet had gone into her heart. It hadn't missed it by much. The ragged, red hole was just below her breast, but off center, toward the left. Where was the doctor? If that cur of a Dryden hadn't called him . . .

He heard the sound of hurried footsteps on the stairs. Two sets. Dryden had come back too. An elderly doctor wearing spectacles and carrying a black case hurried into the room. John stood by his side as he probed at the wound.

"It's Dr. Warner," Dryden said. He was gasping for breath.

"Not too much loss of blood," the doctor said, but the eyes behind the flickering spectacles were worried. "I'll have to fish for the bullet. I'll do it before she comes to. It'll be painful."

"Is there anything I can do?" John asked.

"You can get me a glass of wine."

"No wine! I don't want a drunken mauling at her."

"Be calm, lad. I'm no drinker. I haven't done a job like this in five years. Now settle down. I know what has to be done. I'll need more light."

John lit another lamp and brought it close. He moved the small table to the side of the cot to hold the doctor's equipment. The doctor opened his case and began selecting instruments. "I'll need her lying flat. A pillow under her back would make it easier to operate."

"I'll do it," John said.

He forced himself to icy calm as he gently lifted her body and slipped the pillow under her. It wasn't till the doctor leaned over her inert body, his steel instruments flickering in the lamplight, probing the wound, that the nightmare began playing itself in John's head. The quick fury at seeing Bonnie with Dryden. If he hadn't been half mad, he wouldn't have fired while she was moving. He shouldn't have aimed for Dryden's gun. It was too close to Bonnie. He should have shot the cur in the heart—instead of Bonnie . . . She couldn't die. He wouldn't let her.

Why had he stood like a judge, condemning her for running her parlor? What alternatives were open to girls that had been ruined —by someone like him? No man would marry them. Heedless young men like himself took their pleasure with never a thought to why those girls were where they were. There was something terribly wrong with the world when human beings had to sell their bodies, and their self-respect. If she lived, he'd marry her and be damned. And if she died . . .

"What's taking so long?" he demanded.

"Here we are," the doctor exclaimed, and lifted a spent bullet in the claw of his instrument.

"The bleeding is worse," John said, glancing over the doctor's shoulders.

"I'll just put some basilicum powder on a pad and try to stanch it. Can you get some hot water?"

John went down to the kitchen to hasten the landlady. "What happened?" Mrs. Fellows asked, with the brightly curious eyes of a born gossip. "She was with a man, eh? And her so nice she wouldn't say boo to a goose."

"A man broke into her room. You'd better get your locks attended to. Mrs. Belmont will probably sue you."

"Belmont? She said her name was Banyon. She said she was a widow."

John took the pan of water and left. This new name would be something to conjure with later. There were dozens of questions for which he had no answer. He hadn't a single idea what Bonnie had been doing in this house.

When John returned, the doctor promptly sent him off for the wine, claiming the patient would need it, though it was himself who needed a restorative. He found it enervating, with the young gentleman at his shoulder, nervous as a cat on a griddle. When John returned with the wine, Bonnie had been cleaned and the wound bandaged.

"Can't we get that blood-soaked garment off her?" he asked. It looked grisly.

"A little blood won't kill her. The less she's disturbed, the better. It'll be touch and go for the young lady. There's nothing more I can do tonight. I'll come by in the morning. If she wakes up, you might try to feed her a little broth, but there's no hurry with that. Tomorrow will do. She shouldn't be left alone."

"I won't be leaving," John said.

The doctor stood waiting, and John roused himself to pay the man. When he had left, John turned a steely eye on Dryden.

"You have some explaining to do, Mr. Dryden."

31

Mark Dryden was a man without honor, but he had that animal cunning necessary for survival, and soon realized that the likeliest way to avoid Lord Hywell's wrath was to say nothing against Flora Sommers. The story he told was more or less true insofar as it related to Flora. His own part in the matter of Mother Hyde was whitewashed considerably.

"As Mrs. Banyon—that's Mother Hyde's real name—was my aunt, I naturally expected to inherit when she died," he explained. "Of course, the money was her own to do with as she wished. She chose to leave it to Flora. I may have said a few words I regret, but in the heat of the moment, you know . . ."

"Why did you come here tonight?" Hywell asked.

"I only wanted to borrow a little something from Flora."

"Borrowing done at gunpoint has another name in the eyes of the law, Mr. Dryden."

"Damme, I didn't plan to *shoot* her! You're the one—"

This unvarnished truth was enough to clench Hywell's lips into a grim line. "You don't have to remind me. There's one more thing I must know before you leave."

Dryden heard the delightful word "leave" with a surge of hope. "About Miss Simpson and that note."

Dryden wavered between the expediencies of sticking to his story and turning his colleagues over to the law. He knew by now that Hywell wasn't likely to either swallow the fabrication about a love note or give up until he had achieved his goal.

"My memory might improve if I were offered a pardon for turning evidence against certain parties," he suggested slyly.

He saw the doubt in Hywell's eyes. John knew that speed in rounding up the gang was vital. They'd know by tomorrow that Miss Simpson had been arrested, and fly off in all directions. Dryden had behaved properly in bringing the doctor and returning himself. There was a grain of honor in him still. Hywell was feeling lenient toward people who must scratch for a living, and he knew in any case that Bathurst would leap at the deal.

"I'll see what I can do."

"My part in it was minimal. I truly didn't know what was in the letters at first," Dryden began. Inside of fifteen minutes, he had emptied his budget. Names of anyone he knew, the place where they met and the time. "Can I go now?" he asked when he had finished.

"Not yet. You'll have to help us in capturing the crew tomorrow. Take a note and meet your contact as usual—let him think you have the note you got from Marie. I expect you read it and can write it up again?" Dryden nodded. "We'll follow him and round up the rest of them."

John went to the door and called for the landlady. "I want you to send a note off to Lord Bathurst," he said. "I'll need a pen and paper. There's a hackney cab parked at the corner of Swallow and Glasshouse Street. Your servant can use it."

"The cab driver! That was you!" Dryden exclaimed.

"You didn't really think Bathurst was conned with that story of a love letter?" John sneered. "There's just one more thing you have to do, Dryden. Forget the name Flora Sommer. It was Bonnie Belmont who worked at Mother Hyde's, and later opened the Aviary. If I ever hear of you breathing the name of Flora Sommers, I'll come after you and finish you."

Dryden looked at the icy determination in Hywell's eyes and felt a tremor down his spine. "Do you understand what I'm saying?" Hywell asked.

"Yes."

"I've killed worthier men than you. That they didn't happen to be Englishmen is irrelevant. If you besmirch that woman's name, I'll kill you."

Mrs. Fellows came with the stationery and roused up her servant to deliver the message. John outlined in his letter what he had learned and asked for a guard to take Dryden away, to be sure he was available for the morrow's job. In less than an hour two armed guards arrived and Dryden was led out.

When these necessary details had been taken care of, John drew a chair close to Flora's cot and sat watching her all through the night. Every flicker of her eyelids, every slight moan or twitch was carefully observed. Every one caused a twinge of guilt. He thought of calling Dr. Halford, the city's most prominent physician, but Dr. Warner seemed to know his business. He had extracted the bullet well, and it had been deeply imbedded. To call Halford would attract unnecessary attention.

As John sat holding Flora's limp hand and occasionally touching her hair, he thought of their past. A million regrets came to bedevil him—a hundred occasions when he had been less than kind, and a few when he had been cruel. He had never been able to keep his head when he was around Flora. That was the trouble. He wanted her—loved her—too much. He had been a damned patronizing brute at best, and he prayed that he'd have the chance to make up for all his wrongs. As the first streaks of rosy orange lit the sky, he gave up recriminations and began to plan for the future.

At seven-thirty, Dr. Warner returned. "How is my patient doing?" he asked, and went forward to examine Flora, with John hovering at his shoulder. "She hasn't regained consciousness?"

"No, she's moaned a little. Doctor, is she going to—" The word caught in his throat. He was afraid to ask the overwhelming question.

"Since she's lasted the night, there's hope."

"When can I move her out of here?"

"Be patient, lad. Be patient. That won't be for a while yet, unless you want her taken out in a coffin." The doctor looked around the room. "That doesn't meant you can't enliven the surroundings," he added. "A fire in the grate wouldn't do any harm. But I suggest you find a bed for yourself before you do anything else. You look like death. Has the young lady no relatives that could come and relieve you? I don't want her left alone."

Relatives in Bradbury were of no immediate help. John knew that Flora wouldn't want to worry them in any case. Her new "family" on Riddel Street must be informed, though. There were so many things he should be doing. A part of him wanted to help arrest the Frenchies. But Bathurst had

dozens of men who could do that as well as
he. His place was here, with Flora. For as
long as she was here, he didn't plan to be far
away.

When the doctor had finished his
examination and outlined what to do if Flora
regained consciousness, he left. Mrs. Fellows
came to the door with a breakfast tray, and
John arranged with her to hire a room in the
house. For a little pourboire, she thought the
lady next door would be agreeable to move to
another room. Indeed, the lady had already
demanded to be removed if last night's noisy
activity was to continue. The whole house
was abustle with speculation, but Mrs.
Fellows barred the door and kept the tenants
at their distance.

John sent a note off to his own house
calling for a footman to bring him clean
clothing, a razor and money. As he sipped the
scalding coffee, it felt as if it were entering a
vacuum. His whole body felt empty, with the
hot liquid burning in him. Then he went to
the cot again and gazed down at Flora. Such a
feeling of love swelled in him that his eyes
were glazed with tears. She had to live. He
wished he could open his own veins and
pump life into her still, pale body, which
looked so terribly like a corpse. How could
he go on living if he'd killed her?

At eight-thirty John's extremely curious
valet arrived with a small trunk. His name
was Pounder. He was no dandified city valet
—though he aspired to be one—but John's

batman from Army days. In fact, he resembled the ex-pugilist that he was. His nose had been broken and lay in a mash of tangled flesh and bone on his face. His bright blue eyes pulled into a scowl as he surveyed Hywell's state of disarray, for he prided himself on keeping his master impeccably groomed.

"A footman you're calling for!" he accused. "Your valet is what you need. You look as though you'd crawled a mile in them duds."

"Hush, Pounder," John said, and looked to the cot.

"Eh, what's this, then?" Pounder demanded, and walked softly to see the cause of this freakish behavior on his master's part. "Gorblimey, what happened to her?" In times of stress, Pounder's speech reverted to the low.

"I shot her," John said through clenched teeth.

"Is she dead?"

"No, she's not going to die," Hywell stated firmly, as though stating a fact could make it so. He was still unreasonable where Flora was concerned.

"Were it in the line of business you plugged the young lady, or was it what you might call an affair of the heart?"

"Both."

"Aargh." Pounder knew that his master had been on the fidgets for some time now, and as he cast a knowing look at the desperate man beside him, he knew he had discovered the cause. "We'll want to be looking fit when she wakes up. I've brought along your blue superfine and the biscuit trousers. I suggest the Oriental style to your cravat. But first a shave—"

"Put the things in the next room, Pounder, and call for hot water. But first, I think you'd best take a note over to the lady's house explaining a few things. It's on Riddel Street, just a block over. Ask for Mrs. McMahon."

Pounder had no familiarity with the higher class of brothel. A very genteel house the young lady had on Riddel Street, in his opinion. Mrs. McMahon too struck him as a fine sort of chaperone, barring the fact that she was flying around like a chicken with its head off. She had noticed Flora's empty bed, and in the aftermath of the other doings of the night, she was very worried.

Pounder regretted having to give her the note. Mrs. McMahon read it and turned pale as paper. "Oh my!" she gasped, and stood there, turning circles in the middle of the hallway. "Willie! Tom!" Then she looked again at the note urging her to keep the matter secret. But Willie must be told. She handed him the note and darted downstairs to take the shortcut to Swallow Street.

Willie read the note and sighed. "I feared she'd come to harm," he said, shaking his head.

Pounder stood waiting for Mrs. McMahon, till he was told she had already left by the back way. He returned to Swallow Street and began laying out Hywell's vestments.

Mrs. McMahon came flying into Flora's room, wringing her hands and blaming herself for everything. "I shouldn't have let her come here. What happened, Lord Hywell?"

She was put in possession of the facts as she stood with tears in her eyes, gazing at Flora. "It's all my fault. She never wanted to open that cursed house. I urged her to do it. She that wouldn't hurt a hair of anyone's head, to end up like this. Oh if she dies, Lord Hywell—"

"She's not going to die," he stated flatly. "And the fault isn't yours; it's mine."

Who was to blame was discussed for several minutes. The fault was so widely dispersed—Mother Hyde and Hywell, Mrs. McMahon and Dryden, and a set of deplorable circumstances that could send an innocent girl into the world to fall prey to its vagaries. Maggie pushed Hywell out of the room. She wanted to be alone with Flora, and Hywell looked ready to collapse.

At the doorway he looked all around the little room. "Why did she hire this place?" he asked.

"To survive. Sometimes things just seemed to be closing in around her, she said. She got to hate the Aviary so. She couldn't sleep. She told me this little room reminded her of home. Her folks were not well to do, you know. She sends most of her money home to them. She called this her little haven. It was all that kept her sane."

"I think I understand," John said sadly. "In the Peninsula, I used to climb into my tent after a battle and close my eyes and pretend I was home."

Throughout that long day, they shared the chore of sitting with Flora, looking at her pale, motionless form. The doctor came at noon and in the afternoon. Willie couldn't bear the suspense and came to see for himself that Bonnie was still alive—barely. A tear gathered in his eyes and trickled down his rough face. "Ah, she were a bonnie lass," he said sadly.

Maggie went back to Riddel Street around dinner time. At seven-thirty, John was alone with Flora when Dr. Warner returned. Shortly after, Flora sat up and started talking. Her voice was light, hardly more than a whisper, and her glazed eyes were staring into the distance. "Don't worry, Mama. I'll be fine. What can possibly happen? It's only a drive to London. I'll go directly to Mr. Leadbeater."

John looked at Warner with a wild eye. "She's delirious! Isn't that a bad sign?"

"It's a sign of life, at least."

Flora turned her head slightly and continued babbling. "Perhaps I shan't go after all, Lily. I had the most wretched dream last night. I dreamed I got lost in London and was wandering through the streets alone at night. It was so horrid!" A shudder shook her body, and her head returned to the pillow, where she mumbled incoherently. John wanted to weep for the nightmare of Flora's life.

"I think we might get a bit of that broth into her, if we go carefully," Dr. Warner said. "I don't want her to go much longer without any nourishment—a liquid at least."

"I'll do it," John said.

A pot of broth was simmering on the hob. He filled a bowl and tried to get Flora to sip it. He spoke in soothing tones. She looked right at him and said, "I'm sorry to be such a bother, Papa. I'll help you correct the lessons when I'm better."

"Yes, Flora, but now you must drink this."

She drank half a bowl, then fell back on the pillow. Before Dr. Warner left, he felt she was going to pull through. "The fever's broken," he said. "We can have her woman come and clean her up now. I've put on a clean bandage. The wound is clotting up nicely."

John paced the corridor while Maggie tended to the personal chores necessary in the patient's room. She carefully replaced the stained gown with a clean lawn nightie and washed Flora. When she came out, John said, "Can I go back in now?"

"No, you cannot. She's sleeping. I'll stay with her. For God's sake, go to bed, Hywell. You look worse than Flora. I don't want two invalids on my hands."

Pounder came stomping up the stair. "There's a note for you," he said, handing Hywell a letter.

He scanned it quickly. "The crew of spies were captured this afternoon," he said. "There were a dozen of them, living in hired rooms in Long Acre. It seems Marie Simpson is well known to Bathurst by another name. She's Mrs. Dupuis, the wife of the ringleader."

"I never did trust that wench. She's French, is she?"

"Her mother was French. She grew up in England, but spent some years in France. Well, thank God that's over."

"Now perhaps you'll be able to sleep," Maggie said.

She knew by the surprised light in Hywell's eyes that it wasn't the matter of the spies that had him on thorns. He turned to Flora's door. "I want to see her," he said.

She felt a stab of pity for him. His face was haggard and pale. She could sympathize with the haunted air of guilt he wore. She felt the same herself. She wouldn't let Flora go back to the Aviary. They'd sell it or close it down, but she wouldn't let Flora ever set foot in that cursed house again.

32

It was a few days before Flora was fully conscious and strong enough to sit up and talk. She first became lucid in the evening while John sat with her. Hazy flashes of memory told her he had been there for some days, or she had dreamed it. Perhaps she was still dreaming. She looked at him from partially closed eyes. He noticed it immediately and leaned forward, squeezing her fingers.

"Flora! Flora—can you hear me?" His voice was eager.

She didn't speak—not yet. If this were a dream, she wanted it to continue. It was a soothing dream, after the nightmare of the recent past. Strange, confusing images swirled in her head—time was all distorted, people were in the wrong places. Lily working at Mother Hyde's, and John talking to Papa, who had been dead for years.

"Flora, darling, can you hear me? Talk to me. Tell me you can find it in your heart to forgive me. You were trying to save my life, and I nearly took yours. And I love you so."

I love you so. Of course it was a dream. But the voice was clearer than before, and her understanding was sharper too. She lay still, hardly daring to breathe.

"Can you drink something? The doctor says you must drink. Here, try this broth."

A cup was at her lips, John's hands cradling her as he tilted it to her. It tasted good. It was her own cook's brew. Was she back at the Aviary? She looked around the room. No, she was in her little haven. She drank the broth and sighed, utterly fatigued from the slight exertion. John laid her head gently back on the pillow and went to tell Maggie the good news.

Later, John left and Maggie took up the vigil. Flora opened her eyes then and spoke in her own voice, frail but clear. "Maggie, why am I so weak?" she asked.

"You're lucky you're alive. Don't you remember what happened, Flora?"

"I woke up, and—was Dryden here?"

"That he was. He came to borrow money— he said."

"Oh—and John came. What happened?"

"Dryden was the man Marie was working with. I'll tell you all about it later. Just rest now. You mustn't try too much at first."

"Is John all right? Dryden didn't shoot him? He was going to."

"No one was hurt but yourself. Hywell was trying to shoot Dryden, and you got hit by mistake. The poor man's half crazed with guilt."

"Yes, that's what it is," Flora said. Then she closed her eyes wearily and thought. John had shot her—how odd. He must feel terribly guilty. But she'd get better, and then John wouldn't have to worry. "How are the girls? And Willie and Tom?"

"They're fine. We're looking after them."

"Can I go back to Riddel Street soon?"

"We'll see," Maggie said, but her expression firmed to obstinacy. Never again, my girl!

"You didn't tell Mama?"

"I knew you wouldn't want that."

"No. Don't tell her."

"You rest now, Flora."

Flora closed her eyes. She didn't open them till morning. John was in the room, talking to some man. He called him doctor. "How soon can we get her out of this place? I thought the sea air at Brighton might be good for her."

Brighton! There'd be no happy holiday there now. She couldn't handle the reins with this sore chest.

"A week or so, if you use a well-sprung carriage and keep her well bundled up. You'll want to have another doctor look at her when you get there."

"Of course I'll take every precaution. I mean to see that she has every help money can buy."

Everything money can buy. But money can't buy love. He meant to send her off to Brighton—and from there to a cottage in Chelsea? No, it was better to make a clean break. Flora wanted a whole new life. The business must be wound up, but after that, she'd go far away. Maybe to Ireland. Maggie said Ireland was beautiful, the whole world soft and green. And it was cheap too. With her share of Mother Hyde's money, she could probably buy a little cottage and have a cow and a few chickens.

The doctor left, and John approached the cot. Flora opened her eyes and looked at him. How tired he looked, and how worried. Dear John. She studied his face a long moment while he gazed at her. He saw by her eyes that she was alert.

"Welcome back, Flora," he said gently. He knelt by her little cot and kissed her lips, a swift, fleeting brush. "My darling, can you ever forgive me?"

Flora? He knew, then—Maggie had told him everything. She was too tired to be angry. Flora firmed her resolve to withstand the weakness her love caused. "I know it was an accident. There's nothing to forgive," she said in a dispassionate voice.

"There's a world to be forgiven, if you can find it in your heart—" He thought of Mother Hyde's and that night when he had possessed her. It was too early to speak of that. Even without it, he could see that Flora was only being polite. The ardor was gone from her.

She looked at him as though he were a stranger.

"The doctor says I can remove you to the seaside soon. You'll like Brighton. I hope you'll accept my hospitality there. Maggie says she'll go with—you." He wanted to say "us," but that was taking a good deal for granted.

"I want to go back to Riddel Street," Flora said. "I have things to be done there. I must make some arrangement for the girls. I'm going to close the house, John."

"Yes," he said, with a great feeling of relief. "Maggie is already looking after that."

"I'd like to speak to Maggie. Is she nearby?"

"I'll call her soon. We must talk, Flora."

"Please don't apologize any more," she said wearily.

"But I want to talk about the future—our future."

"I've decided against that" was all she said. She had made up her mind to do an unpleasant duty, and wanted to have it over and done with.

John wanted to rant against it, but Flora's condition had to be taken into consideration. "I don't blame you, darling. I've been an unforgivable disaster in your life, but I do love you," he said. "Don't decide yet. Think about it a little."

"Will you call Maggie?"

"Of course."

Over the next two days, Flora began to sit

up and eat, then to take a few steps around the little room. She was determined to get well as soon as possible. When Maggie arrived the next morning, Flora had her pelisse and bonnet on over her nightdress. "I'm ready to go home, Maggie," she said.

"Flora! You're not well enough! Wait till the doctor comes!"

Even as she stood, the room began to move in circles, and Flora was obliged to sit down again. A cold perspiration broke out on her forehead. "Well, perhaps I'll wait till Dr. Warner comes," she said weakly.

Maggie went running to Hywell. "She wants to go home today, and half the girls are packing to leave. Elsie has already left. What can I tell her, Hywell? She'll see all the card tables—she'll know something is afoot."

"She won't mind that you and Captain Cameron are turning the place into a gambling den. She said she planned to close it."

"I should have discussed it with her. She'll be angry I didn't let the girls come to say goodbye," Maggie fretted. "She says she won't go to Brighton with you."

"Where else can she go? I'll waylay Dr. Warner before he goes upstairs. He'll have to tell her sea air is absolutely vital to her recovery. Thank you for offering to go with us. Why don't you go on down today and make sure the place is ready? You can take my carriage and have it returned."

"I'll do that, but I can't remain for long,

Hywell. Cameron needs me here to oversee the renovations."

"With luck, you won't have to stay long," he said. "Will you have the servants pack up all Flora's things?"

"I already have. I'll take them with me to Brighton."

John gave her the address and waited to meet Dr. Warner as he came in. When the doctor left, Flora felt that her life depended on going to Brighton.

"But there are no houses to be hired so late in the season," she told him.

"Young Hywell has a place that's standing idle. Go there. It's the least he can do for you," he added. By this time, Dr. Warner had some idea of what had caused Miss Sommers' condition. "It'll do his conscience some good to be of use."

Flora decided it wasn't too high a price for John to pay, and agreed. She was curious to see his house. It would be nice to walk along the ocean with Maggie too. Perhaps Maggie would invite her to go to Ireland with her, now that she was an invalid.

The next morning, Flora was wrapped in blankets and carried to John's waiting carriage. "Where's Maggie?" she asked. When John climbed in with her, her surprise turned to alarm.

"She went ahead to Brighton to see that everything is in order."

"But you aren't coming with me, John!" she exclaimed.

"I have to go and speak to the servants. I shan't stay—if you don't want me to," he said, and looked at her from his brooding eyes for her decision.

She saw the concern, and knew that if he remained for an hour, she might change her mind. "It will be better if you return to London," she said coolly.

There was little conversation as the carriage sped into the country. It seemed incredible that summer was dying. Already the leaves had lost their new freshness. They drooped dispiritedly on the trees. Crops were turning to gold. How quickly the seasons passed, and a person's life drifted away with them. Flora looked out the window for an hour, then closed her eyes and slept.

When she awoke, the tang of sea air was in the carriage. They had stopped in front of a fine brick house. John gathered her into his arms and carried her to the door, where Maggie was waiting to receive them.

"How was the trip?" she asked, looking with concern to see Flora's condition.

"It was fine. I slept most of the way," Flora said.

"I've put you in the south wing, Flora, with a view of the sea," Maggie explained. "My room is right next door. Perhaps you should take her up there right away, Hywell. We don't want to overtire Flora. The doctor will come this evening."

"I'm not tired," Flora objected, but she was taken upstairs all the same. She fought the urge to rest her head on John's shoulder as he held her in his strong arms, so tenderly.

"If you're not tired, then I'll join you for tea," John said as he placed her on the bed.

His simple announcement filled her with consternation. Why didn't he just leave? Every minute he stayed made the parting harder. "All right," Flora said primly. "You'll want to eat before returning to London. You might as well eat with Maggie and me."

John didn't say a word about remaining in Brighton. He behaved like a proper host while they had tea with Maggie, and that evening he forced himself to stay away from Flora's room. He talked to the doctor after his visit, and was cheered to hear that Flora was out of danger. All that had to be done now was to build her health up again with good food and rest.

The next morning when Flora announced to Maggie that she was well enough to spend the day downstairs on a sofa in the drawing room, it was John who came to her room to carry her down.

She turned a cold stare on him. "I'm well enough to walk downstairs, if you'll lend me your arm," she said.

Again, John scooped her into his arms and carried her down to the handsome saloon. "I thought you would be leaving yesterday," Flora said when he had bundled her into a blanket and surrounded her with books, games and quiet pastimes suitable to an invalid.

"I managed to get a few days free from work. I haven't been to Brighton at all this summer. A little stint by the sea won't do me any harm either." It went against his instincts for John to hang on when he was palpably not wanted, but he knew this was his last chance. He couldn't leave, but he didn't push himself forward as a lover. He spoke in the calm manner of a friend.

Flora could see that John did look exhausted. With Maggie to play propriety, there was no real harm in his being here with her. But she would have to be on her guard against him. She couldn't say he was trying to change her mind. John behaved like a proper host, thoughtful in the extreme, but not encroaching. If the conversation took a turn she disliked, she had only to yawn and claim fatigue, and he immediately left her alone. The trouble was that he also pulled Maggie away, and left Flora lying alone on the sofa to face the next few hours by herself. She dreaded being by herself as much as being with John. Either way, he filled her thoughts.

33

Flora knew her health was returning when she became bored with idleness. She wanted to go out and walk along the beach, to smell the bracing air and feel the wind in her hair. The next morning, she asked to see Maggie alone after breakfast. John cast a quick, worried glance at her, but he left without argument.

"Maggie, I'm worried about the girls," Flora said. "We've been gone a week. Willie can't handle all the details."

"We closed the house, Flora," Maggie said.

"I suppose you had to when we're both away, but isn't it time to go back and close it officially? Some provision must be made for the girls."

Maggie took a deep breath. "I hope you're not angry with me, Flora, but everything has been done."

"What do you mean, done?"

"I paid them all their share, and have the receipts to prove it."

"I'm not doubting your honesty! But tell me—"

Maggie outlined her arrangements. The girls who insisted on continuing in their chosen line of work had gone to Johnson, or to live with a lover. Others had gone home. "And a few of them are staying on to work for me and Captain Cameron," Maggie announced. She gave Flora a leary look. "Not as hostesses! That is, as *real* hostesses in our new gambling den. That's what we've done with the Aviary, Flora. You put so much money into fixing it up, and the place was only hired. We would have lost all that if we'd terminated the lease. The captain thought a gambling den would be a good, profitable business. Not exactly top of the trees, but not so bad as—as what we did before."

"I thought you were going back to Ireland! I thought—I thought I might go there too," Flora said.

"Oh, Flora, there's hardly anything I'd like better, but Captain Cameron wants me to marry him. He went behind my back and searched through records for my husband, trying to convince me to get a divorce. Jerry was killed ten years ago, so I'm a widow and didn't know it. I'm going to get married, Flora."

Flora felt deserted. "You should have told me. I would have liked to see the girls before they left."

"They all left you their love, and Elsie said she'd write from Jamaica. The doctor didn't want you disturbed. You were too weak. That's why I haven't told you all this sooner. We thought it would be best if you never had to go back to Riddel Street, Flora."

Flora was honest enough to admit she was glad, as long as the girls hadn't been abandoned. But she felt abandoned herself. What was to become of her? "How much money is left for me?" Flora asked.

"Six thousand pounds."

"There can't be that much!"

"There is. I took the furnishings and renovations to the Aviary as part of my share. You got a little more than the others—and you deserve it, Flora. You're the one who did all the work, you ran the place. Bonnie left it all to you, really. That'll give you three hundred a year if you invest in Consols. You could live well on that."

"Yes, and still send money home. Oh, Maggie, I haven't even congratulated you on your engagement! I am happy for you."

She threw her arms around Maggie, her best friend, whom she was losing. "You should be in London with your captain," she said. "Here I've been keeping you in Brighton, and there are a thousand things you need to be doing."

"I would like to get away soon," Maggie admitted. "How much longer do you think—"

Flora tossed the blanket aside and stood

up. "No longer," she announced firmly. "I'm perfectly well enough to travel. Well, perhaps just one more day, to give me time to arrange something."

"Hywell won't let you go so soon!"

"Lord Hywell is my host, not my jailer!" Flora said, with a spark of anger in her eye.

John chose that inauspicious moment to return to the room. He had heard the remark, but it was Flora's bright eyes and healthy complexion that he noticed as he entered, and of course the fact that she was standing up.

"I would like to borrow your carriage, John," Flora said imperiously. "I want to go downtown and see a traveling agent."

"Very well," he answered mildly. The moment he dreaded had come. She was planning to leave, and he still hadn't had a chance to win her over. "I'll send for your bonnet and pelisse." And he would go with her. It might be his last chance.

When the carriage arrived at the door, Hywell stood with his curled beaver in his hand, obviously intending to accompany her.

"It will be best if you not go out alone, in case you have a weak spell," he announced calmly.

"Very well."

Flora swept out the door past him. John gave the groom directions before entering the carriage, where he sat across from Flora. The driver snapped the whip and the carriage lurched forward.

Flora was too full of her grievances to remain silent, as she had intended to do. "You might have told me what was going on behind my back," she snipped.

"We thought it wiser not to disturb you."

"Did you think it wiser to pull my life out from under me, to leave me stranded with no business and no friends, no place to go?"

John leaned toward her and grabbed her hands. "Flora, you know you will always have a friend, and a place to go, as long as I am alive." His voice throbbed with emotion, and his eyes felt like live coals burning into her.

Frustration, disappointment and worry combined to raise Flora's temper. "Thank you, but your friendship in the past has proved a very mixed blessing. And the place you offer me is not what I have in mind for my future. I've given up any connection with that sort of life."

"You don't know how happy I am to hear it!"

"I said *any* connection," she repeated. "I don't plan to be your mistress. And why are we going into the country? I said I want to see a traveling agent!"

John didn't answer her question. He moved to the banquette beside her. "Flora, how can I begin to make up to you for what I've done?"

"What you did was an accident. I've recovered, thanks to your help. You've

provided everything that money can buy,"
she added grimly.

"I'm not just talking about the accident.
I'm talking about the innocent girl I
seduced." Pale from her illness, Flora
resembled that girl more closely than in the
recent past. He writhed to think of having
hurt her.

"So Maggie told you! I wish she had not.
And you didn't seduce me."

"But why didn't you tell me?" he asked.
She saw the pain and regret in his eyes. His
hands gripped hers so tightly it hurt. "I had
no idea—"

"It was a long time ago. That was an
accident of sorts too. I was—in the wrong
place, at the wrong time—you couldn't know
how I came to be there."

"I know now, Flora. I must make it up to
you or I'll go mad. You could have told me
any time since then. Why did you hide behind
that mask, and pretend you were someone
else?"

"Because I was ashamed of myself. I
behaved like a—a—what you called me. A
whore." Flora waited for the familiar
warming of her cheeks, and felt nothing.

"Did I call you that?" he asked sadly. "Talk
about a pot calling a kettle black. I'm the one
to blame. You behaved like a girl who had
been poisoned with brandy, I fancy. If I
hadn't been half drunk myself, I would have
known it. I really had no idea that night,

Flora."

"It was more than brandy. Mother Hyde had some poison she used—"

"Good God! You mean she actually used an aphrodisiac?"

"Something like that. She used it when the girls didn't want to—oh, what's the point of talking about it? She's dead and gone now."

"If she were alive, I'd kill her," he said grimly. "This is all I needed! As if I didn't have enough on my conscience."

Flora wrenched her hands away. "Don't include me in the weights your conscience has to bear. I'm a survivor. I'm still here."

"Flora, I'm not offering you friendship based on a guilty conscience. All that is past. I want a new beginning for us. I love you as I've never loved before, and never will again."

Flora saw the love glowing in his eyes, and withdrew into the safety of her shell. "No," she said.

"But the night you were wounded, you—why did you do that? I think you loved me then."

The memory of that night was strong, and the love had grown even stronger. "Yes, I loved you," she admitted.

"Love me again!" he urged eagerly. "I haven't changed, darling."

"I've changed, John. I've told you, I'm through with all that. Don't ask it of me."

"Are you saying you're through with love—with any association with a man? Is that

what my love has done to you?" The word
convent was in his mind.

Flora sighed. "Perhaps one day, like
Maggie McMahon, when I'm old and gray, I
shall find some man undemanding enough to
marry me."

He blinked. "Why wait till you're old and
gray? Why not marry me now?"

"*Marry you!*" She stared as though he were
insane.

"Of course. What did you think I meant?"

"You mentioned a cottage in Chelsea. You
said you didn't mean marriage."

"That was before I knew the truth."

"The truth is that you can't marry me—a
woman out of a —"

His lips stopped her words. They closed
over hers in a fiery kiss that left her weak
with longing. When he stopped, his lips were
at her ear, breathing words of love. "Flora,
my heart. Don't remind me of what I did to
you. None of this would have happened
except for me. And despite it all, I can't be
completely sorry. If we hadn't been at
Mother Hyde's that night, we might never
have met at all."

"But you can't marry me. What would your
family say?"

John gazed into her dark eyes till he felt he
was drowning. His voice was husky when he
spoke. "I'm not a child. I live my own life—
with you, if you'll have me."

"A man in your position is expected to
marry a fine lady, John."

"That's exactly what I hope to do. I want to marry the finest lady in this or any other country. You, Flora Sommers."

"Oh, John!" A sob shook her body as she clung to him. "How could we? You'd be a laughing stock."

"I don't care if the whole of London dies laughing, but who actually knows about you? You always wore that mask."

"Dryden knows."

"He won't be talking," John said firmly. "The only others who know are Maggie and a few of the girls. Maggie won't talk, and you're not likely to run into the others since you won't be attending Johnson's palace of pleasure."

"I have no idea how to be a lord's wife."

He gave her an encouraging smile. "You, who were the Duke of Clarence's hostess? You've run a large house before. As for the rest of it, I think you know what this lord would like." His smile faded, and in his eyes she read uncertainty, and fear, and love. His voice was resonant with passion. "I don't mean to lose you again—not if you love me. That's the only thing you have to tell me. Do you love me, Flora?"

She could do it. She could be a fine lady, if John believed in her. "Yes," she said on a sigh of joy. She had always loved him. Ever since he had walked into the room and said, "Good evening, Flora," with his black eyes smiling at her. John was right. Despite all the trials, she was glad it had happened. She would go through it all again, for this moment of peace, and all the bliss that would come after. "Yes, John. I love you."

"Then it's settled, Lady Hywell," he smiled, and pulled her into his arms to kiss her.

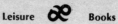